COMMUNITY

Michael is involved in a car crash which kills his girlfriend. He wakes to find himself in the hospital of a small town in Montana. There he convalesces and gradually becomes acquainted with the local community, most of whom seem to be clever and charming, although some are arrogant and difficult to get on with.

COMMUNITY

Graham Masterton

Severn House Large Print
London & New York

This first large print edition published 2014
in Great Britain and the USA by
SEVERN HOUSE PUBLISHERS LTD of
19 Cedar Road, Sutton, Surrey, England, SM2 5DA.
First world regular print edition published 2013 by
Severn House Publishers Ltd., London and New York.

British Library Cataloguing in Publication Data

Masterton, Graham author.
  Community. -- Large print edition.
  1. Montana--Fiction. 2. Horror tales. 3. Large type books.
  I. Title
  823.9'2-dc23

ISBN-13: 9780727896735

Severn House Publishers support the Forest Stewardship Council™
[FSC™], the leading international forest certification organisation. All
our titles that are printed on FSC certified paper carry the FSC logo.

Printed and bound in Great Britain by
TJ International, Padstow, Cornwall.

ONE

The pick-up first appeared in Michael's rear-view mirror about twelve miles north of Weed. It kept its distance at least a half-mile behind them, too far away for Michael to make out what kind of pick-up it was, but its halogen headlights were fixed on high beam, and so even at that distance they were irritatingly bright.

'Inconsiderate schmuck,' said Michael, but only to himself, under his breath, because Tasha was sleeping. He flipped his mirror to anti-glare, but even that didn't stop him from being dazzled.

About eight miles north of Weed, it started to snow. Not thickly, just light whirly stuff that flew into the windshield and skipped diagonally across the highway. The sky was slate-gray, but as they came around the next curve, the pine trees thinned out, and Mount Shasta appeared, its snowy peaks shining orange in the very last light of the day.

'Hey,' said Michael, giving Tasha a nudge. 'Mount Shasta.'

She opened her eyes and blinked at him. 'What did you say?'

'Mount Shasta. Right there.'

'Oh my God, it's *amazing*. It doesn't even look real.'

5

'Fifth highest peak in the Cascade Range,' he told her.

'You *would* know that.'

'I also happen to know that it's four thousand three hundred twenty-two meters high, with an estimated volume of eight hundred fifty cubic kilometers.'

Tasha punched his arm. 'Why do you always have to reduce *everything* to numbers? Look at it, it's so spiritual.'

'Excuse me, I can do spiritual. The Modocs believe that the sky spirit Skell came down to live on top of Mount Shasta. Not only that, a race of aliens called Lemurians are supposed to have made their home inside it, in a network of tunnels. And those New Age people are convinced that it's one of America's principal hubs of psychic energy.'

'I just think it's beautiful. It's so serene.'

Now and then, the mountain disappeared behind the trees, and each time when it reappeared its orange glow had faded a little more, until the sun went down and all they could see was its upper slopes, chilly and white in the gathering darkness. Mount Shasta was as lonely as God, somebody had once written about it, and as white as the winter moon.

Michael hadn't intended to drive through Siskiyou County after nightfall, especially if it was snowing, or windy, but they had blown a tire just outside Yreka and they were running over an hour behind schedule. He had booked a room for them at the Comfort Inn in Weed for six pm, and it was already a quarter after seven.

Tasha stretched herself. 'You shouldn't let me go to sleep like that,' she complained. 'I won't be able to sleep tonight now.'

'Who said anything about sleeping?'

She punched his arm again and said, 'Who do you think you're kidding? I know you. Ten-thirty precisely and you close your eyes and not even the Mormon Tabernacle Choir could wake you.'

Michael checked his rear-view mirror again. The pick-up was still behind them, still with its headlights on high. If he hadn't been so anxious to make up time he would have slowed down and let it pass.

He didn't argue with Tasha because he knew that she was right – he did zonk off as soon as his head hit the pillow. To be fair to him, though, he had been driving nearly three hundred miles every day, all the way up coastal highway 101 as far as Renton, near Seattle, to visit Tasha's sister Rody and her boring husband David. Now they were heading back home to San Francisco the quicker way, on Interstate 5. This trip was what they jokingly called their 'jumping-the-guneymoon'. They had decided to move in together two weeks ago, but they weren't planning to get married until April at the earliest.

'I'm so hungry,' said Tasha. 'I don't know why. That cheeseburger we had at the Black Bear Diner – that was just *enormous.*'

'I don't know where the hell you put it,' said Michael. 'You're so darned skinny, when you eat something that size I'm amazed you don't look pregnant.'

'I have an incredibly efficient metabolism,

that's why. Everything I eat turns into pure energy.'

Michael couldn't disagree with that, either. Tasha was tireless. She ran her own craft store on Mission Street, Tickle Your Fancy, selling scented candles and handmade greetings cards and hand-knitted baby clothes. She was small and pretty in a sharp, Slavic way, with straight blonde hair and blue-gray eyes and a little snub nose, and Michael had fallen for her on the very first evening that they had been introduced, even though they couldn't have been more different.

Michael liked sitting in silence and thinking and analyzing stuff. Tasha liked running and Zumba and making things with her hands. And singing. She was always singing. Usually high, wistful songs like 'I Can't Make You Love Me'.

The halogen headlights flashed in Michael's mirror and he lifted his hand to shield his eyes. 'Dumb ass has been following me for miles with his lights full on.'

Tasha twisted around in her seat. 'He probably doesn't realize. Why don't you let him pass?'

'Because I'd have to slow down and we're late already.'

'What does it matter? It's not like we're meeting anybody. Anyhow, it looks like he's gaining on us.'

Michael checked his mirror again, his eyes narrowed against the glare. 'You're right. And it's about time, too.'

Not only was the pick-up gaining on them, it was gaining on them fast. Now it was only twenty-five feet behind them and the whole

8

interior of Michael's Torrent was filled with blinding white light.

Michael moved as far over to the right-hand side of the highway as he could, so that the pick-up would have plenty of room to pass. But it continued to tailgate them, and now it was so close that it was almost touching the Torrent.

'What's he doing?' Michael protested. 'Guy's some kind of a lunatic!'

He jammed his foot down harder on the gas, and they began to pull away, but within seconds the pick-up had closed the distance again. He swerved left, and then right, and then left again, so that the Torrent's tires howled in a high-pitched chorus, but the pick-up kept after them like an attack dog.

'Oh my God!' Tasha cried out. 'He's going to kill us!'

Michael touched the brakes, but when he did so the pick-up bumped into them, with a deep, hollow thud. For a split-second he lost control, and the Torrent snaked from side to side.

'Michael!' screamed Tasha, gripping the door handle tightly with one hand and pressing the other hand flat against the glove box.

The pick-up bumped into them again, harder this time. The Torrent slewed sideways across the blacktop, with Michael frantically spinning the steering wheel. All he could see was revolving headlights and flying snow. He stood on the brake pedal, trying to slow them both down, but the pick-up rammed into the passenger-side door and forced them right off the blacktop and on to the median strip, which was all rough grass and rocks.

A deafening bang was followed by a series of jolts and groans and screeching noises. Michael and Tasha were thrown violently from side to side, and then the Torrent rolled over and over and over, three times, with its roof buckling and its doors caving in and its windows bursting.

Michael saw Tasha's arms and legs flailing. He felt as if they were being flung around in a giant tumble-dryer, and the tumbling seemed to go on and on as if it would never stop. Their shoulders collided, their heads knocked together, and then he saw Tasha's head hitting the roof.

The Torrent rolled right over on to the north-bound side of the highway, where it tilted on its side and then rocked to a standstill, upside-down.

It was almost completely dark. Michael, hanging twisted in his seat-belt, could see only Tasha's left side, with one thin arm in its pale blue sleeve caught crookedly between the arm-rests. He levered himself upward with his knees, trying to reach his seat-belt catch. As he did so he glimpsed the back of her head. Her blonde hair was glistening with blood, and he thought that he could see a triangular fragment of white bone sticking out.

'Tasha?' he said hoarsely. His seat-belt was pressing across his throat and he could hardly breathe. 'Tasha, can you hear me?'

She didn't answer. He lifted himself up again, and this time he managed to grope around with his left hand and grab hold of the seat-belt catch and hang on to it. He pushed the release button with his thumb but it was jammed.

'Tasha?' he said again. 'Tasha, just tell me that you're OK, darling. Please.'

Very gradually, the crushed and misshapen interior of the Torrent began to fill up with light. Part of the vinyl roof-lining was hanging down so Michael found it difficult to see anything out of his window. *Don't tell me that pick-up's coming back. Haven't they done enough to us already?*

He jabbed at the seat-belt catch again and again, but still it refused to budge. Either it had bent, or he was hanging from it too heavily, so that it couldn't unlatch.

The light grew brighter and brighter. He could clearly see now that Tasha's skull had been smashed, and from the way that she was hanging there, motionless, she looked very much as if she were dead. *Even so – people with serious head injuries often survive, don't they? She could be still alive. Oh dear God, please let her still be alive. I don't care if she needs looking after for the rest of her life. Just please let her still be alive.*

Michael managed to lean forward as well as lever himself up a little, so that his left shoulder was wedged hard against his door. He heaved himself sideways to take some of his weight off the seat-belt catch, and the third time he pushed the release button, it clicked open and he fell heavily on his hands and knees on to the upturned roof.

Immediately, he turned to Tasha. 'Tasha, can you hear me, sweetheart? Tasha, it's Michael.

11

Wake up, darling, please!'

He carefully extricated her skinny wrist from between the armrests, and drew back the sleeve of her sweater, so that he could feel if she still had a pulse. He couldn't detect one, but then he told himself that he wasn't a paramedic, so he didn't know for sure if he was feeling in the right place, and she did still feel warm.

He took hold of her seat-belt catch in both hands, ready to try and release her. He didn't want her to drop down to the roof as hard as he had, in case she knocked her head and worsened her head injury, or in case she had fractured her spine.

'Here we go, darling,' he said. 'Easy does it.'

But suddenly the light brightened to such an intensity that it bleached the color out of everything, and the inside of the Torrent was turned into an overexposed photograph. Before Michael could unfasten Tasha's seat-belt, he was overwhelmed by the four-trumpet blast of an air horn, and the stentorian bellow of a diesel engine. The horn blasted again and again, and then he heard the rubbery slithering of locked wheels on asphalt.

The slithering seemed to go on endlessly, growing louder and louder, until it began to sound like high-pitched, staccato laughter – *hee-hee-hee-hee-hee-hee!* Then Michael felt a massive collision and the Torrent was slammed across the highway, spinning around and around in circles on its roof.

It ended up by the side of the interstate, crumpled up like a badly wrapped parcel.

The driver of the huge red Kenworth tractor-trailer parked his rig by the side of the highway and then shut down his bellowing engine, so that the only sound was the wind blowing the snow between his wheels. He unhooked his CB handset and said, 'Bear Baiter, this is Bear Baiter, do you copy? I have a real bad mess-'em-up just past the six-mile marker north of Weed on I-Five! These folks are going to be needing a meat wagon, and fast! Better inform the Boy Scouts, too!'

As soon as he had made his call, he swung himself down from his cab and jogged across the scrub toward the wreckage. He was less than halfway there, however, when he heard an ambulance siren whooping and scribbling, and saw red and white lights flashing through the snow.

TWO

'Well, good *morning*!' said a warm, woman's voice.

Michael tried to lift his head to see who it was, but he couldn't. His neck was held fast in a high pink polythene collar, and when he tried to raise his hands, he found that he couldn't move his arms, either. His ankles were fastened, too.

He was strapped flat on his back, so that all he could see were pale green ceiling tiles, with diagonal stripes of wintry sunshine across them, and two fluorescent light-fittings, and part of a curtained screen with large green water lilies printed on it.

'Where am I?' he croaked. His throat was dry and his tongue felt as if it were three times its normal size, and coated with very fine sand.

He heard a man talking in a deep, soft mumble, and then a woman's face suddenly appeared, looking down at him. She was ginger-haired, green-eyed, with a sprinkle of freckles across the bridge of her nose. Michael would have guessed her age at early forties. She was wearing a white overall with the italic initials *TSC* embroidered in green on the breast pocket.

She smiled at him and said, 'How do you feel? Or should I say *"what* do you feel"?'

Michael stared at her for a long time, trying to work out if he knew her. His vision was blurry and he found it hard to focus on her clearly. There was something familiar about her – but, no, he didn't know who she was. She looked like a doctor or a nurse.

'I feel ... tired, still,' he told her. 'Have I been asleep for very long?'

She brushed back his fringe with her fingertips, almost as if he were a small boy. 'Yes ... you have. But you're awake now. That's the important thing.'

He heard the man talking again. He was speaking very quietly, but Michael distinctly heard him say '...*Yes, I believe he will ... but not for some weeks yet.*'

'Where am I?' he asked, straining again to lift up his head. 'I don't know where I am.'

Now the man appeared. He, too, was wearing a white overall with *TSC* on the pocket. He was tall, rather Arab-looking, with a shiny bald head but luxuriant black eyebrows. He was quite handsome, even though his nose was rather fleshy, and his eyes were very dark brown, but glittery, as if he had just been counting out gold coins in Ali Baba's cave.

He said, in his thick but reassuring voice, 'This is the Trinity-Shasta Clinic, near Mount Shasta, and I am Doctor Hamid. You have been involved in a serious accident, my dear sir, and it is something of a miracle that you are still with us.'

'An accident? What kind of an accident?'

'A traffic accident, on the interstate. Your car overturned and you were almost killed.'

Michael tried for a third time to lift his head, but the doctor pressed the palm of his hand against his forehead. 'Please to lie very still. Your neck was dislocated. We had to operate on you to fuse together two of the vertebrae in order to achieve realignment of your spinal column. We have every hope that you will recover completely, but I have to warn you that this usually takes some months.'

'I feel like somebody's been beating up on me, and then kicking me while I was down.'

'That doesn't surprise me at all,' said Doctor Hamid, smoothly. 'One of the common symptoms of a serious neck injury such as yours is chronic pain in many different locations all over your body. But we have been giving you intravenous analgesics to ease your discomfort, and we will continue to do so for as long as you need

15

them.'

Michael frowned, and said, '*Where* did you say this was?'

'Trinity-Shasta Clinic, near Mount Shasta.'

'Mount Shasta? What the hell am I doing way up here?'

The red-haired woman drew up a chair close to his bed and sat down. 'This is the nearest trauma clinic to the location where you had your accident,' she said. 'You were lucky. Well – you weren't lucky to have your accident, I'm not saying that. But Trinity-Shasta has one of the most advanced spinal units in the country. If you'd been taken in to some small-town emergency room, you could well have died, or been paralysed from the neck down for the rest of your life.'

'I'm still trying to think what I'm doing near Mount Shasta. The last thing I remember I was...'

He stopped. What *was* the last thing that he could remember? Talking to somebody about something in some bar. He could remember the stained-glass window over the door, and the raucous sound of people laughing, but he couldn't think where it was, or who he had been talking to, or what they had been talking about.

The red-haired woman said, 'Don't worry about it. It's not important. It will all come back to you. Are you thirsty? Maybe you'd like some water or some cranberry juice.'

Michael said, 'We were talking about ... something to do with light. That was it. The speed of light. Why were we talking about that?'

'Who were you talking to?' the red-haired woman asked him.

Michael squeezed his eyes tight shut and tried to visualize the stained-glass window and the face of the man who was sitting underneath it, talking to him. But all he could see was a featureless blur, and all he could hear was a muffled blurting sound.

'No,' he said. 'It's no good. I just can't remember.'

'My name's Catherine, by the way,' the red-haired woman told him. 'Catherine Connor. *Doctor* Catherine Connor.'

'Oh, right,' said Michael. He was beginning to think that she was quite attractive, in a gingery way, even though she must be four or five years older than him. 'Doctor of what, exactly?'

'Post-traumatic therapy, both physical and psychological. I help people to get over traumatic events in their lives, like severe shocks or brain damage or spinal injuries, which is why I'm here talking to you.'

'Nothing personal, Doctor, but you sound expensive. How am I going to pay for all of this?'

Dr Connor smiled and shook her head. 'Don't worry. You won't be charged. The Trinity-Shasta Clinic is a non-profit research foundation, privately funded. You may not believe it, but we'll be getting a whole lot more out of *you* than you'll be getting out of us.'

'How long do I have to stay strapped down like this? I feel like Frankenstein's monster.'

'That depends on Doctor Hamid. When your

vertebrae were dislocated, that injury also tore your neck muscles, your blood vessels, your ligaments, your nerves and your esophagus. But of course we'll be taking regular CT scans, and as soon as we're confident that you can move without causing yourself any further injury, we'll get you up on your feet. I personally believe that patients should start movement therapy as soon as possible.'

'OK. Thanks,' he coughed. 'Maybe I could have that drink now. What do I call you – Doctor Connor? Or Catherine?'

'We're going to be seeing a whole lot of each other, so Catherine is fine.'

'Sorry I can't shake your hand, Catherine. I'm...'

He stopped. He felt as if a black shutter had slammed down inside of his head. He simply couldn't think what his name was. Not only that, he couldn't think of *any* names, so that he could run through them and try to remember which one was his.

He stared at Doctor Connor in complete bewilderment, blinking. How could he not remember his own name? But there was nothing.

Doctor Connor reached out and stroked his fringe again. 'Your name is – *what?*' she coaxed him, very softly. 'Don't try too hard to remember it. Think of your mother instead, calling you. Think of what your friends used to sing, when it was your birthday.'

She paused, and then she sang, *Happy birthday, dear la-la-la! Happy birthday to you.* Can you remember the cake, and the candles? Can

18

you hear them singing, inside your head?'

Michael listened and listened, but there was nothing inside his head, only blankness and silence. He couldn't remember his mother. He couldn't remember the sound of her voice. He couldn't even remember what she looked like.

After a while, he gasped like a swimmer coming up for air. 'I don't know, Catherine! I just can't think of it!'

'Don't get upset,' she told him. 'It's not at all unusual for people to suffer from amnesia, after an accident. There are ways of rebuilding your memories, and that's one of the things that you and I will be doing together, little by little.'

'But how the hell can I not even know my own name?'

'It's really not uncommon. I worked with young marines who came back from Iraq, suffering from just the same problem. Your brain has suffered from such a shock that it has simply shut down, like somebody hiding under the bedcovers and refusing to come out.'

'Tell me some names.'

'What?'

'Tell me some names and maybe I'll be able to tell if one of them is mine.'

'That won't work. You may pick a name simply because it rings a bell. It might not be your name at all, and that will only confuse you even more.'

Michael lay there staring at the ceiling. Then he glanced sideways at Doctor Connor. The sun was shining in her hair so that she looked almost like an angel. He had only just met her and yet he

19

felt desperately dependent on her. How else was he going to find out who he was and what he was doing here, up near Mount Shasta?

The strange thing was that even though he couldn't think of his name, he knew that he didn't belong around here, and that he lived someplace far to the south. It was where that bar was – that noisy bar with the stained-glass window, where he had been talking about the speed of light.

'My accident,' he said. 'Do you know what happened?'

'Not in any detail, no. The paramedics said that your SUV crossed over on to the wrong side of the interstate, and got hit by a truck coming the other way.'

Michael closed his eyes again, and tried to imagine it, but he couldn't. The black shutter remained firmly shut. How can you get hit by a truck and not remember it?

But then he suddenly thought: *Surely I must have had some ID on me, when the paramedics brought me in here? A wallet, with credit cards and a driver's license? A cellphone? And what about my license plate? The police would have been able to check my identity with the Department of Motor Vehicles.*

'Catherine,' he said.

She had been jotting notes on a yellow legal pad, but now she looked up, and he could tell by her expression that she knew what he was going to say.

'You know my name already,' he said.

Catherine nodded. 'I do, yes. But encouraging

20

you to remember it yourself – that's an important part of your cognitive therapy.'

'Tell me what it is.'

'It won't help.'

'I don't care if it helps or not, Catherine. Please. I have to know what my name is. Not just that – who am I? Where do I live? Do my family know what's happened to me? Are any of them coming to visit?'

Doctor Connor flicked back a few pages in her legal pad.

'I shouldn't really be telling you this. It's *much* against my better judgment. I should really be giving you an AMI – that's an Autobiographical Memory Interview. By doing that, I can test how severe your retrograde amnesia really is, and treat it accordingly.'

'Please – just tell me what my name is!'

'All right,' she said, and read from her notes. 'Your name is Gregory John Merrick. You live at ten forty-four Pine Street, San Francisco. You share an apartment with a work colleague, Kenneth Geary. You are a marine engineer working for Moffatt and Nichol. Your sister Sue lives in Oakland with her husband Jimmy and their two children. Your father died two years ago. Your mother now lives in Baywood Apartments close to your sister. Your sister brought her up here to see you soon after your accident and they regularly call to check on your progress.'

She turned over two pages and said, 'As a matter of fact, your sister called only yesterday afternoon, and spoke to Nurse Sheringham.'

After she had finished, Michael said nothing.

'Does any of that help?' asked Doctor Connor, after a while.

Michael was unable to shake his head, because of his high plastic collar, but tears slid out of the side of each eye.

'I still can't remember,' he told her. 'I still don't know who I am.'

'I'm sorry,' she said. 'It's the way your brain works. It *can* re-route your memory paths, so that they bypass the shocked or damaged areas, but it needs you to initiate it.'

She stood up, and tugged a Kleenex out of the box beside the bed, and dabbed his eyes for him, and helped him to blow his nose.

'How long was I asleep for?' he asked her.

'Well, let's put it this way, you've been quite the Rip Van Winkle.'

'How long, Catherine?'

She looked at him steadily, and this time she didn't smile. 'Your accident happened on November eleventh. Today is February sixth. That makes it two months, three weeks, and four days.'

THREE

The first day that Catherine took him outside, it was bright but bitingly cold. The sky was almost completely clear, except for a few wispy mares' tails over Mount Shasta.

Michael was surprised to see how close the mountain was. He guessed that it couldn't have been more than five or six miles away.

'Did you ever climb it?' he asked Catherine.

'Once, yes, two summers ago. We got together a party from the clinic. Everything they say about that mountain is true. What can I say? It's very serene up there. You feel closer to God, or Buddha, or whoever you believe in.'

'It's the fifth highest peak in the Cascade Range,' said Michael.

He did an exaggerated double-take, and then he twisted around in his wheelchair and said, 'How the hell did I know that?'

But then he held up his hand and said, 'Wait ... I also happen to know that it's four thousand three hundred twenty-two meters high, and that it has an estimated volume of eight hundred fifty cubic kilometers.'

'Well, there you are,' said Catherine. 'Little bits and pieces are starting to come back to you. You're an engineer, aren't you, so it's not surprising you're good on statistics.'

She pushed him along the red-brick path to the far end of the clinic's rose garden. The rose beds were lumpy with snow, and the roses themselves looked like nothing more than frozen sticks. Michael was wearing a padded navy-blue jacket with a hood, and insulated boots, and he had a thick plaid blanket tucked around him. Catherine was wearing a brindled fox-fur coat and a bobbly white knitted hat.

They stopped, and Catherine sat down on a bench. Their breath was smoking in the cold, so that it looked from a distance as if they were taking a cigarette break.

'Did you talk to Doctor Hamid this morning?' asked Michael. 'Does he have any idea how much longer I'll have to stay here?'

Catherine shook her head. 'It's really hard to say. Physically you're doing pretty well, although Doctor Hamid is still concerned about the shock sustained by your spine. That can take months to heal completely. It's your amnesia that worries us the most. We can't send you home yet because you simply can't remember where you live or where you work or even what it is that you do.

'Your sister Sue has offered to look after you, but you need highly specialized amnesia therapy, which you can only get here. You could hardly commute from Oakland every day.'

'So you simply don't know how long it's going to take?'

'Based on previous patients, Gregory, I'd say three to four months. I can't be more precise than that. It may be that your neural pathways suddenly open up, and you start to remember everything in a flood. To be honest with you, though, I've only known that to happen very rarely.'

Michael sat back in his wheelchair, which creaked under his weight. He still felt chronically tired, and he ached all over, especially his shoulders and his back, and when he tried to stand up his knees gave him such jabs of pain that he had to bite his lower lip to stop himself from shouting out loud.

What tired him more than anything, though, was not being able to remember who he was. He felt as if he were banging his head against a wall, again and again, as if he were autistic. By the end of the day, he was mentally exhausted, and his brain ached as well as his body.

Even though it was partially screened by the leafless trees that surrounded the rose garden, he could clearly see the dazzling white peaks of Mount Shasta. For a split second, the sight of them brought back a flash of feeling. Not a fully formed memory, but a flicker of light and shade, a snatch of somebody's voice, and – most evocative of all – the briefest hint of some light, flowery perfume.

'Are you all right, Gregory?' Catherine asked him. 'You look ... I don't know. You look puzzled.'

He gave her a quick, dismissive shake of his head. 'I'm OK. Just kind of disoriented, I guess. Remember, this is the first time I've been outside in over three months, even if I was asleep for most of them.'

'Well, I want to show you something,' said Catherine. 'In fact, this is the whole reason I brought you out here.'

She stood up and continued to push him along the bumpy red-brick path. If he had been a small child, he would have said *errrrrrrrrrrrrrrrr*, so that his voice wobbled. He wondered if *that* were a memory from his childhood, his mother pushing him in a baby buggy, and in his mind's eye he tried to turn around to see his mother's face, but he couldn't.

Catherine pushed him through the brick archway at the end of the rose garden, and down a small wet concrete slope. Now they were outside the white concrete walls of the clinic, in a curving street of neat single-story houses, some of them pastel pink and some of them pastel yellow, with snow-covered roofs, all set well back from the road behind their own snow-covered front lawns. All of them had cars and SUVs parked in their driveways, but all of these were covered in snow, too, and there were no tire-tracks across the sidewalks, so it looked to Michael as if none of the residents had been out today.

The road itself had been gritted and cleared of snow, so Catherine pushed Michael along the middle. The street was sunny and almost completely silent, except for the very faint sound of a television show from one of the houses, with occasional bursts of studio laughter.

There were trees on either side, but all of these were bare. Michael thought of the words *'Thus in the winter stands the lonely tree'* but he

26

couldn't remember why he knew them or where they came from.

'This is Trinity,' said Catherine. She stopped, and took a tissue out of her pocket, and dabbed her nose. 'This is our local community.'

'Looks pretty quiet,' said Michael. 'In fact, I'd say "sleepy".'

'That's why people come to live here,' said Catherine, resuming her wheelchair-pushing. 'They want peace, and fresh air, and good neighbors. And more peace.'

'So where do they work? Where's the nearest town to here?'

'Some of them are retired, but most of them work from home. One or two of them have businesses in Redding or Yreka. I think one of them is a personal injury lawyer. But of course nobody's at work today because it's Saturday.'

She kept on pushing him along the street, around the curve, until they came to a wide-open area like a playing field, with houses all around it. A young girl in a red duffel coat was walking a shaggy white sheepdog around the edge of the field, while another young girl in a pink windbreaker was circling around and around her on a bicycle.

The girl on the bicycle pedaled up to Michael and Catherine and began to circle around Michael's wheelchair. She had frizzy brown hair fastened with wooden beads into bunches. Her face was very pale and she had a livid pink lightning-flash scar on her left temple. It almost looked as if somebody had hit her with a machete.

'Who are *you*?' she asked Michael. 'I never

27

saw *you* before. Are you a cripple?'

Catherine said, 'His name's Gregory, Jemima, and he was hurt in a car crash. But he's getting better and soon he'll be walking again, so you'd better watch what you say to him or else he's going to come after you when he can walk and give you a pasting.'

Jemima kept on circling around and around. 'He'd better not *try*! I'll tell my mom, else.'

The girl with the sheepdog called out, 'Come *on*, Jem! We're going to be late!'

'Where are you going?' Michael asked her. 'Anyplace exciting?'

Jemima tapped the side of her nose with her finger and said, 'Mind your own beeswax, Mr Nosy Parker Cripple!'

With that, she furiously pedaled off to catch up with her friend.

'Kids!' said Catherine. 'Mind you, I was probably worse than that when I was her age. I was always getting myself into scrapes!'

Michael would have liked to have been able to say 'me, too!' but he couldn't remember his childhood at all. Nothing. He couldn't remember if he had ever owned a bicycle, or roller-skates, or even if he had ever climbed trees.

Thus in the winter stands the lonely tree.

Catherine continued to push him around the playing field. The sun was shining on the snow so brightly that it was difficult to look at it without being dazzled. As he lifted his gloved hand to shield his eyes, Michael had another momentary flash of feeling, like the sensation he had experienced in the rose garden. The sound of a voice –

maybe a woman's voice. A flicker of light, and the faint smell of some floral perfume. Then it was gone.

Looking across the playing field, he saw two forlorn basketball posts, their nets clotted with snow. What he thought was strange, though, was that there were no footprints in the snow, none at all, human or animal. No ski-tracks or sledge-tracks, either, which he would have expected, especially so close to a winter resort like Mount Shasta, where almost everybody must own a pair of skis or a sledge or at least a child's toboggan.

He thought of mentioning the playing field's pristine condition to Catherine, but he decided not to, although he didn't quite know why. Instead, he said, 'So, Catherine! Where are you taking me? Or are *you* going to tell me to mind my own beeswax, too?'

'I'm taking you right *here*,' said Catherine. She pushed him up the snowy slope in front of a pale yellow house and then maneuvered his wheelchair through the narrow space beside a snow-covered Jeep Compass. As they approached the front porch, the door opened, and a young woman appeared, smiling and lifting her hand in greeting.

'Isobel! Hi!' called Catherine. She turned Michael's wheelchair around so that she could heave it backward up the two front steps. The young woman took one side of it and helped her to lift it over the ledge into the hallway.

'Now I *do* feel like a cripple,' said Michael.

'Oh, don't be so silly,' Catherine scolded him. 'You're just recuperating, that's all!'

She turned the wheelchair around and pushed Michael through to the living room. There was a wide bay window, with a window-seat, but natural-colored calico blinds had been drawn right down to the window sills, so that the light in the living-room was pale and muted.

Michael looked around. The room was furnished with two traditional armchairs and a bulky couch, all upholstered in a busy floral fabric. On the left-hand wall there was a sandstone fireplace with a gas log fire blazing in it, and over the fireplace hung a large framed print of a log cabin, in a gloomy forest, with three or four trappers gathered outside it.

Below the print, on a varnished pine shelf, stood a collection of small china figurines, most of them dogs or Native Americans in buckskins or Disney characters like Bambi and Thumper – although, if anybody had asked him, Michael wouldn't have been able to remember what their names were.

'Here, why don't I help you take off your jacket?' said Isobel. 'It's real warm in here, isn't it, but I do like to keep it toasty.'

She came up to him, untucked his blanket and lifted it off his knees. Then she started to unfasten the stud at his neck. He said, 'Hold up, Isobel. I *can* stand up, just about. That will make it a darn sight easier.'

It took him two attempts, but he managed to heave himself out of his wheelchair into a standing position, and balance himself unsteadily in front of the fire, shuffling his feet every now and then as if he were drunk. Isobel smiled and tugged down the zipper of his padded jacket.

'You'll be walking before you know it,' she told him. 'And that *will* be useful, especially in the fall, when the leaves need sweeping.'

When she said that, Michael blinked his blurry eyes and made a first effort to focus on her more acutely. She was slim, about five-feet-four, with a shiny brunette bob that was cut up high and angular at the back of her neck, but with a heavy fringe. She was actually quite pretty, with high cheekbones and big, brown, wide-apart eyes. She had a small, straight nose and a well-shaped chin, and full pink lips that looked as if she were pouting, or just about to blow him a kiss.

She was wearing a clinging purple roll-neck sweater and tight black slacks. She had very large breasts for a woman so small and so slim, but very narrow hips.

'I'm sorry, Isobel,' he said. 'I can't introduce myself for the simple reason that I can't remember who I am.'

Isobel helped him to drag his arms out of his sleeves, and then she folded his jacket over and laid it down on the window seat. 'Catherine told me that your name is Gregory. Or Greg, according to your sister.'

'Well, she told *me* that, too. But I don't *feel* like Gregory. I don't remember anybody calling me Gregory, or Greg, not ever, or signing my name *Gregory*. If you gave me a pen right now and asked me to give you my autograph, I wouldn't know where to start. I really wouldn't.'

'What's in a name?' said Isobel. 'You know what W.B. Yeats once said?'

31

'No, I'm sorry, I don't. Who's W.B. Yeats?'

'He was a famous Irish poet. He said that the creations of any writer are nothing more than the moods and passions of his own heart, to which he gives Christian names and surnames, and then sends off to walk the earth.'

'I'm not sure I understand what that means.'

'But I believe that's what *we* are, Gregory – us human beings. All of us, we're nothing more than the moods and passions of God, to which He has given names, and then sent out to do what He wants us to do. What really counts is what kind of a mood we happen to be in, or what kind of a passion – not what we're called.'

'Well, I guess that's one point of view,' Michael agreed. 'But I'd still like to know what my name is. I'm ninety-nine per cent sure that I *am* Gregory. I must be. That's the name in my driver's license, and the name embossed on my credit cards. But I don't *know* that I'm Gregory, not in my head, and not in my heart, either.'

'But it won't upset you if I call you Greg?'

'Of course not. You can call me anything you darn well like, so far as I'm concerned. But you said something about your leaves needed sweeping, in the fall.'

'Oh, I was only joking. That's unless you really like gardening, then you're more than welcome.'

'I don't remember if I do like gardening or not. But I don't think I'll still be here in the fall. At least I very much hope not.'

There was a long, awkward silence. Isobel looked across at Catherine and then Catherine said, 'I'm afraid it's more than likely, Gregory.'

'What? You're not serious!'

'I didn't want to depress you before I brought you to meet Isobel, but Doctor Hamid thinks he probably won't be able to discharge you until the late summer at the earliest.'

Michael sat down heavily in his wheelchair. 'That long? I thought you said three or four months! Surely I'll start to get my memory back before then?'

'We're hoping you do, of course. But that's why I brought you here today, Gregory. I wanted to prepare you.'

'Prepare me for what, Catherine? I don't understand.'

'I wanted you to meet Isobel. As soon as you're physically well enough not to need twenty-four-hour care, you'll come to live here, with her. That way, you'll be able to live as normal a life as possible, but still be close enough to come to the clinic twice a day for post-traumatic amnesia therapy.'

She held up both hands. 'If you don't like the idea, or if you think that you and Isobel won't get on together, please tell me now. We did everything we could to select somebody compatible for you.'

'I'm sure we'll get on wonderfully,' smiled Isobel. 'I hope you like lasagne, Greg! That's my specialty.'

Michael slowly shook his head. 'I don't know if I do or not, Isobel. I don't remember. I don't think I can even remember what lasagne actually is.'

'But you don't have any objections to coming

to live here?' asked Catherine.

'I suppose not, no.'

'OK, then. If you could wait here just a couple of minutes, please, Gregory. I have to have a quick word with Isobel about some of the arrangements.'

'Sure,' said Michael. 'I'm not going anyplace.'

Catherine and Isobel went out of the living room and through to the kitchen. Michael heard them talking for a few seconds, something about 'not expecting too much'. Then they closed the kitchen door and there was silence.

He sat in his wheelchair for a while, looking around. He thought that Isobel was good to look at, and very likeable, although he wasn't at all sure about her taste in home decoration. She couldn't have picked a bleaker and more depressing picture to hang over the fireplace, and as for all of her china figurines...

But maybe *he* had china figurines over his fireplace, back at his apartment on Pine Street, and pictures hanging on his walls that were even bleaker and more depressing than this one. He just couldn't remember.

In the opposite corner of the room stood a small side table, with a crochet mat on top of it, and on top of the crochet mat stood a framed color photograph of a sallow, solemn-looking man with rimless eyeglasses and swept-back gray hair. Maybe it was Isobel's father, although Michael couldn't see much of a family likeness. In fact the man in the photograph looked Hispanic.

After a few minutes' more waiting, Michael

thought that he might as well put his jacket back on. Grunting with effort, he hoisted himself out of his wheelchair and limped across to the window seat. He bent over stiffly to pick up his jacket, but as he did so he heard an engine running, right outside. He reached over and lifted up the calico blind, so that he could see what it was.

A black Escalade was parked in the street right in front of Isobel's house. Its windows were all tinted black, but the passenger-side window had been lowered halfway down, so that he could see a white-haired, white-faced man in sunglasses sitting in it. When he lifted the blind a little higher, however, so that he could have a better look, the passenger-side window was immediately closed, and the Escalade drove off, leaving nothing but a ghostly cloud of exhaust fumes.

FOUR

Doctor Connor knocked on his open door and said, 'Surprise! Guess what?'

Michael was sitting in the armchair beside his bed trying to solve a general knowledge crossword. 'Sorry,' he said. 'I have no idea. I can't even guess ninety-nine per cent of this goddamned crossword.'

So far he had managed only to fill in the word *mesa*, in answer to the question *'Large flat-topped mountain on which standing water may be found, and cattle grazed?'*

He knew that it was a *mesa* with even more certainty than he knew his own name. He also knew that a larger flat-topped mountain was a *plateau* and a smaller flat-topped mountain was a *butte* – but he had no idea *how* he knew it, or why.

'Your sister Sue is coming to visit you this afternoon. She should be here around three. Isn't that great?'

Michael looked up. 'I guess so, yes. I just wish I could remember what she looked like.'

'Well, that's the main reason she wanted to come. She thought that if you saw her it might spark some memories.'

'You showed me that picture of her. That didn't help.'

'Maybe when you see her in person, and hear her talking.'

Michael folded up his newspaper and tucked it into the rack at the side of his nightstand. 'I hope it helps, for her sake. It must be taking her at least five hours to drive here from Oakland.'

'See? You know that much. She's staying overnight in our hospitality suite, so you'll be able to see her again tomorrow before she drives home.'

When she had gone, Michael eased himself out of his chair and went to look out of the window. His room was in a wing at the south-east side of the clinic, and so he could see the front entrance with its covered portico and its two snow-topped bay trees standing guard by the doors. He could also see part of the parking lot, with a fluorescent orange snow-sweeper being driven slowly up and down between the rows of parked cars.

So, his sister Sue was coming to see him. He supposed that he ought to be pleased, and excited. After all, she was the first member of his family to come see him since he had regained consciousness. The problem was, he didn't feel anything at all. He simply felt adrift, like the sole survivor of a yacht sinking in mid-ocean, without a single landmark in sight. Doctor Connor had shown him a picture of Sue printed from her Facebook page, a tall blonde in a blue-and-white dress, squinting at the sun, but he hadn't recognized her, and neither could he remember growing up with her, or anything that they had done together when they were children. The name 'Sue' meant nothing.

Still – it was possible that Doctor Connor was right, and that when he saw her in the flesh, and heard her talk, he would remember her.

He was still standing there, looking out of the window, when he heard somebody coming into the room behind him, without knocking.

He turned around and saw that it was a tall, gray-haired man in a silvery-gray suit. He had a long, narrow face, with that slightly yellowish look of a faded suntan. His eyes were hooded and he had a thin, curved nose, which gave him the appearance of an elderly bird of prey.

He gave Michael a lipless smile and held out his hand.

'Mr Merrick! Gregory! It's very good to see you up and about! My name is Kingsley Vane. I'm the medical director of Trinity-Shasta

Clinic.'

Michael hesitated for a moment and then shook Kingsley Vane's hand. It was a strange handshake, dry and elusive, as if a snake were slithering out of his grasp.

'I've been watching your progress closely, ever since you were brought in here,' said Kingsley Vane. 'Do sit down; I know that you've been suffering some pain in your knees.'

Michael returned to his armchair. Kingsley Vane leaned back against the side of his bed, with his arms folded.

'How are you feeling in yourself, Mr Merrick? You don't mind if I call you Gregory, do you?'

'Confused, mainly,' Michael admitted. 'Confused and kind of depressed. I want to get out of here and get on with my life but since I can't remember anything about my life, not a single goddamned thing, I don't see how I can get on with it.'

'I do understand,' said Kingsley Vane, nodding. 'I remember that one of our amnesia patients described his condition as being like losing his place in a book he was reading, only he had lost the book, too.'

'Yes. That sums it up pretty well. Except that I can't even remember the *title* of the book, so that I can order another copy.'

Kingsley Vane said, 'Believe me, Gregory, we're doing everything we can to restore your memory, and our expertise in post-traumatic care is second to none. As you'll discover when you leave the clinic and take up residence with Mrs Weston, several Trinity residents are former or ongoing patients of ours. That's part of the reason they live here, to have continuing access to our aftercare facilities.'

He gave Michael another thin smile. 'From our point of view, Gregory, we *care* about our patients, not just while they're here in the clinic proper, but long after they've been discharged. Post-traumatic care never really ends, ever.'

'I guess it ends when you die.'

Kingsley Vane said nothing to that, but continued to smile at him. After a while, he unfolded his arms, stood up straight and said, 'Anyhow, I very much hope that you'll be comfortable with Mrs Weston. If you're not, for any reason at all, please let Doctor Connor know immediately, won't you? We need you to be stable, and positive. Your amnesia therapy will be much more effective if you are.'

'OK, thank you,' said Michael.

Kingsley Vane turned to go, but then he stopped, and turned back, with a very concentrated expression on his face, and said, 'By the way ... the other residents of Trinity that I was talking about ... those who have undergone treatment here at the clinic ... How shall I put this? Some of them still bear the scars, so to speak ... if not physically, then mentally. So if their behavior on occasions is a little *off-key*, I trust that you'll understand, and respond with sensitivity.'

'*Off-key*?' asked Michael.

'Well ... some of them have been through a lot, and it's taken them months if not *years* of therapy to come to terms with it. We're always very anxious not to set them back.'

'OK,' said Michael. 'I get it. I'll be sensitivity incarnate. And don't worry about me and Isobel Weston. She seems like a real nice person.'

'One more thing,' said Kingsley Vane. 'I gather your sister is coming to see you this afternoon. Do give her my good wishes. And I very much hope that her visit rings a few bells.'

He left the room, calling out as he did so to an intern who had just passed the doorway, 'Newton! A word, please!'

I hope her visit rings a few bells. For some unaccountable reason that made Michael think of the bells which people who were fearful of being buried alive would have suspended above their graves, with a string that was connected to their casket and knotted around their finger. He knew that was where the term 'graveyard shift' had first come from – a verger who would sit up all night in a cemetery, listening for the sound of bells. He also knew that the people who rang those bells were called 'dead ringers'. Not that any of them ever did.

Now, what the hell made me think of that?

They brought him his lunch on a tray – three slices of roast chicken with green beans, sweetcorn, hash browns and gravy. It tasted microwaved. Outside his window, as he ate, a light snow began to fall.

When he had finished eating, he went into his bathroom to make sure that he looked presentable for his sister's visit. He stood in front of the mirror and stared at himself. He couldn't remember what his sister looked like, but the strange thing was that he couldn't really remember what *he* looked like, either. Was this really him? This pale, skinny young man with tousled brown hair and worried brown eyes and a thin, rather studious-looking face. He thought he looked like a not-very-successful tennis player.

He put on a fresh green-and-white striped shirt, washed his teeth and brushed his hair. He couldn't think why, but looking at himself in the mirror made him feel lonely, as if there ought to be somebody standing next to him, smiling.

Again, he experienced that split-second flash of light and shadow and sound, and this time he thought he heard a girl's voice say, *you shouldn't*. He thought he could smell that flowery perfume, too, but that faded so quickly that he couldn't be sure.

You shouldn't. Shouldn't *what?*

He went back into his room and sat in his chair and switched on the TV. He flicked through the channels, but he had a choice only of *Max & Ruby*, *Charmed*, *Squawk on the Street* or *Plaza Sésamo*, so he switched it off. Outside, the snow was falling thicker and thicker, as if God were in a hurry to bury the world forever.

He was still staring out of the window, thinking about nothing much, when he became aware of somebody standing in the corridor outside his open door. As soon as he turned around, she stepped inside, smiling. A tall, blonde woman wearing a red beret and a thick red-and-orange duffel-coat, and brown leather boots. She pulled off her beret and shook her curly hair and said, 'Greg!'

He started to get up, but she gently pushed him

41

back into his chair and said, 'No, you don't have to. I know your knees were all smashed up.'

She had a thin face like him, and he thought that she was quite attractive, although he couldn't really tell for sure if there was any family resemblance. She had very large pale-blue eyes with sleepy eyelids, a straight Pre-Raphaelite nose and full, bow-shaped lips. As attractive as she was, he had no feeling at all that he knew her, even from her voice.

'You're Sue,' he said.

'That's right, baby brother.'

'I'm sorry, I'm not going to pretend that I recognize you, because I simply don't. They showed me your Facebook picture, and they told me you were coming to visit me, but that's the only way I know who you are.'

She dragged over another chair from the opposite corner of the room and took off her coat. Underneath she was wearing a long red knitted dress with a wide red patent-leather belt. She sat down next to him and laid her hand on top of his. He noticed her wedding-band and her engagement ring, white gold set with a large solitaire diamond.

'I know you don't recognize me,' she smiled. 'Doctor Connor has told me all about your condition – what you can remember and what you can't, which is pretty much everything. But she's very optimistic. She thinks that given enough time, it'll all come back to you.'

'Well, I'm glad she's optimistic, because I'm not. I can't even remember my own name.'

'You're Gregory.'

'That's what everybody keeps telling me. But I don't *know* I'm Gregory. It's really hard to explain.'

Sue gave his hand a squeeze and said, 'When you were very small, you used to call yourself "Weggy". You used to have a bright blue teddy bear and for some reason you called him "Numby". Mom used to see you coming up the path and say, "Here they come, Weggy and Numby."'

Michael shrugged. 'Sorry, it means absolutely nothing. It doesn't bring anything back at all. I know all kinds of irrelevant stuff, like facts and figures and random bits of general knowledge. I knew how long it was going to take you to drive here. But the rest of my mind ... it's like an empty room, with the light off.'

'You don't even remember Gemma?'

'Unh-hunh. Who's Gemma?'

'Your very first girlfriend. She was the love of your life – well, the love of your life until you met Rhoda. And then Rhoda was the love of your life until you met Holly.'

Michael shook his head. 'No. You didn't bring pictures of them, did you?'

'I will next time. But listen, I have an idea. Why don't we call Mom?'

'You can call her, sure. But what am I going to say to her?'

'Just say, "Hi, Mom, it's Greg ... I'm calling from the clinic. I just want you to know that I'm getting better every day, and that I'll come to see you pretty soon."'

'OK. If you think it might cheer her up. But I don't like the idea of lying to her.'

'It's not *her* I'm concerned about. It's you. If you hear Mom's voice, maybe it'll bring something back.'

She took a cellphone out of her big red purse and prodded a number. She lifted it to her ear for a moment, and then smiled and said, 'Mom! Hi, Mom! It's Sue! Guess who's sitting here right next to me?'

She passed the cell over. Michael reluctantly took it and said, 'Hi, Mom! This is Greg!'

'Oh, *Greg*!' said a quavery voice. 'It's so good to hear from you, my darling! How are you feeling?'

'I'm still in the clinic, Mom, but I'm very much better. I should be out of here before too long and then I'll come see you.'

'Make sure you get out of there by July second.'

'Oh, yeah? What's so special about July second?'

'It's my *birthday*, Greg! Fancy you forgetting that! I want to see you on my birthday!'

'OK, Mom. I'll pass you back to Sue.'

Sue was rummaging in her purse for something, so Michael held on to the cell for a moment. He was about to tell his mother to hold on for a moment, when he heard her say, 'Oh, shoot, George! Look at that snow! I wanted to go to Ray's Food Place this afternoon!'

Sue said, 'Aha! Here it is!' She lifted up a yellow photo wallet, and Michael handed the cell back to her. Sue took it and said, 'Hi, Mom – look, I'll be back around this time tomorrow afternoon. You have that doctor's appointment, don't you? OK, no problem. OK. Lots of love, then. Greg is blowing you a kiss. Bye.'

'Well?' she asked Michael. 'Anything?'

'If you're asking me if I recognized Mom's voice, then the answer is no. She sounded like some old woman to me, that's all.'

'Try these, then,' said Sue. She passed over the photo wallet, which contained about twenty glossy pictures. Michael looked through them, while Sue gave him a commentary, tapping each one with her red-varnished fingernail.

'There's you and me, on the beach. I was seven then, which means you must have been five. There's you with your first bike, when we lived in Emerald Lake Hills. There's you with your friend Carl. Love the hairstyle! You were inseparable, you two; you didn't need a brother, you had Carl. And that's you the day you graduated from Cal Maritime Academy.'

Michael examined the photographs carefully. There was no doubt that it was him, or some boy who looked uncannily like him. He turned some of them over, and they had scribbled captions on the back like *Gregory and Carl, Roy Cloud Elementary, April 1989* and *Greg at Moss Beach, September '91.*

He handed them back. 'Thanks, but they still don't bring anything back. Even if I can't remember it, though, it looks like I was pretty happy. I mean I wasn't half-starved and dressed in rags and I didn't have to beg for money on the streets.'

Sue said, 'Come on – let's try to stop remembering things for a while. Doctor Connor told me that prompting you with photographs and remi- niscences was all very well, but it's your own brain that needs to do all the work, and that you need plenty of rest as well as people like me trying to jog your memory.'

'What do you want to do then?'

'Anything you like. I'm happy just to sit here and watch TV. It's going to take us some time to get used to each other. There's no point in us trying to swap stories about childhood if you can't remember any of it, is there?'

'No, I guess not.'

He switched on the TV in time for *Days Of Our Lives*. Sue held his hand again, to show him that even if he didn't remember her, he was still her brother, and she loved him. It was a strange feeling, watching TV while holding hands with a woman he didn't know, but it was unexpectedly reassuring, too. Before, he had felt that he was adrift in the ocean, without any landmarks in sight. Sue, at least, was some kind of landmark – some point of reference from which he could start to rediscover who he was.

He suddenly woke up. The TV was still on, but it was mute, and Sue's chair next to him was empty. He must have dropped off halfway through *Days Of Our Lives*.

He gripped the side of the bed and lifted himself out of his chair. He felt stiff all over, especially his neck and his spine. He was often dozing off like that, but he supposed it was all part of his brain and his body trying to conserve his strength.

He looked out of the window. It was still snowing, but only lightly. He was about to sit down again when he saw the revolving door in the middle of the clinic's main entrance catch the light, and Sue stepped out, wearing her red beret and her red-and-orange coat.

She hesitated for a moment at the top of the steps and then she started to cross the forecourt toward the parking lot. As she did so, another woman appeared from around the side of the clinic and started to walk toward her. This woman was wearing a long black coat and a knitted black Peruvian beanie with strings hanging down. Although Michael couldn't hear her, she obviously called out to Sue because she raised her arm and at the same time Sue stopped and turned around and waited for her to catch up with her.

The two women embraced and kissed as if they were old friends, and immediately started talking to each other, with the snow falling on their hats and their shoulders. Michael couldn't see clearly at first who the other woman was, but then both of them laughed at something, and stepped back a little as they did so, and he recognized her as Isobel Weston, the woman with whom he was going to be staying.

He stood watching them, frowning. According to Doctor Connor, Sue had been up here to see him only twice since his accident, and it seemed extraordinary that she had made such a good friend of Isobel in only two visits. Still, she had probably stayed overnight on each occasion, which could have given the women the opportunity to get to know each other quite well.

After they had talked for three or four minutes, they kissed and embraced again, and Sue continued on her way to the parking lot, while Isobel walked around the side of the south-east wing and out of sight.

Sue appeared out of the parking lot a few seconds later, driving a silver Lexus SUV. She looked left and right, and then drove out of the clinic and turned right, away from Trinity and towards the interstate.

That night, Michael suddenly opened his eyes and sat bolt upright in bed.

It was 3:23 am, according to the digital clock on his nightstand, but his room wasn't totally dark because the lights were always left on in the corridor outside. He could hear the night orderlies talking and the squeaking of trolley wheels.

Look at that snow! That's what his mother had said. *Oh, shoot, George! Look at that snow!*

But wasn't his mother supposed to be living in a rest home in Oakland, close to his sister? And although it occasionally snowed on the high ground around San Francisco, it *never* snowed in the Bay area ... or hardly ever.

So if his mother had looked out of her window and seen that it was snowing ... where the hell was she?

FIVE

The next morning he had an early breakfast with Sue in the clinic's commissary. They sat at a green Formica-topped table next to the window, looking out over the snow-covered rose garden. The reflected light from the snow made them both look unnaturally pale.

Sue had tied her hair back with a red silk scarf with patterns of golden stirrups on it, and was wearing a red roll-neck sweater and black jeans. Michael thought she looked like the owner of a riding stable for tourists who didn't know one end of a horse from the other; and there was no doubt that she did have that air of bossiness about her.

'When are you setting off back to Oakland?' he asked her. 'The forecast said it's going to start snowing again later this afternoon.'

'Oh, I shall go as soon as I've finished this,' she said. 'In any case, I doubt if it'll be snowing at all, south of Redding.' She was cutting up waffles with the edge of her fork. Michael had ordered only a cup of black coffee. He usually liked waffles, too, or pancakes, but this morning he didn't feel at all hungry.

'Will you be seeing Mom when you get back?'

'Oh, not until tomorrow, probably.'

49

'You *will* give her my love, though, won't you?'

Sue, with her mouth full, looked at him narrowly.

'Is something bothering you?' she asked him.

'I don't know. Should it be?'

'You mustn't get depressed, Greg, just because you have to stay here for a while. I've talked to Doctor Hamid and Doctor Connor, and they both have your very best interests at heart. And I'm sure you and Mrs Weston will get along fine.'

'Well, you know her a whole lot better than I do.'

Sue swallowed and took a sip of lemon tea. 'Excuse me? I don't know her at all.'

'Oh. I got the impression that you did.'

'What gave you that idea? I've never even met the woman. All I know is what Doctor Connor told me about her.'

'Oh. And what was that?'

'She used to be an English teacher – in Portland, I think it was. She had some kind of accident which was why she was brought here to Trinity-Shasta. Her partner was quite a lot older than she was, and he passed away not too long ago.'

'I see.'

Michael thought: *Why did you just lie to me, and say that you had never even met her? I saw the two of you talking to each other like old friends.*

However, he bit his lip, and said nothing. *I'm confused*, he thought. *My brain isn't firing on all eight cylinders.* Maybe he had simply misinterpreted what he had seen and heard. Maybe that *hadn't* been Isobel that he had seen with Sue – although, if it wasn't, who was it? What other woman did she know at Trinity-Shasta well enough to kiss and embrace and spend nearly five minutes chatting to?

Maybe his mother hadn't said, *'Look at that snow!'* He could easily have misheard her.

In any case, what was so sinister about Sue being friendly with Isobel, or his mother saying 'Look at that snow!' Maybe it *had* snowed briefly in Oakland, without it settling.

Doctor Connor had warned him that post-traumatic amnesiacs often get feelings of paranoia. They have no memory of how things used to be, and so they have no concept of how things *ought* to be. Something that appears to them now as strange or threatening may be perfectly normal and completely harmless, if only they could remember why.

As they were finishing their breakfast, Doctor Hamid made his way toward them between the commissary tables, with a smile on his face.

'Good news, Gregory!' he announced. He opened the yellow Manila folder that he was carrying and said, 'That CT scan you had yesterday morning shows me that your spine is in very much better shape now.'

'That's wonderful,' said Sue, reaching across the table and taking his hand.

'Oh, yes, surprisingly good improvement!' said Doctor Hamid. 'There is now hardly any subluxation of the neck vertebrae and subsequently a great deal of pressure has been taken off your nerves. Physically, you are healing much more quickly than I had expected.'

He closed his folder and said, 'You will of course need continuing spinal therapy for some months to come, and of course your psychological therapy, which is much more difficult to predict. However we think we can release you today, back into the big, bad outside world. Well – when I say "big, bad outside world", I mean of course Trinity.'

'So you're moving me in with Isobel Weston?'

Doctor Hamid smiled at Sue, and Michael was sure that some flicker of understanding passed between them. Nothing more than a twitch of the eye, but that could be enough to communicate something which they both already knew. Or again, maybe he was just being paranoid.

Before she left, Sue drove Michael around to Isobel's house, although he had only one overnight case to carry. She promised him that she would go round to his apartment on Pine Street and collect all his clothes for him, and bring them up to him next weekend. Maybe her husband Jimmy would come next time, as well as their two little girls, Felicity and Alyson.

'Well, thanks for coming,' said Michael, as she pulled up behind Isobel's Jeep. 'It's a hell of a drive just to see somebody who doesn't even remember who you are.'

Sue leaned across and kissed him. 'I know who *you* are, Greg, and that's all that counts. You'll start to remember stuff before too long, I'm sure.

You're in the best possible hands.'

At that moment, Isobel appeared at her front door and came down the driveway to greet them. Both Michael and Sue climbed down from the Lexus to shake hands with her.

'Oh – Isobel, this is my sister Sue,' said Michael. 'Sue, this is Isobel, who I'll be lodging with for a couple of months, if she can put up with me for that long.'

He glanced quickly from one to the other as they shook hands, to see if either of them gave any indication that they knew each other already, but if they did they gave nothing away. Sue said, 'I'm pleased to know you, Isobel. Doctor Connor told me all about you, and I'm sure you'll take real good care of Greg.'

'I'll do my very best,' smiled Isobel. 'So long as he likes my cooking, and doesn't mind watching *Two Broke Girls*.'

'Don't you worry,' said Sue. 'Even if *he* can't remember how easy-going he is, Greg is Mister Tolerant. Even when he was a little kid you couldn't rile him. You could drop caterpillars down the back of his neck and all he did was laugh and say that they tickled.'

Michael opened the hatchback and lifted out his case. 'OK, Sue,' he told her. 'Thank you for coming all of this way to see me, and maybe I'll see you again next week. Hopefully by then a few more pieces of the puzzle will have come together.'

Sue hugged him and kissed him, but there was still nothing familiar about the way she felt or the perfume she was wearing.

He and Isobel stood on the snowy sidewalk while Sue turned her SUV around and drove away. They both waved as she blew her horn and disappeared from sight around the bend in the road.

Isobel turned to Michael and said, 'Well ... welcome home, Greg. I really want you to feel that it *is* your home. Come along in. I made minestrone soup this morning, if you're hungry.'

Michael looked up through the naked branches of the trees at the piercing blue sky. Even the white peaks of Mount Shasta had no clouds around them. Home? He felt as if he didn't belong here at all. He felt so alone and such a stranger that a lump began to rise in his throat, and his eyes prickled with tears, and he had to give a noisy cough to control himself.

He followed Isobel inside. It was warm in the living room, and it smelled of soup.

'Here,' she said, taking him across the hallway. 'This is your room, at the front. It gets the sun first thing in the morning, and you can see Mount Shasta. I hope you like it.'

The room was plain, with pale green walls and a dark green carpet, with a shaggy sheepskin rug beside the double bed. There were two tired-looking armchairs, and a portable TV perched precariously on a stool. In front of the window there was a desk, with a clock on it, and a mug full of pencils, and a china figurine of a woman in a long dark green cloak.

Hanging on the wall beside the bed was a framed print of a wolf catching a wild turkey in its jaws. The wolf's eyes were bulging with greed.

'This will do me just fine, Isobel,' said Michael, setting his suitcase down on the bed. 'Much cozier than a room at the clinic, anyhow.'

Isobel touched his arm. 'If there's anything you need, Greg, anything at all, don't hesitate to ask. Like I said, this is your home now. This is where you live.'

He woke up in the early hours of the morning. The clock on the desk in front of the window did not have a luminous dial, so that he was unable to tell what time it was until he switched on his bedside lamp. It was about seven minutes after three.

He switched his light back off and lay there in the darkness. The house was silent except for the soft, persistent rattling of the television antenna on the roof as it was shaken by the wind.

Maybe if I just lie here, and empty my mind altogether, some of my memories will rise to the surface. How can I have forgotten so completely who I am, and where I live, and what my job is? I'm supposed to be a marine engineer, but I know nothing at all about marine engineering. I don't even know what marine engineers actually do.

How can I have failed to remember my own sister, when she says that we were so close? How come I couldn't recognize my mother's voice? Worst of all, how come I don't really know who I am? Everybody else seems to be so sure that I'm Gregory Merrick, but I'm not sure at all.

He repeated the name *Gregory Merrick*, *Gregory Merrick*, over and over, but it still didn't sound like him.

As he lay there, he had another of those very brief flashes of recollection. That female voice saying *you shouldn't* – but in a blurry, stretched-out way, like a Doppler effect. And that elusive perfume.

He lifted up his head and sniffed the cold bedroom air, but the perfume had gone.

He drew back the bedcover and sat up. He stayed there for a few moments, still trying to keep his mind empty. *Think of nothing. Think of the wall. Think of the darkness. Think of the snow outside.*

He stood up and walked across to the window. The drapes were thick, dark green brocade, with patterns of leaves on them. He drew them back with a noisy scraping of brass rings and there was the snow-covered front yard, and the street beyond it. The moon was nearly full, and the sky was still completely clear, so that everything was lit up in a cold, bone-white light.

What Michael saw outside made his scalp and his wrists tingle, as if he had touched a bare wire. Although the street was silent, it was far from deserted. Standing on the sidewalks and scattered across the road were at least a hundred people, maybe even more. They were all staring back at him, with their arms by their sides, not moving.

Most of them were men, but he saw at least a dozen women. They were all wearing nightwear – a few of them in bathrobes, but the majority in pajamas and nightshirts and nightgowns. As far as Michael could tell, their ages ranged from their early twenties to sixty or seventy or even older.

But what the hell were they doing out there, in the middle of the night? The temperature couldn't be higher than minus five, and it probably felt colder with the wind-chill factor. Yet there they all stood, completely still, their pajamas and nightgowns rippling in the wind.

Michael stepped back from the window. In the darkness of his bedroom, he wasn't sure if they could see him or not. But even if they couldn't, they continued to stare in his direction, and not one of them showed any signs of moving.

He thought of waking up Isobel, but then he didn't want to frighten her. He was disturbed enough himself, even though it didn't look as if any of these people meant to do him any harm. They weren't armed, and they weren't making any moves toward the house. They were simply standing there, utterly silent.

No, he thought. The only thing to do was to go out there and ask them what the hell they were doing. After all, there was no way that he would be able to get back to sleep, knowing they were still gathered outside the house.

He opened his closet and took out his thick blue sweater and his khaki corduroy pants. He also sat on the bed and pulled on a pair of thick white socks.

As quietly as he could, he went out into the hallway and took down the navy blue overcoat which the clinic had given him, and put on his Timberland boots. He went right up close to the front door and peered through the hammered glass window in it, to make sure that none of the people were standing directly outside, but the glass was too bumpy and distorted for him to be able to see anything clearly.

Anyhow, even if somebody *were* standing right outside, and they went for him, he was sure that despite the fact that he was still convalescing, he was more than a match for some oddball in pajamas.

He opened the door. The wind that blew in was bitter, and made the glass chandelier in the hallway start jingling. He stepped outside, but he couldn't completely close the door behind him because he didn't have a key, and the last thing he wanted was to be stuck outside here in the freezing cold, surrounded by all of these people in their nightwear.

He turned around. The street was deserted. There was nobody in sight – not even a last straggler running around the corner.

Frowning, he made his way past Isobel's Jeep down to the sidewalk. He looked left, and then he looked right. Somehow, over a hundred people in their nightclothes had completely disappeared.

He walked out into the middle of the street. It had snowed only lightly since Sue had left, so he could still see her tire tracks and the footprints they had made when they had climbed out of her SUV to talk to Isobel. But there were no other footprints anywhere. The snow across the rest of the street was smooth and untouched, apart from the cross-stitches of a few bird tracks.

I must have dreamed those people. Either that,

or I was hallucinating. Catherine warned that the meds she had prescribed for me might give me some strange ideas. She didn't tell me that I would imagine crowds of people standing outside my bedroom in the middle of the night, though.

He walked back up to the house. As he reached the porch, Isobel appeared in the doorway, clutching a silky pink bathrobe up to her neck.

'Greg! Where have you been? You left the door wide open and it's *freezing*!'

'I'm sorry, Isobel. I thought I saw somebody outside.'

'Well, hurry up and come back in! You'll catch your death of cold.'

Michael came back into the house and Isobel closed the door behind him and bolted it. 'You probably saw a deer,' she said. 'They sometimes come down here, during the winter.'

'Yes, maybe,' said Michael. *Even though I didn't see any deer tracks, either.*

'Come on, it's your first night in a strange house. And you're not one hundred per cent yet, are you? How would you like some hot milk? Would that help?'

She had released her hold on her bathrobe and it had opened a little at the front to reveal that underneath she was wearing a thin white satin nightdress. It was low cut, edged with lace, so that Michael could see her very deep cleavage. Although her hair was tousled and she was wearing no make-up, there was no doubt that she was a very attractive woman – physically, any-how.

'I'll be OK,' Michael told her. 'Like you say – it's my first night here, and I've been having some pretty strange dreams lately.'

'Listen...' she began. She came closer and laid her hand on his sleeve. 'If anything like this happens again – you know, if you think you see something in the middle of the night or you have a bad dream – don't hesitate to wake me up, will you? I'm not your landlady. I'm your housemate. I'm your friend.'

'Thanks, I appreciate it.'

'No more than I do, Greg. It's been very lonely here since Emilio passed.'

'Emilio? Is he the guy in the photograph in the living room?'

Isobel nodded. 'He was such a gentleman. And such a good companion. When he passed, I thought there might be a chance ... but no, it doesn't work that way.'

'Excuse me? You thought there might be a chance of what?'

'Oh my goodness, look at the time!' Isobel exclaimed. 'I have my community meeting to go to tomorrow. I don't want to show up with bags under my eyes! Come on, you and me ought to get back to bed!'

She bobbed up and gave him a quick kiss on the cheek. As she did so, he glimpsed her right breast bouncing. Then she wrapped her robe around herself again and hurried off along the hallway to her own bedroom, which was at the back of the house.

Michael took off his coat and unlaced his boots. Then he returned to his room and closed the door, pressing his back against it for a moment.

He turned his head toward the window, half-expecting to see all those people standing out there, but the street was still empty, and a little light snow was falling, whirling around the street lights like swarms of moths.

He undressed and climbed back into bed. He couldn't stop thinking about Isobel. For some reason that he couldn't understand, he felt guilty that he found her so attractive. Why should he feel guilty? He wasn't married, or engaged. And even though he shared an apartment with a man, he was pretty sure that he wasn't gay, or bisexual. Or maybe he was. Maybe that was something else that he had forgotten, along with the rest of his life.

He slept, and the TV antenna on the roof continued to rattle in the wind, like an endlessly repeated message from another planet.

SIX

The following morning, when he had hobbled slowly back from his first therapy session with Doctor Connor, he found Isobel in the hallway, wearing her long black coat and her Peruvian beanie, winding a thick white scarf around her neck.

'I'm just off to my community meeting,' she

61

said, as he hung up his walking-stick. Seeing her dressed like that, Michael thought: *That* was *her that Sue was talking to so intimately on her way to the parking lot.* It must have been. So why, he wondered, had she insisted that she didn't know the woman, and greeted her when she had dropped him off here as if she had never met her before?

'OK,' said Michael. 'When will you be back?'

'Well – normally these meetings only go on for about an hour, but then we have a buffet lunch and socialize. I expect you're very tired, but why don't you come along? You can meet the neighbors. Some of them are real nice people. I think you'd enjoy it.'

'I'm not too sure if I'm feeling very sociable.'

'Oh, come on,' Isobel coaxed him, tugging at his arm. 'While you still have your coat on.'

Michael *was* feeling tired, and his knees were aching, but the coquettish way in which Isobel tilted her head to one side and fluttered her eyelashes made him think: *Why not?* It would be good for his ego to walk in anywhere with such an attractive woman on his arm.

They left the house and walked around the curve and down a long slope until they reached Trinity's Community Center, which stood in a hollow, surrounded by laurels. It was a plain, modern building with a curved, snow-covered roof. The parking lot outside had been cleared of snow but there were no vehicles parked there. A few residents were walking down the slope from the opposite direction, all of them wearing overcoats or quilted parkas. They looked about the same age range as the people who had been standing outside the house last night – one or two younger faces, but most of them middle-aged or elderly.

As Michael and Isobel approached the porch, arm in arm, one or two of them lifted up their gloved hands in greeting, and Isobel waved back. They reached the doors where everybody was filing inside, and one elderly man came up to them and said, 'Hi, Isobel! This must be your new companion.'

Isobel said, 'That's right, Walter. His name's Gregory Merrick. Greg, this is Walter Kruger. Walter's our community accountant, aren't you, Walter? Keeps the books in order.'

Michael took off his glove and shook Walter Kruger's hand. It was stunningly cold.

'Pleased to meet you,' he said, but at the same time he had a feeling that he had met him before, or seen his picture someplace. He was square-faced, with tangled white eyebrows like snow-covered briars, pale gray eyes, and rimless eye-glasses perched on the end of his nose. For no explicable reason, Michael thought: *atom scientist*.

'Emilio was a very good man,' said Walter Kruger. 'One of the best. Unselfish wasn't the word for Emilio. Kind, thoughtful, considerate. God rest him. I'm afraid you have a lot to live up to, Gregory.'

'Well, I don't think I'm going to be here for too long,' Michael told him. 'I have a few difficulties remembering stuff, but once I've sorted those out...'

Walter Kruger gave him an odd look with those pale gray eyes of his, as if he couldn't really understand what he was talking about, but then he patted Isobel on the back and said, 'We'd better get inside. We don't want Kingsley getting impatient, do we?'

'Kingsley?' asked Michael. 'Is that Kingsley Vane, from the clinic?'

'That's right,' said Isobel. 'He's the chair of the Trinity Community Association. He lives here too, of course. He has a big house out near the lake.'

They entered the hall, which was already crowded with at least two hundred residents. Isobel led Michael to two seats near the front. After all that walking from the clinic, and then from Isobel's house, he sat down with relief, propping his walking-stick against the seat in front of him.

Considering there were so many people here, the hall was strangely hushed. Michael twisted around in his seat to see if he could recognize any of those people who had been standing out in the street last night. Maybe it was his eyesight, which was still somewhat blurry; or maybe it was the white winter light that was coming in through the tall windows which lined the hall on either side; but he found it difficult to focus on any of their faces. There was only one – a pretty girl who was sitting at the opposite end of the row of seats immediately behind him – and she was so familiar that he turned around twice more to look at her.

He nudged Isobel and indicated the girl with a

64

nod of his head. 'That girl at the end, the one in the blue knitted hat with the bobble on top. Do you know who she is?'

Isobel was about to take a look herself when a door at the back of the hall suddenly opened and Kingsley Vane appeared, casually dressed in a white reindeer-patterned sweater and red corduroy pants. He stalked over to the rostrum with a slit of a smile on his face, carrying a large black folder under his arm.

He laid the folder on the rostrum and opened it, and then he slowly swiveled his head from side to side to take in his audience, so that to Michael he looked even more like a bird of prey than he had when he had first met him.

'A warm welcome to all of you,' he said. He paused for effect, and then he said, 'I won't pretend that the winter months have been at all easy for the residents of Trinity, and I know that for some of you these months have brought loss, and tragedy. I look around this hall today and there are several familiar and well-loved faces missing. We mourn them, as we mourn the passing of all those who brought richness and love and meaning to our lives.

'Today, however, I also see some new faces – people who will bring to our small community both freshness and vibrancy. We greet them with open arms, and thank them for the contribution that they will be making to our existence here, even if they are not yet aware of how valuable that contribution is going to be.

'Now – to get down to business – I have here a list of all the social events which are scheduled for the next three months, plus all of the committee meetings and special discussion groups that have been organized. The first of these will be tomorrow afternoon at three pm, a symposium on today's economic crisis, by invitation only.'

Kingsley Vane went through a long list of community activities, and then he finally closed his folder and said, 'Any questions? Any problems?'

One middle-aged man with a gray buzz-cut immediately raised his hand and said, 'My stepdaughter and me, we haven't been getting along too good lately. She keeps talking about leaving home. I mean, what happens if *that* happens? Doesn't she understand? How can I make her understand without scaring her any?'

Kingsley Vane said, 'It's Jeff, isn't it? Jeff Billings? And your stepdaughter's name is Tracey, if I recall?'

'That's right, Tracey. Should have been christened "Trouble", if you ask me.'

'Well, don't you worry, Jeff. Sometimes our younger residents don't quite grasp the implications of leaving Trinity. They're not mature enough to understand the concept of mutual support, and how important it is to all of us. But I have people at the clinic who can talk to Tracey for you and put her choices into perspective without causing her overdue anxiety. If you see me afterward, we'll arrange something.'

After a few more questions about mundane problems like frozen pipes and interrupted broadband connections and dogs fouling the footways, the formal part of the meeting broke up. Everybody shuffled through to a smaller room at the back of the hall, where a buffet had been laid out on a long table – chicken wraps and slices of pizza and corn chips and various dips, as well as cookies and brownies. At the far end of the room, two elderly women were serving tea and coffee and soda.

Michael took a slice of pepperoni pizza and then looked around for the girl in the blue bobble cap. He glimpsed her at the drinks table, waiting for one of the women to make her a glass of Russian tea, and he was just about to maneuver his way through the room to talk to her when a broad-shouldered young man with a shaven head and earrings blocked his way and said, 'Dude! What happened to you?'

'Oh,' said Michael. 'Auto wreck.'

The thickset young man nodded sympathetically. 'Came off my sickle. I was so smashed up they gave me the last rites, right there on the blacktop.'

'Well, it looks like they patched you up pretty good.'

In spite of his shaven head and his bulky build and his earrings, the young man had a broad, friendly face, with expressive brown eyes. He was wearing a black leather motorcycle jacket and a black T-shirt with a color transfer of Jesus on it, holding up one hand in blessing, and the motto *Jesus Waves*.

'Jack Barr,' he said, holding out his hand.

Michael shifted his walking stick to his left hand and shook hands with him. 'Greg Merrick.'

'Kind of weird, this place, don't you think?' said Jack, looking around the room.

'So you're not from round here?'

'Do I look like it? I come from Solana Beach, near San Diego.'

'I don't know,' said Michael. 'I don't think this place is any weirder than any other small community I've ever been to.' Not that he could specifically remember any other small community that he had ever been to, nor any of their names.

Jack said, 'Everybody's pretty friendly, I guess. Especially the family I'm staying with. They treat me like their long-lost son. Well, long-lost *dog*, more like.'

'You're staying here to recuperate? How long for, do you know? Me – they told me at least three months.'

'Yeah, me too. Hit my head when I totaled my sickle so I have some sort of contusion on the brain. Find it difficult to concentrate, know what I mean? Very short span of attention.'

'Tell me about it.'

Jack said, 'You and me, we should get together, have a few beers, see if we can't straighten our heads out. There is no greater cure-all for un-straight heads than a six-pack of Coors.'

'I'm on Piracetam, and about a dozen other meds. I don't know if the doctors will allow me to drink. Besides, does Trinity have a bar? Does it even have a market?'

At that moment, a smiling middle-aged woman came up to them. She had very red lipstick and a dress that looked as if it had been made out of a chintz couch cover. 'You young men, you should mingle! There are so many people here who are dying to meet you! It's not too often that we get new faces here in Trinity!'

'Oh, sure,' said Michael. He patted Jack on the shoulder and said, 'Catch up later, OK?'

'What did she mean "mingle"?' asked Jack.

'It means talking to the first old coot you bump into, followed by the next old coot, and so on, until you're all cooted out.'

'Right,' said Jack, with an undisguised lack of enthusiasm. 'See you later, dude.'

Michael smiled and nodded at the older residents as he weaved his way down the room, but it was the girl in the blue bobble hat who he was headed for. He found her sitting on a plain bentwood chair next to the end of the refreshment table, with a glass of Russian tea and a cookie on the table beside her. She was wearing a blue cable-knit sweater to match her hat, and jeans, and her ankles were neatly crossed.

She looked as if she were thinking about something serious, because she had a vexed little furrow in the middle of her forehead. A gray-haired man in a droopy maroon cardigan was standing close to her, but as Michael approached he shrugged and walked away, as if he had tried to talk to her but she hadn't answered him.

Michael stood in front of her and looked down at her with a feeling like no feeling he had ever experienced before – or no feeling that he could remember, anyhow. He had no idea who she was, and yet everything about her seemed so perfect.

69

Her blue-gray eyes, her high cheekbones, her slightly parted lips.

'Hi,' he said. He put down his half-eaten slice of pizza and wiped his hand on his jeans. 'My name's Greg. You look like you're worried about something and I was wondering if that something was something I could help you with.'

She didn't respond for at least five full seconds. He was just about to repeat himself when she raised her eyes and said, 'What?'

He gave her a smile. 'I said, my name's Greg and you look like you're worried about something.'

She was staring at him with such intensity that he began to wonder if he had tomato sauce on his chin, and he defensively wiped it with the back of his hand.

'Yes,' she said. 'I heard you the first time.'

'And?'

'And, no, I'm not worried. I was thinking about what I have to do when I get back home, that's all.'

'OK. And what *do* you have to do when you get back home?'

Again, there was at least a five-second pause. But then her eyes widened and she let out a terrible ear-splitting scream, her hands clutching the seat of the chair, her whole body rigid. The scream went on and on until she ran out of breath, and then she inhaled with a sound like somebody dragging a saw across a metal drain-pipe, and started screaming again.

'Hey!' said Michael, and took hold of her shoulders, trying to steady her. But she twisted

70

violently out of his grasp and drummed her heels on the floor and went on screaming and screaming.

By now the residents had gathered around them. One of the men said, 'Slap her! *Slap* her! It's the only way! Shock her out of it!'

'Cold water!' croaked an elderly woman. 'That'll do it! That's what my husband always did to me!'

Michael tried to pry the girl's hands away from the seat of the chair but now she was becoming so hysterical that she was bumping the chair up and down on the floor and he had to grab hold of the rungs to stop her from pitching herself backward.

'It's OK!' he kept telling her. 'Everything's OK! Please – try to calm down!'

She stared at him wildly with her eyes bulging. She looked almost as if she hated him. She was obviously exhausted from screaming but she wouldn't stop, with her lungs heaving and spit flying out of her mouth.

'Please,' Michael begged her. 'Please calm down.'

But at that moment Kingsley Vane appeared, moving the residents firmly out of his way. 'Let me through, please. Thank you. Let me through.'

Over the girl's screaming, Michael shouted, 'I don't know what happened! I started to talk to her, and she was fine at first...'

Kingsley Vane didn't reply, but nodded as if he understood exactly. Without hesitation he knelt down on one knee beside the girl and took her into his arms. She was still screaming but he lifted her bodily off the chair and then stood up, cradling her as if she were a child. She stopped screaming almost at once, and nestled her head underneath his chin.

'She'll be all right,' said Kingsley Vane. 'Sometimes the realization is more than they can bear.'

With that, he turned around and carried her out of the room, with the residents all stepping back to let him through.

Jack came up to Michael, shaking his head. 'What in the name of all that's holy was *that* shit about? What did you say to that poor girl to make her holler like that?'

'I don't know,' said Michael. He suddenly realized that he was shaking.

'You must have done *something* to upset her,' said Jack.

Michael turned away. With no warning at all, his eyes had filled with tears, and he didn't want Jack to see that he was crying.

SEVEN

That evening, Isobel served them a supper of spicy chicken casserole and sauté potatoes, which they ate together, sitting side-by-side at the counter in the blue-tiled kitchen. Afterward, Isobel said, 'Go on, you go sit down and watch TV. I'll clear up. Don't worry – next time it's your turn.'

Michael eased himself down on the couch in the living room and switched on the television. He found that he was halfway through an episode of *Unforgettable.*

Isobel slammed the dishwasher door and then came out of the kitchen, wiping her hands. 'How about a nightcap?' she asked him. 'I have a bottle of Shiraz that my neighbors gave me the last time they came to dinner, but we never got around to opening it.'

'Whoa, I'm not too sure I should be drinking alcohol.'

'Oh, come on. One won't hurt.'

'You ever watch this program?' asked Michael. *'Unforgettable?'*

Isobel peered at the screen short-sightedly. 'Can't say that I ever have. It probably makes me sound like a feather-brain, but I prefer comedies, and soaps. Real life is tragic enough already, that's what I always say, without having to watch made-up tragedy on TV. You know what Francis Bacon said.'

'I can't say that I do. Or if I did, I can't remember.'

'He said: "Men fear death as children fear to go in the dark; and as that natural fear in children is increased by tales, so is the other." That's why I don't watch programs about serial killers, or whatever.'

'And you call yourself a feather-brain?'

'Well, I don't know if Doctor Connor told you, but I used to be an English teacher. Until my accident, that is.'

73

'Do you miss it? Would you ever go back to it?'

Isobel shook her head. 'I can't.'

Michael waited for her to explain why, but that was all she said on the subject. Instead, she lifted up her hand as if she were holding up a wine glass and said, 'How about that drink?'

'OK, but just one. Talking of death, Doctor Connor would absolutely murder me, if she knew.'

Isobel brought in two large glasses of red wine and made herself comfortable on the couch, very close to him. She was wearing a plain red needlecord dress with the top three buttons undone to show the sparkling red crystal necklace that rested between her breasts.

'Here's to us,' she said.

Michael clinked glasses with her. Then he nodded toward the TV and said, 'You want me to turn this off?'

'No, watch it if you want to.'

'I find it pretty interesting, that's all. The heroine is a detective who has hyperthymesia, which is like the total opposite of amnesia. She can remember every single detail of every single thing that she ever saw or heard – every conversation, every person's face, every fact, every clue, everything.'

'You wouldn't want to be like that, would you?' Isobel asked him.

'I don't know. I think I'd rather remember everything than nothing.'

'I don't remember *my* accident.'

'What happened?'

74

Isobel shrugged. 'This is only what I've been told. I had just finished a teaching seminar at Raleigh College in Portland. But when we were all leaving for lunch, the elevator doors opened and there was no elevator car. I was talking to my friend and I stepped into the elevator shaft and fell three stories and dislocated my spine. Like I say, though, I don't remember doing it.'

Michael took her hand and squeezed it. 'You're OK now, though?'

'I'm fine. Absolutely one hundred per cent. No pain, no stiffness, nothing. They work miracles at TSC, believe me.'

'I still don't get this community thing. I agree with that guy Jack I was talking to this morning. Like, it's all a little weird. Look at the way that girl started screaming at me like that.'

'There's nothing sinister about it, Greg. The clinic uses Trinity to support people recovering from serious accidents, like me, and like you, and sometimes they're a little off-balance. Trinity is like a convalescent home except that it's a community, and not everybody who lives here is a clinic patient, by any means. There are some very high-end people here. Doctors, lawyers, scientists.'

'I still don't get it. Why would they *want* to live here, people like that, right in the middle of no place at all? There aren't any bars ... not that I've seen, anyhow. There's no nightlife. There are no restaurants. As far as I can make out, you don't even have a market.'

Isobel lifted her hand and touched Michael's cheek, very gently. 'Sometimes, you know,

75

people have no choice.'

'What does that mean? Everybody has a choice of where they want to live. I just can't work out why anybody would want to live *here.* I mean, the natives are friendly enough, aren't they? There's a good warm community spirit. But what the hell are they doing here?'

'You know why *you're* here.'

'Of course I do. I can't remember a goddamned thing about anything, so it's probably the best place for me until I get my memory back. But if it wasn't, I'd be off to San Francisco like a shot.'

Isobel knelt up on the couch and kissed him, first on the forehead and then on the lips. Then she sat back with a challenging look on her face.

'I could give you at least one reason to stay,' she said. 'Even if you do get your memory back.'

Michael said nothing, but looked back at her, directly in the eyes, searching for meaning. He was breathing hard. He noticed for the first time that she had a small heart-shaped mole on her right cheek.

On the television, Detective Carrie Wells was saying, *'March twenty-seventh, nineteen ninety-eight, was a Tuesday. Sunrise was at five forty-six am. Most important of all, on that day, the FDA approved Viagra.'*

Isobel stood up. She unbuttoned her dress all the way down and opened it out, her arms wide apart, as if she were spreading her wings and preparing to fly. Underneath, apart from her red crystal necklace and a lacy red bra, she was wearing nothing at all. Although her breasts were

76

so large and heavy, her hips were very narrow. Her vulva was waxed and completely smooth.

Neither of them took their eyes off each other. Isobel knelt down in front of him, still wearing her open dress like a cape, and reached for his belt-buckle.

'I'm not sure Doctor Hamid would approve of this,' said Michael, hoarsely. 'He told me to be very careful not to strain my back.'

'Then we'll just have to make sure that you *don't* strain your back,' said Isobel. She had licked her lips and they were shining pink in the lamplight. She unfastened his belt and then tugged down his zipper. Reaching inside the top of his shorts with one red-varnished finger, she stretched out the waistband so that she could scoop her other hand inside them, and pull out his rapidly swelling penis.

She gripped the shaft of his penis very tightly, with her pointed fingernails digging into it like needles, and rubbed it up and down two or three times. They were still looking unblinkingly into each other's eyes, almost as if they were daring each other to continue. Then – still gripping his penis just as hard – Isobel reached over for her glass of Shiraz, held it up and said, 'Here's to companionship.' She swallowed a mouthful, and licked her lips again.

Michael tried to lift himself up from the couch, but he felt a sharp twinge of pain in his neck and said, *'Ah!'* Isobel gently pushed him back.

'Let's take it easy, shall we?' she smiled. 'You don't want to go dislocating your neck again, do you?'

Michael said, 'Where's this going, Isobel?'

'Just as far as you want it to.'

With that, she lowered her head and took the purple head of his penis between lips that were still wet with wine. She circled the tip of her tongue around it, around and around, and then she dipped it into the crevice in his glans.

Again, he tried to raise himself up, but he felt another twinge, even more painful this time, and knew that it would be dangerous to try. He looked down at Isobel as she took his penis deep into her mouth, her tongue still circling, her head nodding. Already he felt a tightening sensation between his legs, and he knew that he wouldn't be able to hold off a climax for very long.

She started sucking him harder, and he buried the fingers of both of his hands into her thick, shiny brunette hair, pulling her head down so that she was taking him into her mouth as far as it was possible for him to go.

He started panting as his climax began to rise. Every muscle in his body was rigid and he was seeing pinpricks of light in front of his eyes.

'Oh God,' he gasped, and Isobel lifted her head, so that he climaxed in a loop over the bridge of her nose, and into her eyelashes. She laughed, a high tinkly laugh, like a mischievous fairy, and stuck out her tongue so that she could lasciviously lick the last of his semen.

'Oh God,' he repeated, still panting. 'You are amazing. You are something else, believe me.'

She smiled up at him, her face still decorated with his climax. 'That's companionship, Greg. That's *real* companionship.'

He shifted himself up a little, but as he did so he glimpsed a flash of reflected light over by the window seat. Isobel had failed to pull one of the blinds all the way down, so there was a gap above the window sill of at least six inches. At first he thought that he had seen nothing more than the reflection of the table lamp behind him, as he moved his position. But then he saw another flash and realized that there was somebody looking in through the window, and that the flash had come from the dark glasses that they were wearing.

'Jesus!' he said, struggling to get up from the couch.

'What?' said Isobel.

He yanked up his zipper but didn't bother with his belt. 'Goddamned peeping Tom – spying on us!'

'I don't believe it! Where?'

He hopped and stumbled into the hallway, slid back the chain on the front door and threw it wide open. As he did so, he saw a man in a black coat running diagonally across the snow-covered front yard.

'Hey!' he shouted. 'Come back here, you pervert!'

He grabbed his walking-stick from the hall-stand and started to go after him, even though he had no shoes on. As he did so, however, a black Escalade appeared around the curve, and slewed to a halt right in front of the house. Its passenger door was flung open from inside and the man in the black coat climbed into it.

'Hey, stop!' Michael yelled at him. 'You come

back here!'

He swung himself across the front yard like a one-legged pirate, but he was too late. With a squeal of tires the Escalade drove away and disappeared around the next bend. He heard it drive into the distance and then there was silence. Nothing but the wind, and the frozen branches tapping.

Michael walked back to the house, where Isobel was standing in the open doorway, her dress still unbuttoned but wrapped tightly around her.

'I've seen those guys before,' said Michael, as he closed the front door behind him. 'They were watching the house the first time I came here with Doctor Connor. You don't know who they are, do you? Have you ever seen them before?'

'No. Never. Do you think he saw everything?'

Michael followed her into the living room. He pulled a tissue out of the box on the side table, went up to her and wiped her face.

'I don't know,' he said. 'Probably. But I'm going to report them to the cops. Where's the nearest police station, do you know?'

'I have no idea at all. Weed, I should think.'

'Well, it doesn't really matter. I'll just dial nine-one-one.'

He went across the room and picked up the phone. There was no dialing tone, only an intermittent crackling noise. He tried three or four times, but he still couldn't get a connection.

'Nothing,' he said.

'Maybe the lines are down,' Isobel suggested.

'You have a cell, don't you? Mine got lost

when I crashed.'

'I don't, no. I've never really needed one since I've been here.'

'Great. So to all intents and purposes, we're incommunicado. The only thing I can do is walk up to the clinic and talk to their security staff.'

Isobel came up to him and put her arms around his neck, so that her dress fell open. She looked up at him and said, 'You could leave it till tomorrow, couldn't you? I mean, it's quite a turn-on, don't you think, that somebody was watching us?'

Michael hesitated for a moment. But he was very tired, and his knees were aching, and his socks were cold and soaking wet.

Isobel kissed him, twice, and then she said, 'Come on, it's late. It's time we got some sleep.'

Michael pried her arms away from his neck, walked over to window and pulled the blind all the way down.

'Just in case they come back for an action replay,' he told her.

The next morning, less than five minutes into his therapy session, Catherine put down her clipboard and said, 'What's bothering you, Gregory? You're not even trying.'

'Sorry,' Michael told her. 'I'm kind of distracted, that's all. Something happened last night and I'm going to have to talk to Kingsley Vane about it.'

'All right,' she said. 'What was it?'

He told her about the man in the black overcoat and the dark glasses looking in through the window, although he didn't tell her what he and Isobel had been doing at the time.

'I saw them that first day you took me around to meet Isobel. Do you have any idea who they are?'

'Yes – yes, I do. They're security.'

'*Security?* Come on, Catherine, there's a difference between security and spying. We were sitting on the couch and the guy was peering right in through the window. If he'd wanted to check up on us, he should have knocked on the door and asked us if everything was OK.'

'Well, I agree with you there. But some of the people who live in Trinity need very careful looking after, as you can imagine.'

'The guy ran off! I went out to ask him what he was doing and he was off like a goddamned rabbit!'

'He probably didn't want any kind of confrontation, that's all. Like I say, some of the people who live in Trinity are less than stable, physically or mentally or both. He wouldn't have wanted to make your condition worse than it is already.'

'In that case he should stay the hell away from our windows.'

Catherine picked up her clipboard again. 'If you like, I'll talk to Kingsley Vane for you – just to make sure that it doesn't happen again. By the way, how are you and Isobel Weston getting along? Do you think you're going to enjoy staying with her?'

From the way she looked at him, over her reading-glasses, Michael had the distinct feeling that she already knew what had happened between them. Or *guessed* it, anyhow. She was a highly trained psychotherapist, and people who have enjoyed a passionate night of love-making always find it hard to hide.

'I think so,' he said. 'She's a very interesting woman, isn't she? Really knows her onions when it comes to writers and books and stuff like that.'

Catherine gave him an enigmatic smile, as if to say *if only you knew.*

'What?' he asked her.

'Nothing,' said Catherine. 'Let's get back to these memory exercises, shall we? Try to think what your first pet was, and what you called it.'

EIGHT

The sky that afternoon was as gray as gunmetal, and a light snow began to fall. All the same, Michael took a walk around the streets. He was not only obeying Doctor Hamid's instructions to take regular physical exercise, he was also trying to get a handle on this 'convalescent community' called Trinity and understand why people would choose to live here.

Some of them were obviously TSC outpatients, and had to stay until their rehabilitation was complete, but Isobel had suggested that others had no choice. If that were true, why? What would make it obligatory for anybody to stay in a God-forgotten place like this, when Redding, the county capital, was little more than an hour away, and Sacramento and San Francisco less than five?

He walked past the wide snow-covered recreation area, and then down the slope past the community center. He was breathing hard by the time he reached the top of the slope on the other side, and his left knee was beginning to ache. He stopped for a few moments to rest. There was nobody else in sight. No vehicles rolled past. The whole community was silent as if everybody was sleeping.

As he started walking around the next curve, however, he thought he heard a repetitive chipping sound. He walked on further, and the sound grew louder, and echoed from the houses opposite. Passing a long hedge of laurels, he came to one end of a loop. In front of the second house on the left, a silver Enclave was parked, with snow on its roof. Immediately behind it he saw Jack Barr, in a woolly hat with ear flaps and a thick padded jacket and ski boots. He was using a broad-bladed shovel to chip the ice from the driveway.

'Jack!' he called out, as he approached.

Jack looked up. He didn't seem to recognize Michael at first, but then he said, 'Dude! What are you doing here?'

'Just taking a walk, that's all.'

Jack looked around. 'Taking a *walk*?' he said, as if that were the strangest thing he had ever heard of. 'The folks around here don't take *walks.* So far as I can see, they don't take drives, neither. In fact they don't never seem to go no place at all, apart from the clinic.'

'Well, you know what I said yesterday, about Trinity being not much different from any other small community? Something happened last night and it's really made me change my mind.'

He told Jack about the security man peering in through the window, although again he didn't mention what he and Isobel had been doing when they were being spied on.

'That is not good, man,' said Jack. 'That is not good at all. That is, like, *sinister.*'

'You're not kidding. The longer I stay here in Trinity, and the more I find out about it, the less I understand it.'

'Well, me neither,' said Jack. 'But like you said yesterday, everybody seems real friendly. OK – there was that one girl screaming her head off, but the rest of them don't seem like they're nuts or nothing. They're not some wacky religious sect, are they, like the Church of the Holy UFOs, or some bunch of neo-Nazis, with a secret stock of weapons? They seem normal enough. Maybe they're just *too* normal.'

Michael said, 'No, Jack. They're not. Living in a place like this isn't normal. There's nothing here – no church, no post office, no market – *nothing.* It feels like it's almost completely cut off from the outside world. Sure, some of the residents have to stay here because they're having continuing treatment from the clinic. But the rest of them ... what are *they* all doing here? I mean, would *you* live here, if you hadn't had your accident, and you weren't convalescent? I sure as hell wouldn't.'

Jack sniffed and then wiped his nose on the back of his gray woolly glove. 'I guess not. And I have noticed something. Maybe I'm dumb, but everything that everybody says to me seems to make some kind of sense when they say it, but when I think about it afterward, I think *hunh*? It's like somebody gives you a jigsaw but none of the pieces fit together, if you know what I mean.'

At that moment the front door of the house opened and a man of about sixty appeared, wearing a long camel-hair coat and green rubbers. His long white hair flew up in the wind as he came down the driveway, smiling.

'How it's going, neighbor? I saw you at the community meeting, didn't I, but I didn't get the opportunity to introduce myself. Bill Endersby.'

'Greg Merrick,' said Michael, taking off his glove and shaking hands. 'Good to know you, Bill.'

'Looks like you're making great progress there, Jack!' said Bill Endersby. 'Trouble is, when that snow melts, and then it freezes over again, and then the procedure repeats itself nightly, what you have is your naturally occurring skateway.'

'So, where are you heading off to?' Michael asked him.

Bill Endersby frowned at him as if he had said something in a foreign language. Under his flyaway white hair, he was a very thin man, with a colorless, wrinkled face and pink, watery eyes. His nose was upturned like a character from a Dr

Seuss drawing. Michael thought that he didn't look at all well, and he wouldn't have been surprised to find out that he was suffering from pancreatic cancer, or Crohn's disease, or some other major illness.

'Did I say I was going anyplace?' he asked, with unexpected sharpness.

'Well, no,' Michael admitted. 'I just assumed that since Jack is clearing your driveway, he might be doing it so that you can get your SUV out.'

'Jack's been *great*,' said Bill Endersby. His smile returned and he shook his head benignly. 'We lost our boy Bradley, but now Jack's moved in with us and he's like a son to us, I can tell you that. He does all the chores. My wife, Margaret, she's like a new woman. Always singing these days, and she never sang at all after Bradley went.'

'I guess you're retired now,' said Michael.

'Yes,' said Bill Endersby. 'You could say that.'

'What did you do, before you retired?'

Bill Endersby was silent for a while, sucking thoughtfully at his teeth as if he had a shred of meat stuck between them. Then he said, 'I used to work for Pacific Gas and Electric. Nuclear waste disposal, that was my field.'

'Oh. Sounds pretty high-tech.'

'Yes, it was. Very high-tech. Very good job. But there's a price you have to pay for everything, isn't there?'

Michael had no idea what he was talking about, but he nodded all the same.

Bill Endersby checked his wristwatch, and

said, 'Shoot! Better get myself back inside. I promised Margaret I'd fix the thermostat. One minute we're shivering like penguins and the next minute we're sweating like pigs. Good to meet you, Greg. Keep it up, Jack. You're doing a fine job there, son.'

With that, he walked back up the driveway to the house and closed the front door behind him.

'What did he mean by that?' asked Michael. *'There's a price you have to pay for everything?'*

'Wouldn't know,' said Jack. 'But Bill and Margaret, they always give me the feeling that something God-awful happened in their lives which they can't forget. I don't like to ask what it was. I don't think it was just their Bradley dying.'

He paused, looking toward the house, and then he said, 'Come to that, they have pictures of Bradley all over, but they never specifically say that he died, or even that he passed away. They never use those actual words. They only say that he *went*, or that they lost him, and I guess that could equally mean that all he did was up and walk out on them.'

He started chipping at the ice again, but then Michael said, 'I think we need to find out what's going on here, don't you?'

'I don't know. How do we do that? Supposing there's *nothing* going on and it's just us having the heebie-jeebies? Like I said, supposing they're all just *too* normal, and that's what makes you and me think that they're freaks?'

'I don't think so, Jack,' said Michael, and then he told him about all the people he had seen standing in the street outside Isobel's house.

Jack listened with a serious expression on his face. After Michael had described how he had run out into the street to find that there was nobody there, he said, 'They didn't leave no tracks behind them? A hundred people or more, and they didn't leave a single footprint?'

'Nothing,' Michael told him. 'You may not believe me, but I saw them with my own eyes, and I swear to you that they were really there.'

Jack had a long think about that, and then he propped his shovel against the side of Bill Endersby's SUV and said, 'Come with me.'

He walked up to the side of the house, where there was a yellow-painted gate. He reached over the top of it and slid back a bolt. He beckoned Michael to follow him through to the back yard.

'What do you see here?' he said.

Michael looked around. Immediately behind the house there was a patio with a low brick wall around it and a brick barbecue in one corner. From the patio, three steps led up to a snow-blanketed area which was obviously grassed in the summer. At the very end of this area stood a birdhouse on a pole, with a net bag hanging from it, filled with nuts.

'What am I supposed to be looking at?' asked Michael.

'You see that bag of nuts, on the birdhouse?'

'Yes. What of it?'

'That's fresh, that bag of nuts, isn't it? Like it's only just been hung up there?'

'OK. And...?'

'Margaret put those up there, first thing today.'

'Right. But I still don't see what you're...'

He suddenly stopped, in mid-sentence. The snow-covered area that led to the birdhouse was completely smooth, with not a single footprint on it.

'I was looking out the kitchen window this morning when I was drinking my coffee and I saw the fresh bag of nuts hanging up there but the fact that Margaret hadn't left any footprints didn't hit me till you told me all about those people standing outside of your house. How did she hang those nuts up there without leaving any footprints? Don't tell me she flew.'

The two of them looked at each other, equally lost for an answer.

'I think you're right, man,' said Jack. 'There *is* something weird going down here, and it's not because everybody's too normal. Trouble is, how do we find out what it is? I don't think anybody's going to tell us if we ask them right out, do you?'

'I don't know. I could try asking Doctor Connor.'

'And you really think she's going to tell you?'

'She might.'

'On the other hand she might not. Supposing everybody in Trinity has some really rare disease and they're being kept here so that they don't spread it?'

'Well, you could be right. But that doesn't explain how they can walk around in the snow without leaving footprints, does it? Even people with Ebola leave footprints.'

'Maybe it's us,' said Jack. 'Maybe we're hallucinating. Maybe we're still in a coma after our accidents and this is some kind of drug-induced dream.'

'Two people can't have the same dream.'

'Then maybe one of us isn't real. Maybe one of us is dreaming about the other one. The question is, which one of us is real and which one of us is imaginary? *I* sure feel real.'

'Oh, shit,' said Michael, leaning back against the wall. 'None of this makes any goddamned sense at all.'

Just then, the kitchen door opened and Bill Endersby appeared.

'Jack?' he called out. 'What are you doing back here? Did you finish clearing the driveway yet?'

'It's freaking cold out here, Bill. I was taking a break.'

'If you're cold, the best thing you can do is get on with your shoveling! That'll warm you up!'

He went back inside and slammed the kitchen door. Jack gave him the finger.

'I thought you said they treated you like their own son,' said Michael.

'They do. And if he ran away, that's probably why. No – I'm not being fair. They're very good to me. I guess you could say that Bill is a little old-fashioned, that's all. But Margaret's always fussing over me and baking me cookies and stuff.'

'That still doesn't explain how she can walk on snow without leaving tracks.'

They walked back to the front of the house.

'What are you planning on doing?' Jack asked him. 'Are you going to ask your doctor straight out, or what?'

'I have no idea,' Michael admitted, and he didn't. 'I'll think it over, OK, and then get back to you. Do you have a cell?'

'I do. I called my brother on it a couple of days ago, but now it's on the fritz for some reason.'

'All right. I'll just come round here and knock on the door.'

The snow had stopped falling but the wind persisted, making swirling patterns of snow on the driveway where Jack had cleared it.

Jack said, 'You know something, Greg? I can't explain it, but I never felt so fucking lonely in my whole life.'

Michael didn't answer, but he understood exactly what Jack meant, because he felt the same.

As he walked back to Isobel's house, he saw to his surprise that her Jeep was no longer in the driveway, and that there were tire tracks on the sidewalk to show that she had taken it out. However he was less than fifty yards away when the Jeep appeared around the curve, with Isobel driving, and she blew her horn and flashed her headlights.

She parked and climbed out. 'Hi, baby!' she greeted him, as he approached. She kissed him, and then she said, 'How was your walk?'

'Cold. Boring. Where have you been?'

'I had to go to the market, that's all. You want to help me carry my stuff in?'

'Sure.' He opened up the Jeep's tailgate and found four sacks of groceries and a box of cleaning materials. He passed two of the sacks to Isobel and picked up the other two himself.

'Where's the market from here?' he asked her, as they crossed the snow-covered front yard to the house.

'Weed. Ray's Food Place. It's a really great store. You should come with me next time I go.'

Michael stamped the snow off his feet on the doormat, and then carried the sacks of groceries through to the kitchen. Ray's Food Place? What had he heard his mother saying on the phone? *'Oh, shoot, George! Look at that snow! I wanted to go to Ray's Food Place this afternoon!'*

He stood and watched Isobel take off her Peruvian beanie and shake her hair loose, and then start to unbutton her coat. He had that flickering feeling again, that voice saying *you shouldn't*. Then Isobel turned and smiled at him and said, 'Can you fetch in the rest of it?'

'Oh. Yes. For sure.'

He went back outside. The day was still gray but a watery yellow sunlight was beginning to break through, and as the air warmed up, a fog was beginning to rise. The white peaks of Mount Shasta looked as if they were floating unsupported in the sky.

As he walked back across the front yard, he saw the footprints that had been left in the snow when he and Isobel had carried the groceries from the back of the Jeep. He stopped, and stared at them, and then he turned around and looked back at the house. The front door was open and he could see Isobel in the hallway, hanging up her long black coat. She waved at him, and then disappeared into the living room.

He looked back down at the footprints. *His*

footprints, anyhow – but there were none of hers. She had crossed the front yard slightly ahead of him, on his left, but she had left no impression at all.

Michael stood there for a long time, biting his lip. What the hell was he going to do now? Stalk back to the house and demand to know why Isobel hadn't left any footprints? What good would that do – even if she could explain it?

Maybe Jack had been right, and he was asleep, and dreaming all of this. Maybe he was still in a coma after his accident. But it was all too real. The gradually brightening sky was real. The frost-bitten trees were real.

Thus in the winter stands the lonely tree.

'Greg? Did you get that box yet? I need to close the front door!'

'OK!' he called back. 'Just coming!'

NINE

That evening, Isobel made them a supper of pork, potato and leek stew, with crusty fresh bread.

'You're quiet,' she said, as she watched Michael chasing a potato around his bowl with his fork. 'Don't you like that? I can always make you a sandwich.'

'I guess I'm not too hungry,' he said, putting down his fork. 'I have so much spinning around in my head.'

'Are you beginning to remember things?'

'I get flashes, but nothing really clear. I keep hearing this woman's voice saying *"you should-n't"*, and I see some bright lights, and shadows, and I smell this flowery perfume for a second, but that's about it.'

Isobel looked at him for a while without saying anything. She had her hair tied up in a peacock-blue scarf because she had been cooking, but with her fringe off her face her high forehead and her wide brown eyes were even more striking than usual.

'You don't know if this is real, do you?' she asked him.

He said nothing, but he could tell that his eyes had given him away.

'I felt exactly the same,' she said. 'In the first few weeks that I was here, I wasn't even sure that I was me. Sometimes I thought that I was dreaming. If it hadn't been for Emilio, I don't know what I would have done. Emilio always kept me grounded.'

'So who was he, Emilio?'

Isobel pushed her bowl away. 'He was my companion, the same way that you are.'

'Were you lovers?'

'I don't know whether you have the right to ask me that.'

There was a very long pause between them, but then she said, 'Emilio was much older than you. Seventy-one. But – yes, we were lovers. In a different way than you and me. More ... how can I put it? More like floating down a stream to-

95

gether, on a summer afternoon.'

She stood up, and came around the kitchen table, and stood behind him. She took hold of his shoulders and gently began to massage his neck muscles with her thumbs.

'You're so tense,' she said. 'Maybe you should come to bed.'

Michael said, 'I still have no idea who I am. How can I come to bed with you when I don't even know who I am?'

'You're Greg. You have an apartment in San Francisco and a sister called Sue and a mother who cares about you and you probably have more friends than you can count. What else do you need to know?'

'I need to know if all of this is true. Just like you said, I need to know if all of this is *real*. I'm beginning to suspect that amnesia is the least of my problems. I'm beginning to see things that aren't possible. People keep saying things to me which I can't understand.'

He twisted around in his chair and looked up at her.

'Do I feel real to you?' she asked him.

She took hold of his hand and gently pulled him out of his chair. Then she put her arms around him and kissed him, her tongue sliding into his mouth. Michael closed his eyes while they kissed, and all he could hear was Isobel's breathing, and the hesitant ticking of the electric clock over the range, and the soft clicking of their own lips.

When she had finished kissing him, Isobel brushed back his hair with her fingertips and smiled at him possessively, as if she had won the right to have him. Taking hold of his hand again, she led him through to her bedroom. It was decorated plainly, with magnolia-painted walls and a built-in closet with mirrored doors. The king-size bed was covered with a silky pink quilt, and silky pink cushions were heaped up over the pillows.

Propped up against the cushions was a skinny rag doll, with disproportionately long legs and arms, and a mass of silvery-gray ringlets. Her face was dead white and her eyes were made of black buttons, like a shark's eyes. Her mouth was nothing but a sewn-up slit. She wore a long striped dress in black and gray, trimmed with black ribbons.

'That is one scary-looking dolly,' said Michael.

'Isn't she just? She came with the house, when they moved me in here. I call her Belle, because of all her ringlets. Like, "Belle" as in "bell ringer". But here...'

Isobel picked up the doll, opened the closet door, and pushed her inside.

'That's where she goes at night, because I don't like the idea of her staring at me when I'm asleep, especially with those shiny black eyes.'

She came back over to Michael, and started to unbutton his dark blue shirt.

'You can remember yesterday evening, can't you?' she asked him.

'Of course I can. I don't think I'll ever forget it so long as I live.'

'There you are, then. You may have lost your old memories but already you're making fresh

97

ones. Even if your previous life is only names and photographs, your new life is real.'

She took off his shirt, and then she pulled his T-shirt over his head, so that his hair stuck up. She ruffled it, and kissed him, and said, 'You look about sixteen years old with your hair like that.'

'Oh, thanks.' He nodded toward the bed and said, 'I hope that doesn't mean I'm too young to ... you know.'

She unbuckled his belt and pulled down his jeans. Then she raised her arms so that he could lift off her light gray cable-knit sweater. Underneath she was wearing a lacy white bra through which her nipples showed like two pink rose-petals. He slid the catch apart and her breasts swung free, heavy and soft. He cupped her right breast in his hand, and rotated the ball of his thumb around her crinkling nipple, but even though she was so aroused, she felt surprisingly cold.

'You're freezing,' he said. 'Let's get under the covers.'

'Unh-hunh, I'm fine. And this is *my* bed, so we're going to do what *I* want to do.'

She pushed him so that he fell backward on to the quilt. Then she quickly dropped her short black skirt and stepped out of her tiny white-lace thong.

Naked, she climbed on to the bed and climbed on top of him, until she was sitting astride him. He reached down to push off his shorts, but she gripped his wrist to stop him and said, 'No, not yet.'

She leaned forward, staring into his eyes, until their noses were almost touching. She kissed him again and again, just lightly, and then she said, 'Greg – it doesn't matter if some things seem to be impossible. János Arany said, "In dreams and love, nothing is impossible."'

'János Who? Never heard of him. Or if I have, I've forgotten.'

Isobel kissed him again. 'Arany. Famous Hungarian poet, 1817 to 1882.'

'I never had a history lesson in bed before.'

'How do you know? You have amnesia.'

With that, she maneuvered herself up the bed until she was kneeling astride his face, her shins pinning his shoulders against the mattress. She reached down with both hands and opened the lips of her vulva, so that her clitoris protruded and he could see that she was brimming with clear juice. She looked down at him between her breasts as if she were a goddess on a mountain top and he were a mere mortal on the ground below.

'Go on, Greg,' she coaxed him. 'Taste me.'

Tentatively, he licked her clitoris with the tip of his tongue. He licked it again and this time she shuddered.

'*Ohhhhh*,' she breathed.

He licked her faster and faster. Her clitoris stiffened, almost like the beak of a little bird. She closed her eyes and tilted her head back, and pulled herself open even wider. He pushed his tongue inside her as deeply as he could, and sucked, so that he could taste her. She tasted unusually sweet, but she was still quite cold, even inside.

'Don't stop,' she panted. She was holding on to the bedhead now, and she was so tense that she was hurting his shoulders. But he kept on flicking at her clitoris with the tip of his tongue, and her juice was running down his chin.

There was a moment when he thought he would have to go on licking for hours. His shoulders were beginning to seize up and his jaw was aching from keeping his mouth open for so long. But then Isobel let out a high-pitched cry, and then a snort, and her whole body quaked and shook.

She was still for a few seconds, and then she quaked again, and again. At last, however, she lifted herself off him and rolled over and nestled herself up close, with her shoulder in his armpit. She kissed him, licking her own juice off his face, and panted, 'You're wonderful. You're absolutely wonderful. If only you knew what you do for me.'

She reached down and slid her hand into his shorts. He felt desperately that he wanted to climb on top of her and penetrate her, but she started to rub him, very hard, so hard that it hurt, and he was already so aroused that it took only a few seconds before he climaxed, and filled his shorts with warm semen. Isobel kept her hand inside there, massaging his softening penis and rolling his slippery testicles between her fingers.

He kissed her forehead. 'Don't you want me inside you?' he asked.

'Of course I do. But we need to be careful, don't we?'

'So you're not on the pill?'

She took her hand out of his shorts and then she sat up, sharply shaking her head so that her hair flew from side to side. 'I'm not allowed any medication. Only my regular shots.'

'Oh, yes. And what are *they* for?'

'Just to keep me stable, I suppose. Doctor Connor diagnosed me bipolar. I used to have mood swings like you can't believe.'

'Don't they sell condoms at Ray's Food Place?'

Isobel kissed him and laughed. 'I guess Doctor Connor would supply you with some if you asked her.'

She swung her legs off the bed and walked over to the door, where her bathrobe was hanging. Michael watched her as she turned around and put it on, her breasts swaying underneath it as she tied the sash. He thought her figure was amazing. He hadn't found a woman so irresistible since ... *You shouldn't...*

'What's the matter?' Isobel asked him, sitting back down on the edge of the bed.

He pressed his fingertips to his forehead. 'I don't know. Another flash, I guess.'

'You look like you've seen a ghost.'

'Maybe I have. Or *heard* one, anyhow. It's like somebody's trying to get through to me on a shortwave radio, only there's too much interference.'

'It could be some memory coming back.'

He looked at her. Then he looked across at the closet, with its mirrored doors, and saw the two of them, sitting like two strangers in another

101

room. Isobel had her back to the mirrors and he looked so tired and puffy-eyed that he barely recognized himself.

There was a faint click, and one of the closet doors opened a little way. Obviously Isobel hadn't closed it properly when she had put away her doll, Belle. And there, peering out of the darkness with her black shark's eyes, was Belle herself, as if she were watching him, just to make sure that he behaved himself.

When Michael walked to the clinic the next morning for his therapy session, the sky was clear blue and there were only a few fragmented clouds, although it was still bitterly cold.

He walked in the roadway, because it was only thinly covered with snow from yesterday's snowfall, while the sidewalks were still very slippery. He had always thought that residents had a duty to clear the snow from the sidewalks outside their own homes, but apparently that didn't apply to Trinity.

He was less than halfway to the clinic when the little girl on the bicycle appeared, Jemima, with her frizzy brown hair and her pink windbreaker. She rang her bell as she cycled past him, and then she circled around and came back again.

'Are you staying with Mrs Weston?' she asked, with one eye scrunched up against the sunshine.

'That's right. I am. Only for a while, though, while I get better.'

'My mom says that Mrs Weston is a hoo-ha.'

'A hoo-ha? Is that right?'

Jemima nodded emphatically. 'She goes for

anything in pants, that's what my mom says.'

'Well, I think your mom is being a little unfair. Mrs Weston is a very nice person, and she certainly isn't a hoo-ha.'

Jemima continued to stare at Michael, one-eyed, and then she said, 'What *is* a hoo-ha?'

'Your mom didn't tell you? A hoo-ha is a person who always kicks up a lot of fuss about everything, that's all.'

'Oh.'

Michael carried on walking but Jemima followed him, circling around and around him all the time. Michael thought that the zigzag scar on her forehead looked even more pink and livid in the sunlight.

'Shouldn't you be in school?' he asked her.

'I don't go to school. They don't have a school in Trinity, anyhow.'

'There must be a school in Weed.'

'My mom teaches me. And Mister Bauman comes in from next door to give me math lessons.'

'Don't you miss playing with other kids? You know – what about sport and drama and that kind of stuff?'

'Me and Angela, we play together.'

'Angela – she was the girl walking the dog, right?'

Jemima nodded. 'We do skipping and hop-scotch. And we play "What It Was Like".'

'"What It Was Like"? What's that?'

'That's when we play What It Was Like.'

'I don't understand you. What It Was Like when?'

'*Before*, stupid!'

'Hey, watch who you're calling names, OK? Don't forget what Doctor Connor said – I'll be able to catch up with you soon and give you a pasting!'

'Like to see you try!'

Jemima circled around one more time, well out of Michael's reach. For some reason he remembered a story about somebody stopping a thief by throwing a walking stick through the spokes of his bicycle wheel, but he decided it wouldn't be very wise to try that with Jemima. He watched her pedal off around the curve, provocatively jingling her bell and looking back over her shoulder to stick out her tongue.

Kids. But what had she meant, 'What It Was Like *Before*'? Before what? Before her parents had moved here? Before she had sustained that lightning-flash scar on her forehead? Like everybody else in Trinity, she spoke in riddles.

He carried on making his way to the clinic, leaning on his stick. He was walking between the tire tracks of Isobel's Jeep, which were the only tire tracks that had been made since yesterday's snow. The residents of Trinity certainly didn't get out much.

He reached the clinic, with its white wall around it, and it was here that the road divided – the right-hand fork going directly into the clinic's main entrance. The tilting sign next to the left-hand fork pointed to Route 97, and Weed, and Interstate 5.

Michael was puzzled to see that Isobel's tire-tracks took the right-hand fork, into the clinic.

He followed them through the open gates and into the parking lot, but the parking lot had been swept of snow this morning so he couldn't see where she had left her Jeep, if indeed she had.

This was really bewildering. She said that she had gone to Ray's Food Place for groceries, and she had indeed come back with groceries, some of which were Ray's own brand. But the evidence in the snow was that she hadn't gone there at all.

He stood there for a while, with the chilly wind fluffing in his ears. Then he walked slowly across to the clinic's front doors, climbed the steps and pushed his way inside. It was warm in here, with a shiny marble floor. His senses seemed to be heightened, and the clacking of women's heels sounded so loud that he could hardly hear himself think.

Catherine had not yet finished with her previous patient, so he sat down on the beige leather couch in the waiting area outside her office. A selection of magazines was spread out on the low table in front of him, and he picked up a copy of *Scientific American* and started to flick through it.

He read a few news items about the Large Hadron Collider, and bird flu, and how Alzheimer's patients could benefit from some cancer drugs. Then he turned the page and saw an article about soil erosion.

He thought: *I know all about this. I know all about soil erosion, and what a threat it is to the country's economy. Every year, agricultural topsoil the size of the state of Indiana is washed away down our streams and rivers, drastically reducing our ability to grow crops, and polluting our waterways, and costing us billions of dollars.*

He put down the magazine. He didn't have to read the article because he knew so much about soil erosion that he could have written it himself. He knew all the facts and financial figures.

But I'm a marine engineer. How come a marine engineer is some kind of expert in ecology?

The door to Catherine's office opened and a middle-aged man with his head in bandages came out. He went limping off toward the reception area and then Catherine came out, wearing a smart scarlet suit. She beckoned to Michael and called out, 'Gregory! Come on in! How are you doing today?'

Michael got up and followed her into her office. As she sat down and opened up her casefile, she said, 'You're looking a little tired, Gregory, if you don't mind my saying so. That walk from Isobel Weston's house isn't too much for you, is it? I could always have someone drive down there to give you a ride.'

'No, no, I'm fine,' said Michael, sitting down beside her. 'I'm a little out of it, that's all. You know, inside of my mind. I think maybe my neurons are beginning to regenerate. Isn't that what you said would happen?'

'Well, well, you're becoming quite an expert already!' said Catherine, brightly. 'What makes you think that?'

'I'm beginning to remember things. Not very clearly, but they're definitely coming back. Like

I just picked up that *Scientific American* in the waiting area, and there's an article in it all about soil erosion. Don't ask me how, but I know at least as much about soil erosion as Professor Whatever-his-name-is from Cornell University who wrote that article. Maybe more.'

Catherine pressed her hand thoughtfully across her mouth. Her fingernails were polished scarlet to match her suit.

Michael said, 'Maybe I'm reading too much into it, you know? But inside of my mind it feels like kind of a breakthrough.'

Catherine stood up, and put down her case-file on her desk. 'Will you excuse me for a couple of minutes?' she said.

'Is something wrong?'

'No. Not at all. I forgot to give a message to Mr Vane, that's all. I'll be back as quick as I can.'

She left the office, and hurried away down the corridor, leaving the door open.

Michael sat there for a while, looking around the office. On one side, there was a bookshelf full of books with titles like *Concussion and Brain Injury*, *Simple Salves for Severe Brain Trauma*, *Coup and Contrecoup Injuries* and *Antioxide Therapy for Cellular Brain Damage.*

On the opposite side hung a selection of photographs of Doctor Connor with her family – a serious bespectacled man with pattern baldness who must have been her husband, and two small children. In almost all of the pictures, Mount Shasta was somewhere in the background, snow-covered and remote.

After five minutes, bored, he stood up and

walked over to the door. Outside, in the waiting area, there was a wheelchair with a girl sitting in it, with her back to him. She was wearing a blue knitted bobble hat which he recognized at once. It was the girl who had screamed at him at the community meeting.

He looked left and right. There was nobody else around. He hesitated for a moment and then he walked across the waiting area and stood a little way away from her. He didn't want to surprise her and set her off screaming again.

She was sitting in her wheelchair with her hands clasped together staring at nothing at all. Michael thought that she was beautiful, but he felt that he had only come to recognize how beautiful she was through familiarity, through *knowing* her. Those high cheekbones, that tilt of her nose, those slightly parted lips. Yet how could he possibly know her? The first time he had seen her was at the community meeting.

She slowly turned her head and stared at him. She opened and closed her mouth as if she were about to say something, but then she turned away again.

I know you, he thought. *I know you, I know you, I know you.*

Catherine came back along the corridor. When she saw Michael standing beside the girl in the wheelchair she stage-whispered, *'Gregory!'* and beckoned him urgently back into her office.

Michael said to the girl, 'I'll see you again, OK? Maybe we can talk.'

The girl didn't respond, so Michael left her there, still staring at nothing.

TEN

They spent an hour talking about Michael's childhood, and what he could remember from his earliest days.

He could remember sitting on a wide yellow-painted window-sill, looking out over a sunny back yard. He could remember a red-and-yellow rocking horse, but not clearly, and he couldn't remember if it had been his rocking horse or not, nor where it had been.

One problem was that he kept remembering the photographs that his sister Sue had shown him, and he wasn't able to work out if they were genuine memories or not. Had he really been on Moss Beach that day back in 1991? He thought he could remember the sand, and the wind, and the seagulls crying like lost children, but maybe that was just his imagination helpfully providing background effects for a day that in fact he couldn't recall.

After an hour, though, Catherine said, 'That's enough for this morning, Gregory.'

'I'm fine, Catherine, I truly am. I don't mind carrying on. I think I'm beginning to remember some of the stuff I learned in high school, or college maybe.'

'That's very promising. But it's a mistake to

push yourself too hard. You can start to create false memories, just because you want so much to believe that your life is all coming back to you.'

'Come on – knowing all about soil erosion, that's not a false memory. I *know* about soil erosion. How it happens, what it costs, how to prevent it. You can't just make that up.'

'I know, Gregory. But I don't want you getting overtired. It could undo all of the progress you've made so far. Like I say, the signs are very promising, but we don't want to run before we can walk. Before you go, I'm going to give you a shot of PDT, which is an enzyme designed to increase the blood flow in your brain, and I want you to up your daily dose of Vinpocetine.'

'OK. Anything to speed things up. I'm sure I'm beginning to get better.'

He was about to tell Catherine that he thought he recognized the girl in the blue bobble hat, even though he didn't know *how* he recognized her, or why, or where from. But something stopped him from mentioning her. He didn't know what it was. For some reason, he felt *protective* toward the girl, and he was afraid that if he told Doctor Connor that he knew her, he might never see her again.

Thus in the winter stands the lonely tree.

As he walked out of the clinic gates, he saw Jack bustling toward him up the snow-streaked road, his hands thrust deep into his pockets, his shoulders hunched against the cold.

'Jack!' he called out. 'Hi there, how's it

going?'

'OK, man,' said Jack, doing a little dance to keep himself warm. 'I'm just going in for my physio session. Stretching and pulling and bending and all that shit. I hate that shit. How about you?'

Michael nodded back toward the clinic building. 'That girl who screamed at me, at the community meeting – I saw her just now, in the waiting room.'

'Well, come on, man, that don't surprise me. She's probably being treated for being physically or psychologically fucked up, the same as us.'

'Yes. But I'm sure that I know her. In fact, I'm totally *convinced* that I know her.'

'No shit. Where do you know her from?'

'That's the frustrating part about it. I can't remember. But she's not just some girl I went to college with, or met at some party. I *really* know her.'

'Can't you remember her name?'

Michael shook his head. 'No. I can't. I don't have any idea.'

'Maybe you should ask her. What's the worst she could do? Scream?'

'She didn't scream today. She just stared at me and didn't say a word.'

'Well, like I say, dude, next time you see her, *ask* her.'

'You're right. I should.'

Jack clapped a hand on his shoulder and said, 'Anyhow ... I have to go get my spine stretched and my knees unlocked. Maybe I'll catch you later.'

'That would be good. On your way back, why don't you drop into my place for a drink?'

Michael limped the rest of the way home, and let himself in with the key that Isobel had given him. She was sitting on the couch in front of the TV, her legs curled up under her, watching *The Doctors* and nursing a green pottery mug of herbal tea.

He went over and kissed her, and she lifted one hand and touched his face.

'How was it?' she asked him.

He felt like saying: *I saw your tire-tracks, and you didn't drive to Weed for those groceries, so where in hell did you get them*? But he felt the same sense of caution that he had felt when he had been tempted to ask Doctor Connor about the girl in the bobble hat. He felt that he needed to find out a whole lot more about Trinity and the Trinity-Shasta Clinic before he started to ask challenging questions.

Not only that, he felt that he needed to find out a whole lot more about himself. He still didn't totally discount Jack's suggestion that he might still be in a coma, and hallucinating all of this.

'You hungry?' Isobel asked him. 'I could fix you a sandwich if you are. I have some of that delicious marmalade-roasted ham.'

'Maybe later.' Then he said, 'You don't have a laptop, do you?'

'Sure. It's in the spare room. The Internet connection isn't too brilliant, but you can try it.'

'Thanks.'

She smiled at him, a strangely dreamy smile. Although they hadn't fully consummated their love-making last night, she gave him the feeling that he had satisfied her, and that she was very pleased and comfortable to have him staying here.

He went into the small spare room. It was chilly, and cluttered with cardboard boxes and shoes and suitcases and a vacuum cleaner. Underneath the window stood a cheap pine desk with a silver laptop on it, as well as a mug filled with pencils and ball pens, a clock that had stopped at five after twelve, and a wood-framed photograph of a woman who might have been Isobel's mother, by the look of her.

Michael sat down at the desk, opened up the laptop and switched it on. It seemed to be working, and he made an Internet connection almost immediately. He typed in *Trinity-Shasta Clinic*.

Up came a list of hospitals and clinics in the Shasta and Trinity areas, but no Trinity-Shasta Clinic.

He typed in *Kingsley Vane*. He got nothing.

He typed in *Doctor Catherine Connor*. There were several doctors with the name Catherine O'Connor, but none of them were trauma therapists. Two of them practiced in Dublin, Ireland, and the only Catherine Connor was not a proper doctor but a dermatologist in Cleveland, Ohio.

Next he typed in *Gregory Merrick*, and got nine results, but none of them was a marine engineer in San Francisco, as he was supposed to be. One was the fire marshal at the township of Irondequoit, near Rochester, New York; another was the vice-president of human resources at Canyon Resorts in Salt Lake City; another ran his own communications company in Canada and yet another called himself a 'music professional'.

He was trying to think what to search for next when the laptop's screen went blank. At first he thought it might need recharging, so he plugged it into the socket in the wall. He pressed the *on* button again, but the screen stayed blank, and none of the laptop's indicator lights came on.

He went back into the living room. Isobel was watching *Let's Make A Deal*. Outside the window, it was starting to snow again.

'I think your laptop is kaput,' he said. 'I was right in the middle of checking something and it just went *phut*!'

'Oh, don't worry,' said Isobel. 'It does that sometimes. In any case, I only ever use it for my writing.'

He sat down next to her. 'What do you write?'

'All kinds of things. Articles, stories. Poetry.'

'You should let me read some.'

She reached out her hand and said, 'Come sit down.' He sat next to her and she snuggled up close to him. 'I don't think you'd be very interested in what I write. *Democracy, Sexuality, Death and Immortality in the Works of Walt Whitman*. That was my latest essay.'

'Sounds profound.'

'Believe me, it is. Not that I'm suggesting that you wouldn't understand it. I just think you'd find it boring. I'm sure you'd much prefer to read something technical about boats.'

'I'm not so sure that I would,' said Michael. 'In fact I don't think I'm a marine engineer at all. In

114

fact I don't even believe that my name is Gregory Merrick.'

She sat up straight and frowned at him. 'It *must* be. You had your driving license on you, didn't you, when you had your accident? And your credit cards.'

'I just don't *feel* like "Gregory Merrick".'

'Who do you feel like, then?'

'I don't know, Isobel. I still can't remember.'

She snuggled up close to him again. 'Doctor Connor told me that you would probably have doubts about your identity. Apparently it's common when you have post-traumatic amnesia. Accepting who you are, that can be really hard, especially if you weren't particularly happy before your accident – or you were lonely, or depressed, or you didn't like your job.'

'I couldn't tell you if I liked my job or not. I know absolutely squat about marine engineering. Well – maybe that's what the problem was. Maybe I *was* a marine engineer, but I was really crappy at it.'

'Doctor Connor said I should try to keep you calm and happy.'

Michael looked sideways at her, and then kissed her on the forehead. 'You do,' he said. 'You're a very attractive lady, and you make me feel very, very good – whoever I am.'

A little over an hour later, when Isobel was in the kitchen preparing a chili, the doorbell chimed. Michael went to answer it, and there was Jack, with his hair and the shoulders of his leather jacket covered in snow.

'Hi. You said come round for a drink. Is that still OK?'

'For sure. Come on in. Better take your boots off, though. Isobel's fussy about her rugs.'

'Who's that, Greg?' called Isobel, from the kitchen.

'Jack. You remember Jack from the community meeting? I invited him back for a drink.'

'Of course,' said Isobel. She appeared in the kitchen doorway wearing a red-and-white checkered apron. 'How are you, Jack? How are Margaret and Bill?'

'Oh, they're good, thanks, Ms Weston.' He knelt down on one knee to unbuckle his biker boots. 'I'll tell them you asked after them.'

Michael took Jack through to the living room and then went through to the kitchen to take two bottles of Coors out of the fridge.

'How about you, Isobel?' he asked her. 'Glass of white wine?'

'I don't know why you asked him back here,' she hissed. 'He's not exactly our kind of people, is he?'

'I like him. He's genuine. And who cares what kind of people he is?'

'The Endersbys only took him because they couldn't find anybody else.'

'What are you talking about?'

'They had to have *somebody* when they lost Bradley, so they didn't really have a choice, did they?'

'I don't understand. Why not?'

Isobel didn't answer, but furiously started chopping up onions.

'Bill Endersby seems to like him,' said Michael.

'Well, like I say, he didn't have any choice, did he?'

Michael stood by the door, watching her scrape the chopped-up onions into the skillet. He considered pursuing the subject, but then he thought: *No, leave it. I'm only going to end up with even more riddles than I started with.*

'So – how about that glass of wine?' he asked her.

She looked up at him, and suddenly broke into a flirtatious smile. 'OK, then. I'm sorry. I guess you're entitled to have friends, even if they are a little rough at the edges.'

Michael gave her another kiss. Even if she didn't speak a whole lot of sense, he did like her, a lot. At least she was somebody to talk to, and somebody to share a bed with.

He went back into the living room while Isobel finished off preparing her chili, and handed Jack a beer.

Jack said, 'Going back to that girl, man, I definitely think you need to ask her who she is.'

'It's not going to be easy. How am I going to find her? And she may be the same as me, and have amnesia. Maybe she doesn't *know* who she is.'

Jack took a swig of beer and burped. 'I have a definite feeling that if you can discover who she is, then a whole lot of other stuff is going to fall into place. Like I said, there's so many things in this place that don't click together. Maybe if we can get just *two* things to click together, like who

117

she is and why you know her so good...'

'Well, you could be right,' said Michael. He glanced over his shoulder to make sure that Isobel was still busy in the kitchen. 'Let me tell you something else.'

He leaned close to Jack and in a low voice he told him about the groceries that she had brought home from Ray's Food Place in Weed – except that her tire tracks showed that she hadn't driven to Weed at all.

'There you are, then,' said Jack. He sang the *dee-dee-dee-dee* theme music from *The Twilight Zone*. 'We have to find out what's going on around here, even if we find out that you and me are both bananas, and we're reading things into things that aren't really happening at all. I mean, maybe everybody in Trinity has these special snow shoes that don't leave footprints.'

'Do you believe that?' Michael asked him.

'Of course not.'

'Neither do I.'

Jack swigged more beer, and then he said, 'What we should do is go up to the clinic tonight, walk in and find that girl and ask her straight out. She should have medical notes on the end of her bed, anyhow, and her name is bound to be in there.'

'Oh, I see. We just walk in.'

'We're both patients there, man. We both have ID badges.'

'I don't know, Jack. What do we say if they stop us?'

'Come on, we make some kind of excuse, like one of us wasn't feeling too good so the other one helped him up to the clinic to find a doctor.'

Michael was about to say 'give me some time to think about it' when Isobel came out of the kitchen, carrying her glass of wine and a bowl of pretzels.

'Here, thought you might like something to nibble on. Chili's going to take another forty minutes. Do you want to stay for lunch, Jack?'

'That's real kind of you, Ms Weston, but I think Margaret's cooking me one of her chicken pot pies today. She sure likes to spoil me.'

Michael finished his bottle of beer and went into the kitchen for another one. The chili was bubbling quietly to itself on the hob, and the windows were steamed up. He opened the fridge and took out two bottles, and as he closed the fridge door and turned around, he could see through the steam that the snow was falling on the back yard much more thickly now, like duck down.

He went up to the window and wiped it with his hand.

He said, *'Shit!'* and almost dropped both bottles on the floor.

Standing at the far end of the yard, quite still, were Bill Endersby and a woman whom Michael could only assume was his wife, Margaret. They were both staring at the house, their arms by their sides, making no attempt to brush off the snow that was piling on their shoulders. Neither of them was wearing an overcoat. Bill Endersby had on a dark green cardigan and baggy black corduroy pants while Margaret was wearing a beige sweater and a brown pleated skirt.

Michael stared back at them. He couldn't work out if they could see him or not, because they showed no sign of movement. A black-headed mountain jay landed on the snow right in front of them, and hopped in between them, leaving its fork-like tracks, but around Bill and Margaret there were no footprints at all. Either the thick snow had already covered them up, or else they hadn't left any.

'Greg?' called Isobel. 'Are you OK in there? You're not sneaking a taste of my chili, are you?'

Michael returned to the living room. He looked at Jack and tried to convey by rolling his eyes that he had seen something weird out of the kitchen window, but Jack didn't cotton on.

'You feeling OK, man? You sure you can handle another beer?'

What was he going to tell him? *'We have two uninvited visitors, out in the yard'*? Maybe if Isobel had left footprints when she crossed the front lawn he would have done. But he decided to say nothing for now. If the Endersbys were still there when Isobel returned to the kitchen to check on her chili, she would see them for herself.

On the other hand, what if they were still there but she *couldn't* see them? What would that mean? That he was hallucinating? That he really was still in a coma, after all?

He sat down and tried to smile, and Isobel put her hand affectionately on his knee, but he felt that he was on the verge of madness.

ELEVEN

He waited until Isobel was sleeping. She was lying on her back, her head turned away from him, breathing evenly through slightly parted lips. She was still wearing her pearl earrings.

She had failed to draw the drapes completely together, leaving a narrow gap between them, and so the bedroom was coldly illuminated by moonlight, and by the moonlight that was reflected by the snow outside.

After Jack had left, and Michael and Isobel had gone through to the kitchen together, there had been no sign in the back yard of Bill and Margaret Endersby. No footprints, either – only the cross-stitching of birds' feet.

All the same, Michael had glanced out of the window so frequently when they had been sitting at the kitchen table eating their chili that Isobel had frowned and said, 'What's out in the yard that's so much more interesting than me?'

'Thought I saw a raccoon, that's all.'

'Oh, great. What a compliment!'

They had held each other close when they had gone to bed, but when Michael had started to stroke her breasts and roll her tightening nipples between his fingers, she had gently pushed him away, and kissed him, and said, 'I'm a little tired

121

right now. Is that OK? Maybe later. Wake me up in a couple of hours.'

She had fallen asleep very quickly, within five or six minutes. He had leaned over her for a while, his head in his hand, watching her sleep. He had seen from the way that her eyeballs were darting around underneath her eyelids that she was dreaming. *Maybe she's dreaming of me*, he thought. *Maybe that's who I really am, after all. Nothing more than a character in Isobel's dream.*

He ran his hand gently over her shoulder, and her upper arm. She still felt so cold. He dragged up the quilt and covered her, up to her shoulders, but she didn't feel any warmer.

He felt quite tired himself, but he had arranged to meet Jack outside at a quarter after midnight. He had never seen the numbers on a digital clock change so slowly. When they showed 10:39 he deliberately turned away, and counted to sixty, but when he turned back they were still showing 10:39.

Isobel continued to breathe, and to dream, but her skin still felt chilly.

He could see his pale reflection in the mirrors on the closet doors. *'Gregory Merrick!'* he called out, in a whisper, but the pale reflection did nothing but stare back at him. It didn't wave, or climb out of bed, or bury itself under the quilt. *'Gregory John Merrick!'*

Like last night, the closet doors were slightly ajar, and he could see the black shark's eyes of Isobel's doll, Belle, gleaming at him suspiciously out of the darkness.

At last the clock said 12:02. Michael eased himself out of bed, taking care to cover up Isobel's shoulders with the quilt, but she didn't stir. He tiptoed out of the bedroom, closing the closet door on his way past. It was ridiculously superstitious of him to think that Belle might tell Isobel that he had crept out of the house, but right now he was beginning to believe that anything was possible. If people could walk across deep snow without leaving footprints, who was to say that dolls couldn't talk?

He hurried to his room and pulled on his Levis and his thick black roll-neck sweater. Then he shrugged on his coat and pulled on his boots, and let himself out of the house. After he had opened the front door, he paused and listened for a moment, just to make sure that Isobel hadn't woken up, but there was only silence.

Jack was waiting for him, leaning against the front fender of Isobel's Jeep and chafing his hands together to keep warm. He had wrapped a thick gray scarf around and around his head in a ball, so that he looked like a snowman with leprosy.

'OK,' he said, hoarsely. 'You ready for this? 'Cause if you don't want to do it, man, we don't have to. We can just go back to bed and pretend that everything in Trinity is stone-cold normal.'

Michael said, 'I sure as hell can't do that now, Jack. Bill and Margaret were standing in the back yard when you were there.'

'Ex-squeeze me? What back yard? Where?'

'Isobel's back yard. When I went to fetch that second beer, there they were, the two of them, standing outside in the snow.'

'You're pulling my chain! Doing what?'

'Doing nothing. Just standing there. After you'd gone, they disappeared, too. But they didn't leave any footprints.'

Jack looked bewildered. 'I don't know how that's possible, man. They were both at home when I got back. Margaret was in the kitchen rolling out pastry and Bill was in his den, tying flies. That's one of his hobbies, so he told me, fly-fishing.'

'What were they wearing?' asked Michael. He and Jack were climbing up the gradient toward the clinic now, and they were both slightly out of breath, especially since the temperature was well below zero.

'How should I know? Oh – Bill had on that slime-green button-up sweater he always wears, and Margaret – I don't know. She was wearing an apron. But something brown, probably. That woman does love her brown.'

They walked along beside the whitewashed clinic wall, and in through the main entrance. A gray-haired security guard was sitting in a small illuminated booth on the right-hand side of the entrance, reading a newspaper. He looked up as they approached, but they both held up their TSC identity tags and he gave them a dismissive wave of the hand and let them pass.

'See ... told you we could just walk in,' said Jack. 'They might be hiding something here, man, but what they don't know is that we *suspect* that they're hiding something. So they're not going to be so alert, are they?'

'We haven't gotten inside yet, so don't be too optimistic.'

'Do you know something?' asked Jack, as they approached the front steps. 'You have a real interesting accent. I meant to mention it to you before. You definitely don't sound like you was born and raised in 'Frisco. You sound more like Mid-West, you know? More like Chicago or Milwaukee. I had a girlfriend from Milwaukee – well, Kenosha, really. That's how I can tell.'

'If you're trying to make me more confused than I am already, you're succeeding,' said Michael. The revolving door was locked but they pushed their way into the clinic reception area through one of the side doors.

There was nobody sitting behind the reception desk. The reception area was brightly lit and shiny and very quiet. Somewhere they could hear the sound of a floor-polisher, and what sounded like a television, with occasional bursts of studio laughter, but that was all.

Michael said, 'That girl looked like she'd suffered a head injury, so it wouldn't surprise me if she's located in the same wing where they treated me. If she has brain damage, they'll be giving her psychiatric treatment as well as physio.'

'Well, you know where that is, man. Lead on.'

They passed the reception desk and took the right-hand corridor. It was long and softly lit, with a blue-gray carpeted floor, and framed land-scapes all the way along it, every one of them featuring Mount Shasta in the background.

Along the corridor there were sixteen blue-

125

painted doors, eight on each side. Every door had an oval window in it, so they could peek inside to see if there was anybody in there. Most of the rooms were empty, with nothing in them but stripped-down beds. In two or three of them, patients were sleeping, bandaged and connected up to heart monitors and drug dispensers. In the seventh room they came to, two nurses and a doctor were gathered around a patient's bed, checking his blood pressure and hooking him up to an intravenous drip. Michael ducked his head down quickly so that they wouldn't catch sight of him.

They walked all the way down to the end of the corridor. As they came to the last two doors, Jack said, 'Nah ... looks like they've taken her some-place else, man. Maybe she's not here in the clinic at all.'

But when Michael looked into the second-to-last window, he saw the girl lying on her bed on her back, her head bound with white bandages, fast asleep. Her blue bobble hat was hanging on the chair beside her. He angled his head to the left, and then to the right, just to make sure that there was nobody else in the room, but the girl was alone.

'It's her,' he told Jack. 'I'll go in and try to wake her up. With any luck she won't scream the place down.'

'I'll keep watch,' said Jack. 'If I see anybody coming, I'll give you three knocks.'

'And what if they ask you what the hell you're doing here, in the middle of the night?'

'Don't worry about it, dude. I'll think of something.'

'Like what?'

'Something like we said before. Like, I was woken up by these terrible shooting pains in my back, right? I couldn't take them any more, so I came up here to the clinic to find myself a doctor. But, I kind of got lost, and wandered down the wrong corridor, and that's why I'm here.'

'OK. I guess that sounds plausible. Or plausible-ish.'

Michael took a quick look back down the corridor to make sure that there was nobody in sight, and then he carefully opened the door. He hesitated for a moment, but Jack said, 'Go on. If you're going to do it, go ahead and do it.'

Michael stepped into the girl's room and closed the door behind him. He approached the bed and stood over her. She was attached to a Veris vital signs monitor, which was softly beeping and flashing, and as far as he could tell, her heart rate looked stable. She was very pale, but she looked just as beautiful as she had when he had first seen her at the community meeting, and even more familiar.

I know you. I know you so well. How can I possibly know you so well?

For a split-second, he saw another flash of lights, and heard that blurt of sound again, and that girl's voice saying *you shouldn't*. And he smelled that perfume, too – that elusive, floral perfume.

Maybe it was *her* voice, and *her* perfume.

'Who are you?' he said, but only in a whisper, because now that he was here, standing beside her bed, he wasn't at all sure that he was doing the right thing. It was clear from the bandages around her head that she had sustained a very serious injury. Waking her up and demanding to know who she was and why he knew her so well – who knows what trauma that could cause her, both physically and psychologically? He didn't want to make her worse than she was already.

He heard a single sharp tap at the door, and turned around. Jack was glaring in through the window and jerking his head to indicate that Michael should hurry up. Michael gave him a thumb's-up and mouthed, 'OK.'

He laid his hand on the girl's shoulder and gently shook it. She didn't show any signs of waking up so he shook it again. Maybe the doctors had given her a sedative, and nothing would rouse her.

'Hello?' he said. 'Hello, can you hear me? I need you to open your eyes.'

She licked her lips with the tip of her tongue and murmured, *'Why did you...?'*

'Can you hear me?' he repeated. 'I need you to open your eyes. I need you to talk to me. I need you to tell me your name.'

Again she licked her lips, and then her eyelids fluttered.

'Please,' said Michael. 'Please wake up and tell me who you are.'

He shook her shoulder once more, harder this time. Still she didn't open her eyes.

'Please,' he repeated. 'Please wake up.'

There was another single knock at the door, and there was Jack, giving him the evil eye through the window. He shrugged to show that he was having no luck. Jack pointed furiously to the metal bracket at the end of the bed which contained the girl's medical notes. *Look in there*, he mouthed, silently. *See if you can find her name in there.*

Michael lifted out the folder. It had a stiff pink cardboard cover with the name *Natasha Kerwin* written on it, in black felt-tip pen. Underneath was printed *G. Hamid, Snr Consultant* and – in parentheses – the words (*semi-substantial*).

Michael opened the folder and quickly leafed through the notes. He couldn't make sense of any of them. There were twenty pages or more, crowded with statistics and graphs and comments like 'Temporal dynamics in layers II/III have unusually fast 4–5 Hz oscillation' and 'Cortical trauma could jeopardize prospect of conversion to s.s.'

He closed the folder and touched the name *Natasha Kerwin* with his fingertips, as if by osmosis it could give him some clue as to who she was. Her name seemed faintly familiar, but he couldn't think why. It told him nothing more than those flashing lights he kept seeing, and that girl's voice saying *you shouldn't*, and that tantalizing waft of perfume.

He slid the folder back in its bracket, and looked at the girl again. To his surprise, her eyes were open and she was staring at him.

'You're awake,' he said, coming around to the side of the bed.

She opened and closed her mouth without saying anything, but she lifted up her right hand as

129

if she wanted him to take hold of it. He clasped it between both of his hands, and it was shockingly cold.

'Jesus, you're *freezing*,' he told her. 'Why don't you put your hands under the covers?'

She licked her lips again, and then she whispered, 'You shouldn't let me go to sleep like that.'

'What?'

She looked around the room, frowning. 'Where are we? Is this our hotel?'

'This is a clinic. You've been in some kind of an accident. You've been hurt.'

'Accident?'

'I really don't know. It could have been an auto wreck.'

'But *you're* not hurt, are you?'

'Me? No. I *was*, but that was months ago. I'm pretty much recovered now, except for my memory.'

'Have you come to take me home?'

'I can't,' said Michael. 'You're still having treatment. Your name's Natasha, right? That's what it says on your notes.'

The girl stared at him as if he had said something completely absurd.

'My *notes*? What are you talking about?'

Michael was about to explain when there were three rapid knocks at the door. Jack was pulling faces outside the window and making frantic hand signals.

Michael looked quickly around the room. There was a door on the left-hand side, which was half open. He could see a white-tiled wall inside, so he presumed that this was the bathroom. Next to the bathroom, there was a closet. He went over and opened it and saw that the only clothes hanging up inside it were a pale green toweling robe and a gray dress that was still covered in plastic from Shasta Dry Cleaners.

Jack knocked again, twice, and even more urgently. Michael turned to the girl and said, 'Listen – you haven't seen me, OK? I was never here.'

'But aren't you going to take me home?'

'Later. Not yet. But I will. I promise.'

At that moment he heard voices outside the door. He couldn't make out exactly what they were saying, but it sounded as if somebody was asking Jack what he was doing there, and Jack was trying to explain that he was lost. For twenty or thirty seconds after that, there was silence, and then suddenly the door opened. Michael quickly stepped inside the closet and closed the door behind him, although he had to leave it a half-inch open because the catch was on the outside, and he didn't want to lock himself in.

A deep, accented voice said, 'What's this, Natasha? You're awake!' Michael recognized it immediately as Doctor Hamid. 'Did you have another one of your nightmares?'

The girl didn't answer, but another man's voice said, 'Her heart rate's up. Blood pressure's down.' This voice was sharper, and higher.

'I shall have to give you another sedative, my dear,' said Doctor Hamid. 'You need all the sleep you can get.'

'Maybe we should think about bringing her SS

131

forward,' said the other man.

'No – not yet,' replied Doctor Hamid. 'SS is quite traumatic enough without perceptual impairment at the same time.'

'So, when do you think, then?'

'I don't know. If we can see within the next few days that function is returning to the parietal lobe, then, yes, maybe we can go ahead. Otherwise – well – there's not a whole lot of point, is there?'

'She'll be a good guinea-pig for our drug program.'

'Possibly, yes. But as far as SS is concerned, it's not as though she has anything to offer intellectually, is it? And she won't be much good as a companion, if she's suffering from chronic PTSD. We might as well pull the plug.'

Doctor Hamid and his associate stayed in the room for another five minutes, while Michael remained in the closet, breathing as quietly as he could, his knees aching, his neck growing stiffer and stiffer, praying for them to hurry up and go. They said very little more to each other, and nothing that Michael could understand, although Doctor Hamid spoke to the girl as he injected her with a sedative.

'There, Natasha, this should give you much more pleasant dreams,' he said soothingly.

The girl said nothing at all.

Michael heard a rattling sound, and then a cough, and at last he heard the door opening and closing as the two men left. He waited for a few seconds more, and then he stepped out of the closet. He bent over to rub his knees, and then he stood up straight to stretch his back.

He crossed over to the girl's bedside, but the sedative had already taken effect and she was asleep. He took hold of her hand again. He couldn't believe how cold she was, as cold as if she were dead, although she was still steadily breathing. He tucked her hand underneath the woven cotton cover.

He stood there for a while, just watching her, trying to make sense of the way he felt about her, trying to understand who she was, and what was happening to her.

'Natasha Kerwin,' he repeated. 'Natasha Kerwin.'

Why had Doctor Hamid said that 'we might as well pull the plug'? Had he seriously suggested that they were going to take her off life-support? Because that was what it had sounded like. But why? Because she 'didn't have anything to offer intellectually', whatever that meant? Because she was 'too traumatized to be a companion', whatever that was?

Michael felt such a strong urge to protect her, and take care of her, although he didn't understand why that should be. She had asked him if he had come to take her home, and he wished that he could, except that he didn't know where her home was, and she obviously wasn't well enough to go anywhere.

He leaned over her bed and kissed her on the forehead. Her eyelids fluttered but that was all.

'Natasha Kerwin,' he said, one more time, and then he left her bedside and opened the door to the corridor. There was nobody in sight, so he quickly stepped out and closed the door behind him. Now he had to find out what had happened to Jack.

He walked rapidly back to the reception area. It was deserted. He tried looking into one or two rooms nearby, but they were empty, too. The clinic was totally silent. Even the sound of the floor-polisher had stopped, and the television had been switched off.

Doctor Hamid must have told Jack to go home, and it was so cold outside that Jack wouldn't have waited for him. Michael took one last look around, and then he pushed his way out through the clinic doors. The night was clear and frosty, and the sky was prickly with stars.

He walked back to Isobel's house and quietly let himself in. When he undressed and slipped into bed beside her, she turned toward him and murmured, *'Emilio, it isn't true, I swear it.'*

Michael lay awake for almost an hour after that, and the night was so silent and so still that he almost felt as if he could feel the world turning underneath him.

He could think of nothing but Natasha, her white and perfect face, and Doctor Hamid saying that he 'might as well pull the plug'.

TWELVE

After breakfast the following morning, Michael told Isobel that he was going to take an early walk. Toward dawn, the wind had changed around, and clouds had rolled over, pillowy and gray, with that dull orange tinge that usually warns of impending snow.

'I thought you might want to come back to bed,' she told him, smiling at him over her second mug of herbal tea.

'For sure – well, yes,' he said, although he could feel that his own smile was tight and defensive. 'But maybe later. I don't want to get myself caught out in a blizzard.'

'Well, your loss, lover,' she shrugged. 'But you know that you're more than welcome, any time.' Her pink silky robe was open at the front so that he could see she was wearing nothing underneath, only a shiny silver pendant like a gibbous moon.

He went through to the hallway and pulled on his boots. As he was buttoning up his coat Isobel came out of the kitchen and said, 'By the way, I'm having some friends around this afternoon. Just a little social get-together. I hope you're going to join us.'

'OK. Fine. What else would I be doing?'

'I don't know. I have the feeling you're not very settled, that's all. I just wanted to make you feel at home.'

'I'm fine. Really. It's this amnesia that's bugging me, that's all. I keep remembering bits and pieces but I don't know what they mean, or how they all fit together.'

'How does Doctor Connor think you're getting on?'

'Catherine? She's increased my meds, but I'm not sure that's made any difference. Not yet, anyhow.'

Isobel came up to him and put her arms around his neck. She looked up into his eyes and said, 'You know that I'll do anything for you, don't you? And I mean *anything*. You're my whole life now, Greg. I hope you understand that. I couldn't live without you.'

He gently prised her arms open, and kissed her on the forehead. 'Like I said before, Isobel, I'll be able to give you a whole lot more of myself when I know for sure who I am.'

'I love you,' she said.

Michael knew how happy it would make her if he said the same thing back to her, but he couldn't. He simply smiled that tight, defensive smile and squeezed those chilly hands of hers.

'I won't be too long. I'm only going for a walk around the block, just to keep Doctor Hamid happy.'

He opened the front door and went out into the blustery cold. Already a few snowflakes were whirling around, and they flew into his eyelashes and on to his lips so that he could taste them as they melted. He had taken his walking stick with him, but he was beginning to hobble a little less, and even since yesterday his knees seemed to have lost some of their stiffness. *If my body's on the mend*, he thought, *maybe my memory is, too.*

And then he thought: *Natasha. Natasha Kerwin. I* know *you, Natasha. God knows why, but I don't care why. I know you and there's no way that I'm going to let Doctor Hamid pull the plug on you, whatever that means, and whatever his reason for doing it.*

He walked down past the community center and then up the slope toward the loop where the Endersbys lived. The snow was coming down much thicker now, although the wind was blowing it in wild, unpredictable patterns, as if ghosts were dancing all around him. He went up to the front door and pressed the doorbell. Inside, he heard a two-tone chime, and after a few seconds a light was switched on. Through the hammered-glass panel beside the door he saw the fragmented image of Bill Endersby coming to see who was there.

'Bill!' he said, cheerfully, when the door opened up.

Bill Endersby looked whiter and sicker than ever. He was wearing a baggy green cardigan and gray flannel slacks that must have been three sizes too big for him.

'Yes?' he blinked, as if he didn't know who Michael was.

'It's Greg Merrick, Bill! *Greg* – Isobel's companion.'

'Oh, yes. What do you want, Greg? It's damned cold here, with this door open.'

'I'd like to talk to Jack, if I could.'

'Jack?' said Bill Endersby. He sucked at his dentures, and then he said, ''Fraid that won't be possible. No.'

'Why's that, Bill? Isn't he here right now? I can come back later.'

'He's not here and he won't be here later. He won't be coming back at all.'

'Really? Where's he gone? I only saw him yesterday and he didn't say anything to *me* about leaving. He's OK, isn't he?'

'He's gone, and he won't be living here no more. That's all I know.'

'Any way I can contact him? Did he leave a cellphone number, or an email address? Anything like that?'

Bill Endersby was already starting to close the door. 'I told you. He's gone, and he won't be living here no more, and that's all I know.'

'If you see Jack, or hear from him, tell him I called around, will you?' Michael called out, as the door was closed in his face.

And another thing, Bill – what the hell were you and your wife doing in Isobel's back yard yesterday, staring in through the kitchen window? And how come you left no footprints? What are you – a man, or an optical illusion?

Michael stood in the porch for a few moments, wondering if he ought to try ringing the doorbell again, and pressing Bill Endersby to tell him more. But he decided it was probably a waste of time, especially since Bill Endersby didn't look at all well. He retraced his steps, out of the loop and back down the slope, with the snow clinging to his coat and catching in his hair. He checked his watch, and saw that it was almost 10:30 – nearly time for him to go to the clinic for his morning therapy session with Catherine.

He trudged up the hill, back past Isobel's house. Because the day was so dark Isobel had raised the blinds, so that he could see her inside the living room, still wearing her silky pink robe. She had her arms raised above her head, and she was pirouetting around and around, as if she were ballet-dancing, although he couldn't hear any music. He stopped and watched her for a while, and then continued on his way. Not a single car passed him as he climbed up toward the clinic, and he saw nobody out walking – not even the girl in the red duffel coat with her sheepdog, or Jemima on her bicycle. The snow was so thick that even Mount Shasta was invisible, although he was sure that he could feel its brooding presence.

Catherine said, 'Let's go back to names that you might be able to remember from your childhood. Your teachers, your school friends. Your pets.'

But Michael asked her, 'What's happened to Jack?'

'Jack? Excuse me? I don't know what you mean.'

'You know, *Jack* ... who was living with the Endersbys.'

'Oh, Jack Barr, yes.'

'Well – what's happened to him? I saw him yesterday and he was fine. Then I went around to the Endersbys' house this morning to see him again and Bill Endersby told me he was gone.'

Catherine nodded, and kept on nodding, as if she were playing for time. In the end, she said, 'Sometimes, Gregory, a companion doesn't quite fit in.'

Michael said, 'Really? It seemed to me that Jack fitted in with the Endersbys pretty darn good. He seemed to be rubbing along with them OK, and they were certainly fond of him. Bill Endersby said that he was like a son to them.'

'Yes, I know. But Jack had other problems. Physical, and psychological. We didn't want to jeopardize the Endersbys' well-being. They're quite frail, healthwise, and since they lost their son Bradley, they've both been very vulnerable to any kind of emotional upset. We moved Jack away as a precautionary measure – for all the parties involved.'

'That tells me absolutely nothing. Where have you moved him to?'

'He's having intensive treatment here at the clinic. Then he's going to go back into the community until he's fully recovered.'

'But not to the Endersbys?'

'No. That won't be possible. We're urgently trying to find them a replacement.'

'So where will Jack go?'

'We have two gentlemen living on Siskiyou Drive. We're planning on moving him in with them. You met one of them at the community meeting – Walter Kruger.'

'Walter Kruger's an accountant. Jack's a biker. Do you seriously think that the two of *them* are going to get along together?'

'Getting along together isn't always the point, Greg. It can help, for sure, but it isn't everything. People have other needs which are far more important than simple compatibility.'

'Like?'

Catherine gave him the slightest of shrugs. 'Like symbiosis. Like needing each other, whether they like each other or not.'

'You've lost me again. Why would somebody like Walter Kruger need somebody like Jack, or vice versa?'

'We're getting way off the subject, Greg. Tell me if you can remember the name of your first math teacher.'

'I have absolutely no idea. Even if I didn't have amnesia, I don't think I would have been able to remember something like that.'

'Ms Truman, that was her name. Your sister told me that.'

'Ms Truman? Doesn't ring a bell at all. But if that's what her name was, OK, that's what her name was. Ms Truman. Can I see Jack, since he's here?'

'Not at the moment, no. He's still undergoing treatment.'

'So what exactly is wrong with him?'

'You know I can't tell you that, Gregory. Patient confidentiality. But he should be up and about in two or three days. What was the name of your best friend at school?'

'Natasha.'

Catherine checked her clipboard. Then she said, 'No, that's not correct, I'm afraid. Your

141

sister said it was Bradford Mitchell.'

'Unh-hunh, no way. It was Natasha Kerwin, I'm sure of it.'

Catherine stared at him narrowly. 'Where did you hear that name? Natasha Kerwin?'

'In my head. In my memory. Natasha Kerwin.'

'What you *think* is a memory is more than likely something that you've picked up since you regained consciousness. You probably heard somebody say that name soon after you came out of your coma, and it lodged in your auditory cortex.'

'What makes you so sure? It's perfectly possible that I had a best friend at school called Natasha Kerwin, isn't it?'

Catherine said nothing, but turned over another page on her clipboard. 'How about place names?' she suggested.

It was then that Michael thought: *She doesn't want me to believe that I can remember Natasha Kerwin. She's deliberately trying to make me think that my mind is playing tricks on me. But I do remember her, and I would very much like to find out why Catherine doesn't want me to think that I do.*

'Sure,' he said. 'Place names.'

He closed his eyes tightly and tried to remember houses, and streets, and parks, and shopping centers. In his mind, he could see a dull suburban road, with houses and trees slowly passing him by, as if he were sitting in the back seat of a car. For some reason, he was feeling desperately unhappy, close to tears. At first he had no idea what this road was called, but then he heard a man's

142

voice saying, 'Here we are, folks! Home again! Fonderlack Trail!'

He opened his eyes. 'I think I can remember a name,' he told Catherine.

'You can?'

'I think we must have lived there. It was a road called Fonderlack Trail. I can remember lawns. And houses. And some of the houses were gray. And I can remember feeling really sad there, although I don't know why.'

Catherine laid her clipboard down on her desk. 'I think you might need some alternative medication, Greg. It seems to me like your mind is trying to compensate for your amnesia by inventing memories that never happened to you. I'm going to try you on propranolol. It's a beta-blocker. It may help you to distinguish between real memories and made-up memories.'

'But I *can* remember it,' Michael insisted. 'I can see it in my mind's eye. Fonderlack Trail. I was sitting in the back of a car and I was almost crying.'

'That's the effect of your accident,' said Catherine. 'Your amygdala is creating an emotional experience to explain how you feel. Propranolol will help your brain to erase it.'

'But what if it *is* real? And what if I don't *want* it erased, whether it's real or not?'

'If you allow it to stay stored in your subconscious, Gregory, you may never find your way back to knowing who you really are. And I mean, like, *ever*.'

Isobel was dressed by the time he returned to the

house. She was wearing a tight charcoal-gray sweater and even tighter black jeans. She was laying out side-plates and glasses on the coffee table in the middle of the living room, but when Michael entered she immediately put down the plates she was holding and came over to wrap her arms around him.

'I *missed* you,' she said. 'I think you should realize that making love is just as therapeutic as walking. Even Doctor Hamid will tell you that.'

'OK. I'll ask him next time I see him, just to make sure. What time are your guests arriving?'

'Any minute now. It's not still snowing, is it?'

'Not as much as it was.'

Isobel frowned and said, 'Something's still worrying you, isn't it? It's not *me*, I hope. I'm not coming on too strong for you? I think that's always been my trouble. When I like a man, I can't hide my feelings. I simply can't.'

Michael shook his head. 'No, it's not that. But I think that I'm being lied to. In fact, I'm beginning to wonder if anybody in Trinity ever tells the truth about anything.'

'What makes you think *that*, for heaven's sakes? Everybody here is so friendly. And all the doctors and nurses at the clinic ... they're all so open, and all so helpful.'

'OK,' said Michael. 'Where did you get those groceries yesterday?'

Isobel lowered her arms, her forehead furrowed in a frown. 'I told you. Ray's Food Place, in Weed.'

'You never went to Weed. I saw your tire tracks in the snow when I walked up to the clinic. As a matter of fact, *nobody* had been to Weed, not since the snow started.'

'Well, of course I didn't actually *go* to Weed. Why would I? We all place our orders with Ray's Food Place online and then they deliver to the clinic, because it's so central.'

'Why don't they deliver to your door?'

'They do, when it isn't so icy. It's for safety, that's all. There are too many kids and seniors walking in the roads, because the sidewalks are so slippery.'

'I'm sure you told me that I should come along with you, next time you go there. Which kind of implied that you'd actually been there, wouldn't you say?'

'Well, you should come with me. You must. But not for a week or two. Not until it thaws.'

She paused, and then she took hold of his hands. 'Why would I lie to you, Greg? What would be the point? Why would *anybody* in Trinity lie to you?'

'I don't know,' said Michael. 'Maybe I'm be ing paranoid. I feel like something's badly wrong but I can't work out what it is. Half the time I don't even believe that I'm real.'

'Of course you're real. I can vouch for that. You can't give a man head, can you, if he isn't real?'

'Yes – but supposing *you're* not real? Supposing none of this is real?'

At that moment the doorbell jangled. Isobel kissed Michael on the cheek and said, 'I'll prove it to you later, when all of our guests have gone. Meanwhile, how about being sociable?'

They all arrived at once, nine of them, and crowded into the hallway, taking off their hats and coats and stamping their snowy boots on the doormat. Isobel went out to help them, but Michael stayed in the living room, staring at himself in the mirror.

You're real, he told himself, as he waited for Isobel's guests to come in. The strange thing was that none of them was talking. The only sound from the hallway was shuffling and stamping and two or three coughs.

After a short while the first of them came in, a short middle-aged man with gingery hair that was beginning to turn gray. He reminded Michael of Mickey Rooney. He held out his hand and said, 'George Kelly, my friend. Pleased to know you. Glad that our Isobel has found herself another companion. What would we do without her, eh?'

It was only when Michael saw that George Kelly's bright blue eyes were not focused on him at all, but somewhere behind his right shoulder, that he realized that he was totally blind. He stepped forward and took George Kelly's hand, and shook it. It was, like Isobel's hands, stunningly cold.

'Pretty darn chilly outside,' he remarked. 'When do you get spring in these parts?'

'End of March, if we're lucky, beginning of April. Can't say that I notice the seasons much. Spend most of my time indoors, and when I do go out I don't feel the cold. Don't feel the heat, neither.'

'Where are you from, George?' Michael asked him. 'I mean, like, originally, before you came here to Trinity?'

'We don't talk about the past,' said a large woman in a crimson corduroy dress, flooding into the living room like a tsunami and clamping her podgy hand on George Kelly's shoulder. 'All we care about is the present, here in this community, and the future, too, of course. Some of us have been through experiences that we prefer not to dwell on.'

'Sure, yes, sorry,' said Michael. 'I guess I'd be the same, if I could remember what happened to me, but the plain fact is that I can't. Post-traumatic amnesia.'

'You're a lucky man,' said George Kelly. 'I'd give anything, if I could forget. Anything.'

Now the rest of Isobel's guests entered the living room. They varied in ages from a pretty girl with a ponytail who looked only about fifteen or sixteen, to a bulky man with a black bandanna tied around his head who was probably forty-something. Then in came an elderly woman whose back was hunched and who walked with two sticks, her long amethyst earrings swinging from side to side as she made her way across the room.

Isobel asked Michael to go through to the kitchen and carry in three extra chairs, and then they all sat down around the coffee table. With the help of the girl with the ponytail, Isobel brought in shortbread cookies and brownies and ginger snaps, and poured out coffee or herbal tea or Pepsi-cola.

'Everybody!' she said, clapping her hands. 'I want you all to welcome Greg Merrick, my new companion. Greg was involved in an auto wreck and has temporarily lost his memory, and so he's staying here with me while he recovers. He's a very welcome replacement for dear Emilio.'

'Well, I'm sorry to say that I don't think anybody could quite replace Emilio,' said the large woman in the crimson dress. 'But we're happy to have you here, Greg, for Isobel's sake. We wouldn't want to lose our dear Isobel; she's the life and soul, so to speak.'

Michael didn't know if that was a compliment or an insult, so he said nothing at all, and simply smiled, and raised his coffee cup.

The fortyish man with the black bandanna reached across the table and held out his hand. 'Good to know you, Greg. My name's Lloyd Hammers. Guess you and me are pretty much in the same leaky boat.'

Michael raised his eyebrows to show that he didn't quite understand.

'My truck turned over on the interstate. Well, so they say. Me – I don't recall how it happened. Broke both legs in seven different places and suffered from memory loss, just like you. I got most of my memory back but I was single and unattached and there was nothing for me to go back to Bakersfield for. I couldn't drive a truck no more with my legs, so I decided to stay here. I get housed, and fed, and all I have to do is take care of old Mrs Kroker there.'

The conversations continued, and it quickly became obvious to Michael that this was a regular support group, with everybody discussing their problems and their fears for the future. And there did seem to Michael to be one unspoken fear which haunted them all.

'I don't know what I'm going to do without my Lloyd here,' said Mrs Kroker, her back so bent that she had to twist her head sideways to look up at them all. She reached out with a turkey-claw hand and gripped Lloyd's wrist.

Michael thought: *What the hell is she worried about? She must be eighty-five years old if she's a day. Her Lloyd is going to outlive her by two decades at least.*

But then George Kelly smiled in the direction of a young woman with upswept spectacles and flicked-up brunette hair and a pale green printed blouse. 'I can't imagine life without Hedda. I have nightmares about it, I'll tell you.'

Michael could understand anybody's anxiety about being left on their own as they grew older, but what both Mrs Kroker and George Kelly were saying made no sense. What puzzled him even more was that neither Lloyd Hammers nor the girl in the pale green printed blouse made any comment. They simply smiled dumbly and shrugged.

'Katie, dear, I forgot the paper napkins,' said Isobel. 'Would you fetch them for me, please? They should be in the third drawer on the right-hand side, under the flour jar.'

The girl with the ponytail stood up and went through to the kitchen. Michael stood up, too, and held up his empty soda glass. 'Just going to get myself a refill,' he said, and Isobel smiled

149

at him.

In the kitchen, he found the girl opening and closing drawers.

'Can't find them?' he said.

'No. They're not in any of *these* drawers, anyhow.'

'Greg Merrick,' he said, holding out his hand.

'Katie Thomson,' she replied. She was really very pretty, with a heart-shaped face and pink cheeks and wide brown Betty Boop eyes. She was wearing a shocking-pink sweatshirt with silver sequins on it, and bright red jeans.

'Mind if I ask you what you're doing with *that* crowd of misfits?' he asked her, nodding his head back toward the living-room.

'I don't have any choice, do I?'

'I don't know. Do you? I would have thought living in Trinity was pretty soul-destroying for somebody of your age.'

She let out a little snort as if she thought he had said something funny.

'Where are your folks today?' he asked her. 'Don't they come to these get-togethers, too?'

'My folks?'

'Yes. Your mom and dad.'

Katie Thomson suddenly said, 'Look, there they are! She left them on the window sill!'

She went across and picked up the cellophane pack of blue paper napkins which Isobel had left behind the kitchen faucets. Michael turned around and opened the door of the fridge so that he could take out the bottle of Pepsi.

'It seems kind of strange to me that you should be here on your own, that's all,' he said.

150

But when he turned around again, with his hand on the bottle-top, he saw that Katie Thomson was already back in the living room, handing out napkins to Isobel's guests. She was right on the opposite side of the coffee table, and he couldn't think how she had got there almost instantaneously, without making any sound whatsoever. He hadn't even glimpsed her leaving the kitchen out of the corner of his eye, even though she was wearing those red jeans and that shocking-pink sweatshirt.

He filled his glass with cola and his hand was trembling. When he went back into the living room, Katie Thomson looked up at him and beamed triumphantly, as if she had answered all of his questions by leaving him like that. It occurred to him that he might have reason to be afraid of her. In fact he might have reason to be afraid of *all* of these people.

He sat down next to her. She leaned over to him confidentially, and whispered, 'I'm jealous.'

He looked at her for a long time. Her eyelashes were long and sooty with mascara, and she had very fine hairs on her upper lip.

'What of?' he asked her at last, although his voice was little more than a croak.

'Of Isobel,' she said. 'Of you.'

THIRTEEN

That night, when he was almost asleep, Isobel started gently to rub him.

He turned his head toward her and said, 'Hey...'

'You should have come back to bed this morning. Then I wouldn't feel so frustrated.'

She continued to rub him, harder and harder, and after a while he tried to lift himself up so that he could climb on top of her.

'No,' she said, trying to push him back down. 'Let me do it to you.'

She started to wriggle down the bed, but now Michael took hold of her wrists and pinned her down. He heaved himself up again and sat astride her, gripping her body between his thighs. She struggled, and thrashed from side to side, but he was too heavy for her, and too strong, and besides that he urgently wanted to penetrate her.

'No,' she gasped.

'No? What do you mean "no"? You're the one who's coming on to me!'

'I said I'd do anything. But not that.'

Michael reached one hand down and forcibly parted her thighs.

'Please,' she said, but his blood was banging in

his ears now and he ignored her. He raised himself up, and positioned himself between her legs, with the head of his hardened penis nestling between the lips of her vulva. She was very juicy, even though her juice felt cold.

'Greg,' she said, 'you won't like me if you do this.'

'I won't like you? What do you mean? I do like you. I want you. I want to make love to you properly.'

'Greg, please...' she begged him, and made another effort to twist herself out from underneath him.

But right then Michael wanted to push himself inside her more than anything else in the world, and he did. He leaned his whole weight on top of her and forced his penis into her as far as it would go. She gave a little jump as he touched the neck of her womb, but then she let out a long, breathy *oohhhhhhhhhh* and tilted her head back and closed her eyes.

Michael pushed himself into her again and again. But even as he felt his climax beginning to tighten between his legs, he began to understand why she had resisted him, and why she had said that he wouldn't like her.

Inside, she was numbingly cold. Slippery, yes, but slippery-chilly, so cold that his glans began to ache, in spite of how hard and how fast he was pushing himself in and out of her. He could even feel the cold juice smothering his scrotum and the sides of his thighs.

He released her wrists and she clung to him tightly, digging her fingernails into his bare back. She was gasping now, while he was grunting. His penis was so cold that he could hardly feel it, and he had to push harder and harder to get any sensation out of their love-making at all.

It was Isobel who climaxed first. She gave a high-pitched yelp, and then she began to quake. Her fingernails dug deeper into his back, and she quaked, and quaked, and as she did so, Michael climaxed, too. For a moment he could feel the warmth of his own semen inside her, but then that was chilled, too.

He took himself out of her and rolled over on to his side, his penis shrinking as quickly as if he had waded into the ocean on a January day.

Isobel stayed where she was, on her back, her legs still wide apart, her left forearm resting across her forehead, almost covering her eyes.

'You're so cold,' said Michael, with a catch in his throat. He coughed, to clear it.

'I told you that you wouldn't like me, if we did it that way.'

He leaned across and tried to kiss her but she turned her head away.

'I *do* like you,' he insisted. 'But why are you so cold? Are you sick, or something? Have you talked to anybody at the clinic about it?'

'*I'm* not sick,' she said.

Michael thought for a moment, but then he said, 'What does that mean? *You're* not sick?'

She sat up, and swung her legs off the side of the bed, with her back to him. Her pale, triangular back. He reached out and touched her shoulder blades with his fingertips and then trailed them down her spine. She shuddered, but not as though she didn't like it.

'Are you saying that I'm sick? That there's something wrong with me?'

'I'm not saying anything. If you knew why I feel so cold, it would only spoil things, and I love you, and I don't want to lose you. I don't want to lose *me*, either.'

Michael sat up, too. 'There you go. Talking in fucking riddles again.'

Isobel turned her head around. Her eyes glistened in the half-light, in the same way that Belle's eyes glistened inside the closet. 'The whole of life is a riddle, Greg. From beginning to end. There's no point in trying to work out what it all means. Like W.B. Yeats said, "Life is a long preparation for something that never happens."'

'But why do you feel so cold? That's all I'm asking. If there's something wrong with you, I need to call a doctor. If there's something wrong with me, I need to call a doctor.'

'There are some things, Greg, that no doctor can cure. Like a broken heart, for instance.'

Michael reached out for her again, but before he could touch her she stood up and walked off to the bathroom. On the sheet where she had been sitting he felt cold, prickly crystals, like grains of rock salt. Some of them stuck to the palm of his hand, but almost as soon as they had done so, they melted.

He lifted his fingers to his nose, and sniffed, and smelled the distinctive bleachy aroma of semen. When he had ejaculated inside her, Isobel had been so cold that his climax had actually frozen.

He lay awake almost all night thinking what he should do. Isobel lay in his arms, cold but sleeping soundly, her cool breath playing against his shoulder.

Catherine Connor must have known about Isobel's medical condition before she brought him here to convalesce, and to act as her companion. She must also have suspected what would happen between them. So maybe her coldness wasn't contagious, or life-threatening. But what sickness can make a woman so cold inside that she turns her partner's semen into ice? Why wasn't she dead from hypothermia?

Then again, Isobel had appeared to suggest that the problem could be his, not hers. He felt OK, physically. His knee and elbow joints were still swollen, and he had moments when he felt off-balance, which Doctor Hamid had attributed to the concussion that he had suffered, but he was sure that he was improving every day. He certainly wasn't suffering from any erectile dysfunction.

Maybe his problem wasn't physical at all, but metaphysical. Maybe Jack had been right after all, and what appeared to be happening in Trinity was all to do with reality, or unreality. And what had happened to Jack anyway?

The digital clock beside the bed flicked to 4:46. Isobel was still sleeping in his arms. She had said that she loved him, but he wondered if that was lust, rather than love. All the same, and in spite of her coldness, and the bewildering things that she said to him, he liked her, and he felt strongly protective toward her.

He decided that today was the day when he was going to demand some straight answers from Catherine and Doctor Hamid and he would go to Kingsley Vane, if he had to.

A small voice inside his head said: *What if they're hiding something from you for your own good? What if they tell you something that you wish you'd never known? What if you sustained some injury in that accident that altered your perception of the whole world, and who you are? What if...?*

But he closed his eyes then, and deliberately shut off his thinking, like closing a musical box.

Go to sleep, he told himself. *Tomorrow you'll find out for sure.*

The next morning was sunny and bright, so bright that Isobel pulled down the blinds. She made him French toast for breakfast, and sang 'Somebody I Used To Know' as she fluttered around the kitchen, perking his coffee for him and laying the kitchen table.

She put her arms around him and kissed him, and looked meaningfully into his eyes, but that was all. She said nothing about their love-making last night, and he didn't intend to raise the subject, either. Whatever questions he asked her, she would only give him conundrums in return.

'What are you doing today?' he asked her instead.

'I'm going round to Bethany Thomson's to play bridge this afternoon. You can come if you like.'

'No, I think I'll take a rain check. I don't know how to play bridge, and even if I do, I've forgotten. Bethany Thomson – is she Katie Thomson's mother? That girl who was here yesterday?'

'That's right. Tragic, what happened to that family.'

'Oh, yeah?'

'There was a house fire. Apart from Katie, the Thomsons had twin boys, aged three. Both of them died from smoke inhalation.'

'That's terrible. No wonder Katie's a little off the wall.'

'She took a shine to you, though.'

'That's me. Greg Merrick the Babe Magnet.'

Isobel touched his cheek and smiled. 'It's good to see you relax. One day you'll realize that you don't have to keep on asking questions about the way things are.'

'The day I do that, sweetheart, I'll be dead.'

Isobel's smile immediately faded. 'Don't say that, Greg. Please.'

'Why not? We all have to die someday. You know what I'm going to have engraved on my tombstone? "He Came. He Went."'

'Don't,' she insisted. 'It isn't funny.'

'I'm sorry,' he said, and put his arms around her, and gave her a hug. He kissed her earlobe and it was cold. He nearly whispered 'I love you' in her ear to make her feel better, but he still couldn't bring himself to say it.

He had intended to face Catherine with a barrage of questions about the Trinity-Shasta Clinic, and about his treatment here. He had wanted to ask her why everybody that he had met here in the community felt so physically cold, and how they could appear to leave no footprints in the snow. He had also wanted to find out what was happening to Natasha Kerwin, and what 'pull the plug' meant.

When he reached the clinic, however, he was told by the receptionist that Doctor Connor was away that morning, and that he would be treated instead by Doctor Do Shu-Ji.

He spent a dull and unproductive hour with Doctor Do, who mainly went over the questions that Catherine had asked him so many times before. What color was your mother's hair? What was your favorite toy when you were little? Who was your best friend at school? What sports did you enjoy the most?

Doctor Do was small and polite with a black pudding-bowl haircut and rimless spectacles. He spoke English with hardly any expression at all, so that it was sometimes difficult to know if he was asking a question or making a statement.

'Your mother was good cook.'

'Was she? I don't remember.'

'No ... I am asking *you*, Gregory-ssi. Your mother was good cook?'

'Oh. In that case, I still don't remember.'

When he had finished, he went past the reception desk toward the corridor that led to Natasha Kerwin's room. The receptionist looked up from the magazine she was reading and said, 'Help you, Mr Merrick?'

'Just looking around, that's all.'

'That corridor is off-limits, I'm afraid. Intensive care. That's where *you* were, when they first brought you in here, all smashed up.'

'Oh. OK.'

Michael circled around the reception area for a while, but there was no real point in staying if Catherine was away and he couldn't get to see Natasha. Eventually he pushed out through the revolving door into the sunshine, and stood on the steps outside, tugging on his gloves. It may have been sunny outside, but the temperature was still minus five.

He was halfway down the steps when a clinic orderly in a green TSC jacket appeared around the left side of the building, pushing a wheelchair. Sitting in the wheelchair, all bundled up in a red plaid blanket, was Jack. He was wearing large movie-star sunglasses, but it was unmistakably him.

At the same time, in the parking lot, a large green Chevy Express panel van started up, and came creeping out to meet them. The van pulled up close to the clinic entrance, and then its driver climbed out to open up its back doors. He pressed a button to lower an elevator platform, and the orderly pushed Jack's wheelchair on to it, and locked it into place.

Michael stepped to one side, so that he was mostly concealed behind the bay tree at the right-hand side of the entrance. He didn't quite know why he felt the need to hide himself, but until he knew more about the Trinity-Shasta Clinic, and what had happened to Jack, he thought it would be wiser not to show how inquisitive he was. For all he knew, it might even be safer, too.

Jack's wheelchair was lifted into the back of the van, and the driver slammed the doors. Then the driver and the orderly walked around to the front of the van and climbed in. They drove out through the clinic gates, and turned left, toward Trinity, leaving behind them a sun-gilded ghost of exhaust smoke.

Michael hurried down the steps and followed them out on to the road. He was just in time to see them take the left fork that followed the clinic boundary wall, rather than the right fork which led back down to Isobel's house and the community center.

He started to walk after them, as fast as he could manage. Trinity was only a small community, after all, so they couldn't have gone very far. His leg muscles were aching after his lovemaking, and his sleepless night had left him feeling tired, but he needed to find out where they were taking Jack. The last time he had seen him, before he had gone into Natasha's room, Jack had seemed fine, both physically and mentally. How come he needed to be wrapped up in a blanket and wheeled around in a wheelchair, as if he were crippled?

The road curved around to the left until it reached the end of the clinic boundary, and then it curved to the right, and began to slope downhill. Here, there were houses on both sides of the road, most of them single-story, most of them with snow-covered vehicles parked outside. Again, there were hardly any tire tracks across the sidewalk, which indicated that their owners hardly ever went out – not since yesterday's snowfall, anyhow.

The TSC panel van was parked about seventy-five yards down the road, on the right-hand side, outside a yellow-painted two-story house with a gray stone porch. Its back doors were open, and Jack's wheelchair was being lowered on its elevator platform, although it looked as if the platform had jammed halfway down, because the van driver was banging at it with a wrench. As Michael came hobbling down the slope, he realized that he was very conspicuous in his long black overcoat against the snow, and especially since he was the only other person in the street. However, it appeared that the clinic orderly and the van driver were too preoccupied with unloading Jack's wheelchair to have noticed him. There was a leafless acer tree a few yards ahead of him, and he took four long steps and hid himself behind it.

Thus in the winter stands the lonely tree. He just hoped that they wouldn't notice his vaporizing breath.

The van driver continued to bang at the elevator platform with his wrench, and the banging echoed across the cold and silent street. At last there was a whining noise, and the platform sank down to road level. The clinic orderly pushed Jack's wheelchair across the snowy sidewalk and up the driveway to the house.

As he did so, the front door opened and a woman came out. A tall, blonde woman in a dark blue sleeveless shift dress with a pale blue turtleneck sweater underneath. Michael recognized her instantly, even from this distance. It was his

162

sister, Sue.

He stood stiffly behind the tree, with his back against the trunk, trying to breathe out through his nostrils so that he wouldn't produce so much tell-tale breath. What was Sue doing here, in a house in Trinity, when she was supposed to be living with her husband and her children in Oakland – the best part of three hundred miles away? And if she was only here on a visit, why hadn't she come to see him? Most baffling of all, why was she taking Jack into her house?

He had to wait for over ten minutes before the clinic orderly came back out of the house, and the van U-turned in the middle of the road and drove off back toward the clinic. He waited two or three minutes longer, and then he peeked around the side of the tree to make sure that there was nobody standing in front of the house, or looking out of any of the windows. Then he walked back uphill as quickly as he could.

It was clear to him now that he was being deceived by everybody in Trinity, both at the clinic and in the community. Maybe their intentions were good, but how could he be sure until he knew why they were lying to him? He was almost certain now that 'Sue' wasn't his real sister at all – that's if he even had a sister. And that meant that all of the childhood photographs she had shown him must have been fake, and all of the stories that she had told him about his schooldays were invented.

More importantly, that suggested that the name 'Gregory Merrick' was invented, too, and that he wasn't a marine engineer from San Francisco.

Maybe he didn't even live in San Francisco. Maybe he was somebody else altogether – somebody who remembered Fonderlack Trail and feeling sad; somebody who knew all of the technical facts about soil erosion. Somebody who knew a girl called Natasha Kerwin, and knew her well.

As he reached the long clinic wall, and walked beside it, he began to remember something else.

Thus in the winter stands the lonely tree
Nor knows what birds—

He thought harder, frowning in concentration.

'Nor knows what birds have vanished—'

And then the next words came to him.

'Nor knows what birds have vanished one by one.'

He couldn't think of any more, but he could hear a woman's voice faintly saying, like somebody talking to him through a closed window, 'Well done, Michael! Very well done!'

FOURTEEN

Michael.

Could that be his real name – Michael? Or was he simply remembering the name of a classmate? He didn't feel like a 'Michael' any more than he felt like a 'Gregory'.

He reached the turn-off to walk back down to Isobel's house. As he did so the black Escalade slid silently out of the clinic entrance and drove toward him. He pretended to ignore it, and carried on walking in the road, but the Escalade crept up behind him and then drew level.

Even when it was keeping pace with him, its engine softly burbling, he acted as if it wasn't there. After it had accompanied him about fifty yards down the road, however, its blacked-out passenger window came down with a whine and he was confronted by the white-haired, white-faced man in his sunglasses.

'Take a wrong turn back there, sir?' the man asked in a tensile twang.

Michael looked at him for a long time before answering, trying to give the man the impression that he didn't know what the hell he was talking about, and even if he did it was none of his business. The man looked much younger than he had first imagined him to be. His skin was very smooth and his hair was albino white rather than white with age. Michael was tempted to ask him if he had seen him before, as a sclf-flagcllating monk in *The Da Vinci Code*.

'Just taking some exercise,' he replied. 'As per Doctor Hamid's explicit instructions.'

'Prefer if you restricted your walks to your own locality, sir,' the man told him. 'Some of the individuals who live on Summit View are kind of sensitive about their privacy.'

'Oh ... like it's a "no-go" area? Sorry. Nobody told me.'

'It's just a question of security, sir, and respecting other residents' personal space. We don't have "no-go" areas in Trinity.'

'I'll have to correct you there,' Michael retorted. 'Right outside Mrs Weston's house, with your nose pressed to the fucking window, that's a "no-go" area. Got it?'

Michael continued to walk down the slope and the Escalade continued to creep along beside him. The white-faced man stared at Michael from behind his sunglasses although his face was completely expressionless. After about fifteen seconds, he put up his window without saying another word and the Escalade drove away.

Maybe he hadn't been wise to provoke Trinity's security patrol like that, Michael thought. But here in Trinity, what was wise and what wasn't? It was impossible to judge. Maybe a little provocation would help him to find out what was going on in this community. Maybe there was nothing going on at all, in which case it wouldn't really matter if he made a few sharp remarks.

But if there was nothing going on at all, why had the security patrol cautioned him to stay away from Summit View, and more to the point, what was his sister Sue doing there, with Jack?

When he returned home, he found Isobel in the kitchen, which was warm and steamy. She was stirring a large herby-smelling pot of soup.

'Hope you like minestrone,' she smiled, turning her face toward him so that he could kiss her.

'If it tastes like it smells, then yes.'

'How was your therapy?'

'Useless. Catherine was away so I was stuck with some dopey Korean doctor who kept call-

166

ing me "Gregory-ssi".'

'That's supposed to be polite, in Korean, isn't it?'

'If that's polite, give me insulting any time.'

He watched while Isobel replaced the lid on the pot and turned down the gas. She hung up her apron and then came up to him and put her arms around him.

'After my therapy was finished, I saw something very strange,' he told her.

'Go on,' she said.

He didn't know if it was a good idea to be telling her this, because he had seen her talking to Sue as if they were old friends – even though Sue had denied it. But after being cautioned by the Trinity security patrol like that, he was in a mood to stir things up. Not only that, he felt that he had to tell *somebody*, and Isobel was the only person he could talk to. If he kept it to himself, he would have no way of judging if he was suffering from some sort of delusion. In short, he would have no way of knowing that he wasn't going mad.

'I saw Jack, being pushed in a wheelchair,' he said. He explained how he had followed the TSC van, and how he had hidden behind the tree, and how he thought he had seen Sue coming out of the house.

'You're sure it was her?'

'Pretty sure, yes. I mean, she was quite far away, and I only saw her for a few seconds. But, yes, I'd lay money on it. It was Sue.'

'Why don't you call her? She gave you her number, didn't she?'

'Yes, she did. I didn't think of that.' Michael reached into the back pocket of his jeans and took out his wallet. In the back of it, he found the number that Sue had written down for him. It had an Oakland area code, 501, so if she *did* answer, that would prove that he had been mistaken, and that the woman he had seen taking Jack into her house was only a lookalike.

Isobel took the kitchen phone from its bracket on the wall and handed it to him. He punched out the number and waited. It rang and rang and rang without anybody answering it, and he was just about to hand it back to Isobel when a man's voice said, 'Hallo? Hayward residence.'

'Oh – hi,' said Michael. 'I was wondering if I could speak to Sue.'

'Who is this?'

'It's her brother Greg, calling from Trinity. You must be Jimmy.'

'That's right. Hi, Greg. How are things shaping up?'

'Not so bad. Still having a little trouble with the old amnesia. Is Sue there?'

'Sure thing. Wait up just a second.'

There was a pause, and Michael heard the man calling out, 'Sue! Sue! Your brother's on the phone!' Then footsteps clattering down uncarpeted stairs, and finally Sue saying breathlessly, 'Greg! How are you? Is everything OK? There's nothing wrong, is there?'

'No – no, nothing's wrong. It was just that you said you would come up to see me next week and I've forgotten which day.'

'Well – Thursday, probably. But it may have to

be the week after, because Petey may be chosen for the swim team, in which case I'll have to take him to practice.'

'OK. That's OK. It's my memory, that's all. It still comes and goes. It's like talking on your cell when you're driving through a tunnel.'

'I'll call you, Greg, I promise you, and let you know when I'm coming.'

'Thanks, Sue. Give my best to Jimmy and your kids.'

He gave the phone back to Isobel and she slotted it back on the wall.

'There,' she smiled. 'Does that make you feel better?'

'I guess it does, yes,' he said. But then he paused, and thought about it. 'No, Isobel, it doesn't. In fact, totally the opposite. I'm sure that was Sue I saw coming out of that house, and if I'm so sure, but she's really in Oakland, then there must be something wrong with me. Not just memory loss. Something else.'

Isobel took hold of his hands. 'Greg, there's nothing wrong with you that a few more months here in Trinity won't cure. I promise you. Everything's normal here. Maybe everything's *too* normal, and your brain refuses to accept it. But it will, eventually. Believe me, Emilio was the same as you at first, always having doubts, always having suspicions.'

'The late Emilio.'

Isobel nodded.

'I don't know,' said Michael. 'Maybe I ought to take the bull by the horns and go straight back up to Summit View and knock on the door.'

'Greg, baby, you're just making things worse for yourself.'

'But supposing I knock on the door and it *is* Sue?'

'It can't be. It won't be. You just talked to her on the phone in Oakland.'

Michael stood in the middle of the kitchen and covered his face with his hands. 'I'm going crazy.'

Isobel held him close. 'You're not, Greg. You're not. You've been through so much. You're bound to have days when your mind plays tricks on you.'

Michael lowered his hands and looked at her. 'What if it's not my mind? What if there's something else wrong with me?'

'Like what? Doctor Hamid says you're making wonderful progress.'

'I don't know, Isobel. I don't trust anything that anybody says to me. I don't trust anything that anybody does. Worst of all, I don't even trust *me*.'

Thus.

Isobel kissed him, first the tip of his nose and then his lips. 'Come to bed,' she said.

In the winter.

'It's one-twenty in the afternoon.'

Stands the lonely tree.

'What does that have to do with it? Come to bed.'

Nor knows what birds have vanished.

'It's starting to snow again. Look.'

One by one.

She gripped the front of his jeans and held him

170

tight, her eyes narrowed in lust and amusement. 'Come to bed,' she said.

She led him by the hand into the bedroom and quickly took off her clothes, crossing her arms to lift her tight white sweater over her head, and reaching behind her with her triangular shoulder blades protruding to slide open the catch of her bra.

By the time Michael had taken off his sweater and unbuttoned his shirt, she had already tugged off her jeans and stepped out of her thong, and was sitting on the side of the bed pulling off her nylon socks.

They lifted the covers and climbed into bed together naked. The bedroom was filled with a pale reflected light from the snow in the back yard outside, a light that was almost eerie, as if they were making love somewhere high above the Arctic Circle, or on the moon.

Michael wrapped his arms around Isobel and held her close.

'You're still so cold,' he told her. 'I really think you should go see one of the doctors.'

'I love you,' she whispered, and her whisper was thunder in his ear. She took hold of his penis with her chilly fingers and started to massage him.

He kissed her cold forehead, and ran his fingers into her hair. Even her scalp was cold. He kissed her again, but then her head disappeared under the covers and he felt her icy tongue sliding all the way down his chest and his stomach, and her cold lips closing over the head of his penis.

She sucked him so hard that it was painful, and he gasped. At the same time she cupped his testicles in her hand and her hand was so cold that his scrotum shrank. Then she forced his thighs wide apart and stroked his anus with her fingertip.

Inside his head, he thought: *This is all madness. I shouldn't allow her to do this to me. But what if it's me that's mad? What if she isn't really cold at all, but there's something wrong with my nervous system, and she just* feels *cold? Not to anybody else, just to me.*

If I can see my sister who isn't there – who can't *be there – why isn't it possible that all of my other senses are out of whack, including my sense of touch?*

Isobel continued to suck him and lick him and gradually his penis began to grow numb, like the last time they had made love. But just when he began to think that he would have to beg her to stop, she slid her finger deep inside his anus, all the way past the knuckle. It felt like being penetrated by an icicle, and he immediately climaxed.

She gave him three long sucks, even though he could barely feel them, and then she reappeared from under the covers with a triumphant smile on her face.

'There,' she said. 'Don't tell me you didn't enjoy that?'

He kissed her. 'It was different, I'll tell you that. It was like being raped by a Popsicle.'

'That was the idea. Now – how about you return the favor?'

* * *

They made love for over another hour, until Michael began to shiver.

Isobel touched his lips with his fingertips and said, 'Look at your lips, they're blue. You need to get dressed and get warm and I'll feed you a bowl of my minestrone soup.'

'Sounds like a plan,' he told her. He hadn't felt as cold as this since ... He frowned. He *had* felt as cold as this once, but he couldn't remember when, or where, or why. He thought he could hear young boys' voices calling to each other across a frozen lake, and he thought he could hear a whistle, and a man shouting. But then the voices and the whistle and the frozen lake faded from his consciousness, and he was left lying in the rumpled bed while Isobel climbed out and picked up her clothes.

For a few moments she stood naked against the opaline light of the bedroom window, and he couldn't help thinking what a beautiful figure she had, and how he could probably have fallen in love with her, if only things had been different. If only she hadn't felt so cold (or seemed to him to feel so cold) and if only he hadn't felt that the Trinity-Shasta Clinic and everybody who lived in Trinity was on the wrong side of Alice's looking-glass, himself included.

He stayed in bed for a few minutes longer while Isobel went into the kitchen to heat up the soup. Eventually he got up and went to the window to look at the snow falling.

He was shocked to see Jemima standing outside, with her friend in the red duffel coat.

173

Jemima was wearing the same pink windbreaker that he had seen her wearing before, and the same wooden beads in her frizzy brown hair. The two of them were standing side by side, motionless, while the thickening snowflakes clung to their hair and their shoulders. Michael couldn't work out if their eyes were focused on him or not, but they didn't seem to be perturbed by the fact that he was naked.

He went through to the kitchen. Isobel turned around, wide-eyed, and said, 'Are you going to walk around like that for the rest of the day? Not that I mind, one bit!'

'Look out there,' he told her, pointing to the window.

Isobel looked, and then said, 'What? It's snowing. So what?'

'Can't you see them? There are two little girls out there.'

Isobel put down her soup ladle and went right up to the sink. 'No, there aren't.'

Michael came up and stood beside her. She was right. The back yard was empty. There were no footprints, either, not even jays' footprints, because the snow was so fresh.

Michael shook his head. 'I saw them out there, I swear to God. They were probably out there when we were in bed together. They must have run off.'

'Greg, the gate is locked. There's no way that anybody could have gotten into the yard unless they climbed right over the fence. Do you know these girls? Have you seen them before?'

'I met them on the first day that Catherine

brought me down here to meet you. One's called Jemima but I don't know what the other one's name is. Jemima has kind of a nasty pink scar on her forehead, like a lightning flash.'

'She's not Harry Potter's sister, by any chance?'

'Isobel, get serious. I saw them. They were standing right there, by the bird bath.'

Isobel kissed him and then put her hand down between his legs and squeezed him. 'I believe you. Thousands wouldn't. Now hurry up and put some clothes on before I'm tempted to take you back to bed again.'

Michael went back into the bedroom and started to dress. As he did so, though, he kept staring out of the window, but the two girls didn't reappear.

It is me. If I can see them, but Isobel can't, it must be me. Like I saw Bill and Margaret standing outside, when Jack was here. Like I saw Sue. I'm seeing people who aren't really there. I'm hallucinating. Either that, or there's something devastatingly wrong with me, and nobody has the heart to tell me what it is.

He put on his wristwatch and checked the time. Two thirty-three, well past time to take his midday dose of Vinpocetine. He went along the hallway to his bedroom, which seemed chilly and abandoned now that he had started sleeping with Isobel. He took the blue-and-white carton of pills out of his left-hand desk drawer, and pressed four of them out of their foil backing.

He cupped them in his hand, and took them through to the bathroom. He filled a glass tumbler with water, and was about to swallow them when he saw his face in the mirror over the washbasin.

'*Michael*,' he said. His face looked back at him but offered no indication that he had recognized himself.

'Gregory,' he said. Then, again, '*Michael.*'

He juggled the four pills in his hand. He was about to take the first of them when he thought: *No, if I can't trust anybody in Trinity to tell me the truth, how can I trust them to give me the correct medication? Instead of helping me to remember, maybe these pills are to make sure that I never do.*

One by one, he pushed them down the drain, and then flushed the basin with water. *Let's see what happens now*, he told his reflection. *If my memory doesn't improve – well, it can hardly be worse than it is now. But if it* does *improve...*

If he were to be honest with himself, he had no idea what the implication would be, if he did start to regain his memory. It might mean that Catherine was deliberately keeping him in a permanent state of post-traumatic amnesia, or it might mean that he was regaining his memory in any case, with or without medication.

But he was certain about one thing. He was going to leave Trinity, and he was going to leave Trinity tonight, and for good. Whether he could remember who he really was or not, he would rather face the challenge of the world outside than spend another day in this community, wondering whether or not he was mad – or worse.

* * *

They sat at the kitchen table to eat their mine-strone soup, and it was good, with plenty of celery and carrots and tomatoes and cannellini beans, all mixed up with pasta. However cold Isobel felt in bed, she was a marvelous cook.

'What are you going to do for the rest of the afternoon?' she asked him.

'Take my obligatory walk. Then, I don't know. You're off to play bridge with Bethany Thomson, aren't you? I think I'll just collapse on to the couch and watch one of those soaps you like so much. *The Bold and the Boring*, whatever it's called.'

'*The Bold and the Beautiful*,' said Isobel. 'Like you, my darling.'

After lunch, Michael put on his overcoat and wound his long blue scarf around his neck, and then opened the door and stepped outside. It was snowing so furiously that he was almost tempted to forget his walk and forget about leaving Trinity and go back inside, where it was warm and comfortable.

But he knew that he had to get away tonight. The snow could be even worse tomorrow, and he had the feeling that he might have already left it too late. He started to make his way down the middle of the road toward old Mrs Kroker's house, at the bottom of the slope, next to the community center.

On the opposite side of the slope, about a half-mile away and almost invisible in the snow, he saw the distinctive red duffel-coat of Jemima's friend, and then the pink smudge of Jemima's windbreaker. He supposed he could have called out to them, but he didn't want the snow flying into his mouth, and he had something much more important to do than find out how they had managed to climb into Isobel's yard.

He had to arrange his escape.

FIFTEEN

Mrs Kroker's house stood cater-corner to the community center. It was painted an odd maroon color, with yellow drapes which were all drawn tight, as if nobody outside should be able to look in and nobody inside should be able to look out. There was an old bronze Honda sedan parked in the driveway.

Michael climbed the steps to the front door and knocked. The knocker was tarnished brass and had the face of a snarling wolf on it. For some reason Michael remembered that people whose front doors faced east hung wolf-like knockers on them to keep away evil spirits, which always came from the east.

After more than half a minute there was no answer so he knocked again.

He heard Mrs Kroker call out, 'Lloyd! Where are you, Lloyd? Somebody's banging at the damn door!'

There was a pause, and then he heard Lloyd saying, 'It's OK, Mrs K! I'm getting it! I'm getting it!'

The door opened with a shudder and there was Lloyd in a red bandanna, wearing a red football shirt with *Bakersfield Falcons* printed across the chest in white. When Michael had talked to him at Isobel's afternoon get-together, Lloyd had been sitting down, so he hadn't realized how tall and heavily built he was – at least six-four and three hundred pounds. He was quite good looking, in a roughly sculptured way, with clear blue eyes, but his nose looked as if it had been broken more than once, and he had a livid red scar above his left eyebrow, as if he had split his head open – and not too long ago, either.

'Hey there, Greg!' he said. 'What you doing out on a day like this?'

'I was bored, that's all,' Michael told him. 'Thought I might pay you a visit.'

'Who is it, Lloyd?' screeched Mrs Kroker, from the living room.

'It's only Greg,' Lloyd called back, over his shoulder. 'You remember Greg – we met him at Isobel's.'

'Greg? I don't remember any Greg! What does he want?'

'Just needs to chew the fat about something, Mrs K. Don't worry. We'll go in the kitchen.'

'Well, don't you dare to fetch him in here!'

'I won't, Mrs K, I promise!' Lloyd winked at Michael and said, with his hand half-cupped over his mouth, 'Still in her hair-rollers and her nightdress. I wouldn't wish the sight of that on nobody.'

He beckoned Michael inside and shut the door

behind him. Then he led the way through to the kitchen, which was fitted out Shaker-style, with wooden cupboards and worktops, and wheel-back chairs.

'How about a cup of coffee?' asked Lloyd. 'Or maybe a brewski if you'd rather.'

'Sure, why not? How about a beer?'

Lloyd went to the fridge and took out two bottles of Coors. They sat down together at the kitchen table and clinked them together. 'Here's to swimming with knock-kneed women.'

'I thought it was "bow-legged",' said Michael.

'You have more fun when they're knock-kneed. It's that prying them apart. Just like opening up a clam.'

Michael said, 'I'll come directly to the point, Lloyd. I need your help. I don't want to get you into any trouble, but there's something I need to do and I can't manage it on my own. I need somebody physically strong.'

'Well ... thanks for the compliment,' said Lloyd, flexing his left bicep until the veins bulged out. 'But what kind of trouble are we talking about?'

'I'm leaving Trinity. I'm going tonight. I'm going to take Isobel's truck and I'm getting the hell out of here and I'm not coming back.'

'What's the matter? You and Isobel fall out or something? I think you landed on your feet there, having Isobel to take care of. Look at me, with old Mrs K. Not exactly the screw of the century, is she? Well, she might have been, but which century?'

'I don't know. I don't want to get you too

deeply involved in this, but there's something badly wrong about this place. I have no idea what it is, but some very weird things have been happening. It could be me. You know, hallucinating or something. But I need to know for sure, and the only way I can do that is to get out of here and look back at it objectively.'

Lloyd swigged his beer and wiped his mouth with the back of his hand. 'So why do you need me? All you have to do is get into Isobel's truck and head for the interstate.'

'The thing is, Lloyd, there's somebody I want to take with me. In fact I'm not going to leave unless I can. She's a patient up at the clinic, and at the moment they're treating her in their intensive care wing. I want to get her out of there, but I simply don't have the strength to carry her out on my own.'

Lloyd sat back in his chair, looking serious. 'That's a big ask, Greg. What happens if they catch us doing it? What would that be – patient-napping or something? I mean, they might kick me out of here, and what would I do then?'

'I don't know, Lloyd. Maybe it *is* too much to ask. Maybe I should forget the whole thing.'

'Who is she, this patient?'

'She's a girl I used to know, Natasha Kerwin. I *think* I used to know her, anyhow. I can't specifically remember how, or why, or where from. But I'm sure that she and I were very close, and I need to get her out of here so that I can find out who she is.'

'Hate to say this, but that's pretty darn vague, isn't it? You might be abducting a perfect

181

stranger for all you know. And even if she *isn't* a perfect stranger, you say that they have her in intensive care. What if you take her out of the clinic and she croaks or something?'

Michael said, 'I think she's going to die regardless.'

He told Lloyd how he and Jack had sneaked into the clinic and found Natasha Kerwin's room, and how he had overheard Doctor Hamid saying that he would 'pull the plug' on her.

'The way he said it, it sounded to me like they had no more use for her, and that they were planning to take her off life-support.'

Lloyd said nothing, but sat there looking at Michael and systematically swigging his beer. His face was expressionless.

Michael pushed back his chair and stood up. 'I should go,' he said. 'I never should have asked you in the first place.'

'What?' Lloyd demanded. 'You're trying to say that I'm chickenshit?'

'No, of course not. It wasn't fair to ask you, that's all, but I couldn't think of anybody else. I'll have to work out a way of getting her out of there on my own. Maybe a wheelchair or a gurney or something like that.'

'I'll help you,' said Lloyd.

'You will? Are you sure about that?'

'Sure I'm sure. What else happens in my life, apart from sitting here day after day listening to Mrs K going on about the old days, and how she dazzled all the boys, and how she used to dance until dawn. "Oh! That night at the Peacock Court! I danced until my ass dropped off!"'

Lloyd's imitation of Mrs Kroker was so spot-on that Michael couldn't help smiling and shaking his head.

'But what if they catch us, and kick you out of here, like you said?'

'Well ... I don't know, Greg, do you honestly think that they would? Who would they find to replace me? Besides – even if they did kick me out, maybe it's time that I did the same as you, and went back out to Reality Land.'

'Lloyd!' called Mrs Kroker, from the living room. 'What are you up to, Lloyd? Isn't it time for my temazepam?'

Lloyd said, 'Just a second, Greg.' He stood up and went to the living-room door. 'Me and Greg are talking football scores, that's all. And you don't take your temazepam till seven. I'll fetch you a cup of tea in a minute.'

'Don't forget my ginger thins!'

'Do I ever?'

'Well, no, but you might this time!'

Lloyd came back into the kitchen. 'Jesus. I wish *she* had a plug, because I swear to God I'd be first in line to pull it.'

'But you'll help me?'

'For sure. What time were you thinking of? Mrs K takes her temazepam at seven so she's usually out of it by twenty after.'

'Isobel's not usually asleep till nine-thirty. Why don't I pick you up at eleven? The clinic should be pretty much deserted by then, too.'

Lloyd held out his hand and Michael took it. 'See you round eleven.'

As Michael was leaving, the living-room door

opened and Mrs Kroker appeared, in a droopy pink nightdress, her breasts hanging as flat as two pieces of pitta bread, with her hair all in rollers.

'Who's this?' she squawked. She looked like some species of hunchbacked monkey, with her head on one side. 'Isn't it time for my temazepam?'

They ate a light supper of cold roast chicken salad, but Michael made sure that he kept on refilling Isobel's glass with Zinfandel so that by 8:30 she had drunk more than a whole bottle.

'Cheers!' she said, as she toppled back on to the couch in the living room, raising her glass to him and blowing him a kiss.

'Listen,' he said, 'I'll clear up the supper things. Why don't you undress and get yourself all ready in bed?'

'Yes!' she said. 'Why not? But you can leave the dishes till tomorrow, can't you?'

'No, you know me and my OCD. I can't make love to you if I know that there are dirty plates still stacked in the sink.'

'You're a very strange man, Greg. You're very, very sexy. But you're very, *very* strange. You make me feel all goosebumpy.'

'Well, believe me, the feeling is mutual. I still think you should see a doctor about being so cold.'

Isobel stood up again, swaying slightly, but then she regained her balance and came right up to him. 'I want to see Doctor Greg first of all. I'm sure Doctor Greg can warm me up.'

He kissed her chilly forehead. 'OK. Let me finish clearing up and I'll be right with you.'

She kissed him back, on the lips. 'If you're very good I might let you try out your thermometer.'

She tilted her way into the bedroom. Michael waited for a moment, until he heard her stumble into the bathroom, and then he went back into the kitchen. He took his time clearing the table and rinsing the plates, whistling tunelessly to himself as he did so. He was trying to be nonchalant, but he was so tense that even his jaw was aching. He could easily forget about rescuing Natasha Kerwin. All he had to do was finish the dishes, undress and go to bed, where Isobel would be waiting for him, her legs open, polar-cold but welcoming.

He saw himself reflected in the blackness of the kitchen window. He looked like a ghost of himself, clearing up a ghostly kitchen, out in the night. He wondered which one of them was real, or if they were *both* real, or neither of them.

As he was putting away the knives that they hadn't used tonight, he saw a pair of kitchen scissors in the cutlery drawer, and a thought occurred to him about what he was going to be doing tonight. He took out the scissors and stuck them in the back pocket of his jeans.

When he had finished wiping the work surfaces, he folded up his dish-towel, looked around the kitchen to make sure that he had put everything away, and switched off the light. He went through to the bedroom to find Isobel already fast asleep, her clothes strewn all across the carpet.

He leaned over the bed and whispered, 'Isobel?' but she didn't even murmur.

He looked at her for a while. It was hard to think that he would never see her again. Although she had been so physically cold, she had been an extraordinary lover, and she had become his friend, too, and that was what he would miss about her more than anything else. She had accepted him for who he was, post-traumatic amnesia and all, and made him feel that she really valued his company.

He went into his own bedroom and took his warm black roll-neck sweater out of his closet. The rest of the few clothes that the clinic had given him he would have to leave behind. He put on his overcoat and laced up his boots, and then he took down the keys to Isobel's Jeep. He supposed that taking her SUV was technically theft, but he proposed to leave it in some supermarket parking lot once he had put a good few miles between him and Trinity, and phone her to tell her where she could recover it.

He went out and closed the front door very quietly behind him. Then he unlocked the Jeep and climbed into the driver's seat. The leather was as cold as Isobel's skin. It even *smelled* cold.

He didn't start up the engine immediately, but released the parking brake and put the gear shift into neutral so that the Jeep rolled silently backward down the sloping driveway and into the road. It was only then that he turned the key, and the engine surged into life, and he turned the wheel and headed for Mrs Kroker's house. All the same, he didn't switch on his lights, in case the security patrol were anywhere in the vicinity.

Outside the community center, he turned around and stopped, flashing his headlights three times. All he could do then was sit and wait and hope that Lloyd hadn't changed his mind.

Five long minutes went by, and there was still no sign of Lloyd. Michael put down his window and listened. The silence was absolute. Two or three of the surrounding houses were lit up, but Michael could hear no televisions, no music, not even people talking. He could see no stars, but in the distance he could see the white cold peaks of Mount Shasta.

He began to think that he was going to have to resort to Plan B, and rescue Natasha Kerwin on his own, although he wasn't at all confident that he could manage it. Supposing Lloyd had been right, and he took her out of intensive care and she died, because of him?

He shifted the Jeep into drive, and he was about to release the parking brake when the front door of Mrs Kroker's house opened and Lloyd appeared, wearing a shiny black padded snow jacket, with the hood up. He gave Michael a wave and came jogging across the road.

'Sorry to keep you waiting,' he panted, as he climbed up into the passenger seat. 'The old crow woke up and wanted a drink of water. But she's zonked off again now. Once she's had her temazepam, she sleeps like she's gone to meet her Maker.'

'You're still sure you want to do this?' Michael asked him.

Lloyd clapped his hands together. 'Raring to go, Greg! First time I've been out in the evening for months! Well, except for some gruesome country-and-western party, about two weeks ago. Line-dancing of the living dead.'

They drove up the slope toward the clinic. As they approached the entrance, Lloyd said, 'Pull in here. We don't want Henry to see us.'

'Henry?'

'Henry, the gate guard.'

'Oh, shit,' said Michael. 'I clean forgot about him. I was so busy wondering how we could explain what we were doing if they caught us inside.'

He pulled the Jeep into the side of the road about fifty yards shy of the entrance and parked it at a tilt, with two wheels up on the snowy verge.

'Don't worry about them catching us inside,' said Lloyd. 'All we need to do is walk in there like we own the place. This time of night, there shouldn't be too many people around anyhow. Mealtime's over, and the cleaners won't have come in yet.'

Michael raised an eyebrow, as if to ask Lloyd how he knew so much about the clinic's routine, but Lloyd said, 'I used to do odd jobs for them, before they sent me down to Mrs K's. I volunteered, as a matter of fact. I've never been much of a reader, except for the sports pages, and I can't watch those fucking soaps. I was bored out of my skull, is all.'

'But what do we do if this gate guard stops us from going in – what's-his-name, Henry?'

'He won't. I used to come out here some evenings and Henry and me would play cards together and tell each other off-color jokes. I'll tell him that I've come up here to pick up some new meds for Mrs K. While him and me are shooting the breeze, you sneak in behind me and I'll meet you on the steps.'

He didn't give Michael any time to decide whether he went along with this plan or not, but headed off toward the security booth with a carefree swagger. Michael kept himself well back against one of the pillars to the entrance gate, watching for his moment.

As the gate guard caught sight of Lloyd approaching, Lloyd raised one hand in salute to him. The gate guard put down the paperback that he was reading and stood up to unlock the door of the booth so that Lloyd could join him inside. Michael heard a snatch of conversation, and then the door was slammed shut.

He could see them talking, however, and as they talked, Lloyd put his arm around the security guard's shoulders, as if he were letting him in on some confidential gossip or telling him some really blue joke. As he did so, he half-turned him around so that he had his back to the gateway.

Michael immediately ducked down and ran at a crouch toward the clinic's main entrance. He hurried up the steps and hid himself behind the bay tree where he had hidden himself before, when he was watching Jack being driven away. His heart was thumping and he was sure that so much breath was billowing out from behind the bay tree that anybody could have seen him hiding there.

While he was waiting for Lloyd to finish his banter with the security guard, he took a quick look inside the clinic's lobby. It was deserted, without even a receptionist sitting at the front desk. It began to occur to Michael that the clinic weren't really too hot on security, except for the white-haired, white-faced men in their sunglasses, touring the community in their black Escalade. What was more, those two seemed to be much more interested in keeping an eye on the residents and their behavior, rather than watching out for unwelcome intruders from outside.

He was still kicking himself for not remembering the guard at the gate, especially since they would have to pass him again, on their way out of the clinic with Natasha Kerwin. There was no doubt that Henry would raise the alarm if they tried to do that, and they would obviously be walking painfully slowly. Henry might even be armed, and then they wouldn't stand a chance.

As he waited behind the bay tree, however, shuffling his feet and clapping his gloves together to keep warm, he began to think of a way around it – how they could escape without Henry having the chance to stop them, and without Lloyd getting the blame for helping him. By the time he heard Lloyd stepping out of the security booth, he had it all pretty much worked out.

'See you later, Henry!' Lloyd called out, and Henry called, 'See you later, Lloyd! Superpussy! Ha! That was a doozie!'

Lloyd came walking across to the clinic's front

steps, while Lloyd slammed the door of his booth behind him.

'Looks like there's nobody around,' said Michael, nodding his head toward the clinic lobby. 'And I've just thought of a way that we can get out of here before they can set the dogs on us.'

'What dogs?'

'I'm talking metaphorically.'

'Meta-what?'

'Never mind. I'll tell you once we get inside.'

They pushed their way into the lobby. It was silent, and shiny. Not even the sound of a distant floor-polisher.

'Let's go,' said Michael. Now that he was here – now that he was actually trying to get Natasha Kerwin free – he was all fired up, and much more sure of himself than at any time since he had woken out of his coma. He still wasn't sure what his name was, or where he came from, but he felt a rising sense of self-assurance, as if he were beginning to remember what kind of a man he was. Headstrong, perhaps, and inclined to rush into things without thinking them through, but always determined, and ready to take a risk.

Together, he and Lloyd walked quickly down to the end of the corridor, to Natasha Kerwin's room. He peeked in through the window and there she was, lying asleep. She was still connected to a Veris vital signs monitor, but she didn't appear to be attached to any intravenous drips, although there was a catheter bag half-swollen with amber urine clipped to the side of her bed.

'You ready?' he asked Lloyd. 'If we're going

191

to do it, we need to do it now.'

Lloyd crossed himself.

'You're Catholic?' Michael asked him.

Lloyd shrugged and pulled a face. 'Don't ask me. I can't remember. I'm just doing that in case I am.'

SIXTEEN

Michael eased open the door. Before they went in, though, they waited for a few seconds, listening. The clinic was still silent, except for the soft persistent beeping of Natasha Kerwin's monitor. Not even the padding of feet on the carpeted floors.

'OK, let's do it,' said Michael, and they entered the room, closing the door behind them, and approached the bed. Natasha Kerwin was lying on her back, sleeping, with two oxygen tubes up her nostrils. She looked deathly pale, and she felt so cold when Michael touched her arm that he could have believed she was dead already. Yet her chest rose and fell, and the monitor indicated that her heart was beating steadily and that her blood-pressure was 90 over 60, which was low, but not life-threatening, although Michael had no idea how he knew that.

With a sticky crackle, he peeled off the pad on her chest, which connected her to the monitor. Then he carefully extracted the oxygen tubes from her nostrils, lifting them over her head.

'What about this pee thing?' asked Lloyd.

Michael took the kitchen scissors out of his back pants pocket and held them up.

'Good thinking,' said Lloyd. 'For a moment there I thought we were going to have to take it with us.'

'No way. But I had one of these, when I was in here, and you don't want anybody yanking it out of you in a hurry, believe me, even when you're asleep. *Especially* if you're asleep.'

Michael pulled back Natasha Kerwin's bed-covers, lifted up her pale green gown, and snipped off her catheter as short as he could.

'OK – now help me sit her up,' he said. 'There should be a robe in that closet over there.'

He had hoped that there might be some slippers in the closet, too, but apart from the robe and the dress in its dry-cleaning bag there was only a jumble of empty coat-hangers. At least Natasha Kerwin was wearing long white surgical socks.

She was as floppy as a toy clown, but between them Michael and Lloyd managed to shuffle her arms into the sleeves of the green toweling robe, wrap it around her and tie up the belt.

'Right, let's go,' said Michael. They sat either side of her, each of them holding one of her arms around the back of his neck, and then they lifted her up into a standing position. Her head hung down between them, and as they walked toward the door her feet trailed on the carpet.

Please God, let me be doing the right thing, Michael thought. *Maybe we should just tuck her up in bed again, and get the hell out of here. What if I really do kill her, trying to take her away like this?*

Lloyd opened the door and they dragged Natasha Kerwin out into the corridor. She wasn't heavy but she was so lifeless that it was an effort to keep her up straight.

'What's the plan now, Greg?' asked Lloyd. 'How are we going to get her out of here without Henry blowing the whistle on us?'

'We'll take her to the front entrance, OK? Then I'll borrow your jacket, put up the hood, and jog past Henry and give him a wave as I go, so he'll think you've left.'

'Then what?'

'Then I'll jump into the Jeep, and come screaming in through the gates. We'll lift Natasha into the back seat, and then we'll go screaming back out again, before anybody can stop us. A few yards down the road, I'll let you out. Then I'll go hightailing off to Route Ninety-Seven.'

Lloyd nodded. 'Sounds good. Well, semi-good, so long as Henry gets taken in.'

They reached the lobby. Two red lights were flashing on the receptionist's switchboard, but there was still nobody around. Lloyd held the door open with his back while they maneuvered Natasha Kerwin out on to the front steps. Outside, the cold was instant and razor-sharp, but it was hard to think that she could feel any colder than she did already. Michael supported her in his arms while Lloyd wrestled himself out of his snow jacket.

Her head was tilted back now, and her lips

were slightly parted. Although her eyes were closed he had the feeling that she was aware he was holding her, and that she felt that she was safe. He was more sure than ever that he knew her. He even had the feeling that he loved her.

Lloyd dropped his jacket on the steps and reached out for Natasha Kerwin. As soon as Lloyd had taken her, Michael unbuttoned his overcoat, took it off and draped it over her shoulders. Then he picked up Lloyd's jacket and put it on, pulling up the hood.

'I'll try to make it real quick,' he said. 'Just remember, though – as soon as I pull up, we need to lift her into the back and burn rubber. And you get into the back, too. Lie on the floor so that Henry doesn't see you when we're driving out.'

'I gotcha,' said Lloyd. He was trying to look serious, like a character in an action movie, but Michael could see that he was enjoying this. It was a whole lot more exciting than making sure that Mrs Kroker took her temazepam and cutting up meatloaf for her.

Michael bounded down the steps and started to jog toward the clinic's front gates. As he approached the security booth, he saw Henry looking up from his book and turning around. He ran faster, with his head down, so that Henry wouldn't be able to see his face. As he passed the booth, he lifted his left arm in salute.

Henry opened up the door of his booth and called out, 'Lloyd! Hey, Lloyd!'

Michael stopped, without turning around.

'I forgot to tell you – we won forty-five bucks on that Redskins game!'

195

'Great!' said Michael, trying to sound as gruff as Lloyd.

'I can give it to you now if you like!'

''S'okay. I'll pick it up tomorrow!'

'I got it right here!'

'Gotta rush, Henry! Old Mrs K needs her meds!'

'I got it right here in my hand!'

'See you tomorrow,' said Michael, giving Henry another salute and jogging off out of the gates.

Once he was out of the clinic grounds, he ran back to Isobel's Jeep as fast as he could. Twice he almost slipped over on the icy road. He pulled off Lloyd's coat, and when he opened the Jeep's doors and scrambled in, he tossed it over on to the back seat. He jabbed in the key and started the engine with a *whoomph.*

He pulled away from the side of the road and sped back toward the clinic gates, his tires leaving a snake-like S shape in the snow. As he spun the steering wheel and turned into the entrance, he saw that Henry had only just returned to his booth, and was closing the door behind him. He sped toward the clinic's front entrance and slewed the Jeep around 180 degrees in a parking-brake turn, trying to make sure that he stopped diagonally across Henry's line of sight. As far as he could see, though, Henry had already picked up his phone, and had his back turned. *That's one good thing,* he thought. *If he's calling for assistance, he probably doesn't have a gun.*

He jumped down from the driver's seat and ran up to help Lloyd, who had already started to carry Natasha Kerwin down the steps. Between them, they lifted her as gently as they could into the back seat, sliding her across the slippery gray vinyl. Then Lloyd heaved himself awkwardly in after her, wedging himself down behind the two front seats. Michael slammed the door, ran around the rear of the Jeep and climbed back behind the wheel. He stamped his foot down on the gas, and with shrieking tires they hurtled out through the clinic gates and into the roadway.

Michael drove as far as the turn-off to Summit View, and then abruptly stopped so that Lloyd could get out.

'Thanks, Lloyd,' he said, twisting around in his seat and grasping Lloyd's hand. 'Couldn't have done it without you.'

Lloyd shook his hand and then opened the door and squeezed himself out. 'You just get the hell out of here, Greg. And try to let me know how you get on, you and this sick young lady here. If you two can survive outside of Trinity, then I'll come join you.'

Michael gave him a thumb's-up, and then turneded the Jeep around and headed back toward the clinic entrance and the turn-off that was signposted to Route 97, and Weed, and Interstate 5. As he flashed past the clinic, he glimpsed cars coming out of the parking lot, and several people running this way and that. He accelerated hard, and soon he was driving into near-total darkness. On either side of the road, endless rows of snowy trees stood like some ghostly guard of honor.

After a few minutes he turned his head quickly to check on Natasha Kerwin. She was lying on her side with her face toward him, and as far as he could see she was still breathing. Once he had reached Route 97 he would pull over and stop and make sure that she was comfortable. He had already turned up the Jeep's air-conditioning to maximum heat.

He kept going as fast as he dared, repeatedly glancing into his rear-view mirror to see if any headlights were following him. He didn't know why, but this reminded him of something that had happened to him, something life-changing. It had been over twenty-four hours now since he had last taken the meds that Catherine had pre-scribed for him, and he was beginning to think that bits and pieces of memory were coming back to him, like a shattering mirror filmed in reverse.

After more than twenty-five minutes of driving at sixty miles an hour, he started to feel uneasy. If you drove for twenty-five minutes at sixty miles an hour, that meant you would have cover-ed twenty-five miles. So how far away was Route 97 from Trinity? He couldn't have missed it, because he hadn't passed a single intersection. All he had seen were those ghostly trees. And how far away from Trinity was Weed?

He drove for more than an hour. For a while he sped faster and faster, until the needle was hover-ing just under eighty-five. But then a deer sud-denly ran out into the road right in front of him, and jumped, and then froze, and it was only by braking hard and swerving violently to the left that he missed it.

He sat behind the wheel, his heart beating hard

against his ribcage. He had lost count now of how long he had been driving and how far he might have traveled. There was no satnav in the Jeep, and no maps. He looked again at Natasha Kerwin and she was still very pale. How was he going to get her to a hospital if he couldn't even find a highway?

He parked the Jeep by the side of the road and opened up the back door so that he could check her breathing and her pulse. Her breathing was very shallow, and with each inward breath she gave a little gasp. Her pulse was fluttery, too. What worried him most, though, was that a small dark spot of blood had appeared on the side of the bandages around her head.

He closed the door as quietly as he could and stood looking at her through the window. He was torn by indecision. He had driven so far that he must reach Route 97 before too long. But how long was too long? He knew that if he turned around it would take over an hour to get back to Trinity, and what would happen to Natasha Kerwin there? They had intensive-care facilities at the clinic, but what difference would that make if they had already decided to pull the plug on her?

He looked around. There was a bitter breeze blowing from the north-west, and he was sur-rounded by dark, snowy forest. Standing here, the trees looked less like a guard of honor and more like an army of ghosts, crowded silently all around him. The sky was clouded over because he could see no stars, but he could still dimly see the peaks of Mount Shasta, luminous in the darkness. He was beginning to hate that volcano, as if it would never let him go. He had heard some Japanese saying similar things about Mount Fuji, and that was a volcano, too. They revered it, but they could never get away from it. It was always there, day and night, year after year, watching them happy, watching them sad, watching them die.

Don't lose your nerve now, he told himself. *Route 97 can't be far ahead now. There is no road in America, no matter how insignificant, that doesn't eventually meet up with another, more important road, and then with a highway, and then with an interstate. It's like your circulation. Even the finest capillaries eventually join up with the arteries, and then the heart.*

He got back behind the wheel and pulled away from the side of the road. He checked his rear-view mirror again and there was still no sign of anybody coming after him. Maybe they had been glad to see him go. He switched on the Jeep's radio but all he heard was hissing and crackling, on almost every station. On one station, he thought he could make out people talking, but the reception was too poor for him to be able to catch more than a few words.

'—*can't agree with that*—'
'—*climb it once in a lifetime*—'
'—*caught them together*—'
'—*saying what?*—'

After a few minutes of straining to understand what they were talking about, Michael switched it off. The road continued to unravel in front of him, mile after mile. Darkness in front of him, darkness behind him, darkness all around. He had never felt so lonely in his life. He seriously began to think that he was the only person left on the entire planet.

Maybe he was hallucinating, and he wasn't driving through the darkness at all, but lying in bed next to Isobel, and the sound of Natasha Kerwin's breathing was really the sound of Isobel breathing, and the sound of the Jeep's tires on the blacktop was only the sound of the central heating boiler.

On the other hand, maybe he was still in a coma, because he definitely felt that driving along a road and feeling anxious that somebody was following him were integral parts of his accident.

'—*inconsiderate schmuck*—'

Another ten minutes went by, and he covered yet another eight miles. The feeling that he was being followed grew stronger and stronger, and he checked his rear-view mirror again and again, even though there were still no lights behind him.

'—*dumb ass has been following me for miles with his lights full on*—'

Another ten minutes. He was driving more slowly now, constantly glancing up at his mirror. Another six-and-a-half miles.

It was then that, at last, he saw a sprinkling of lights up ahead of him. *Hallelujah*, he thought. This wasn't a nightmare, after all, or some kind of delusion. He had reached civilization at last. It looked like a small township, and he guessed it was probably Weed.

'We made it, Natasha!' he said, out loud. 'Now we're going to find you a doctor!'

He stopped looking in his mirror and put his foot down, speeding up to sixty again, and the lights quickly came closer and closer. He passed what looked like a public park, and then a traffic sign saying 20, so he slowed right down. Soon he was driving down a road with houses on either side, and street lights. All he had to do now was find a medical center, or a hospital, if they had a hospital in Weed.

He drove for about three quarters of a mile, but there were still no signs for the town center, or a hospital. At last, however, the road curved around to the right, with two signs side by side: one saying Stop For Pedestrians, and the other giving the name of the road.

Michael slowed to a crawl to read it. It said *Summit View.*

He stopped the Jeep, right in the middle of the road. He looked around and recognized where he was now. He had approached it from a different direction before, when he was walking – when he had been following the ambulance in which Jack had been taken away from the clinic, to the house where the Sue lookalike lived.

He had been driving for over two hours in a circle of more than fifty miles, and he had arrived back in Trinity.

SEVENTEEN

He turned around and looked at Natasha Kerwin, lying on the back seat. Her breathing was still shallow and irregular, and she was twitching as if she were dreaming or just about to have a fit. The bloodstain on her bandage had spread even wider.

He knew that he had no alternative. He shifted the Jeep back into gear and steered it around the curve to the clinic gates, and drove in. As he did so, he saw Henry in his security booth pick up his phone.

By the time he had stopped outside the front entrance, six or seven people were already coming down the steps, led by Kingsley Vane. Close behind him came Doctor Hamid, Catherine Connor and another doctor whom Michael didn't recognize. There were two orderlies, too, one of them carrying a folded wheelchair, and a nurse, and one of the two white-faced security men.

Kingsley Vane was wearing a very long black overcoat and a gray cashmere scarf. His face was gray and drawn and unshaven and his gray hair looked as if he had combed it in a hurry. Catherine was wearing a red overcoat which fleetingly reminded Michael of some movie he had seen, or thought he had seen.

Michael climbed out of the driver's seat and opened the back door. Immediately the two orderlies reached inside and carefully lifted Natasha Kerwin out. They opened up the wheelchair and sat her in it, and then carried her up the steps and in through the front doors.

Kingsley Vane came up to Michael, with Catherine and Doctor Hamid on either side of him. His eyes looked even more hooded and predatory than ever.

'Are you all *right*, Gregory?' he asked him, in a grit-dry voice.

'I didn't take a wrong turn, did I?' Michael challenged him. 'That road doesn't go to Route Ninety-Seven, or Weed, or the interstate, does it?'

'No.'

'Then how the fuck do you get out of this place?'

Kingsley Vane took a deep breath, as if he were trying his best to be very patient. 'That road is for your own protection. We put up the signpost to reassure our patients that one day they *will* be well enough to leave Trinity for the outside world. You're not a prisoner, after all. But you're not ready yet, Gregory. You still have a long way to go, physically, and your amnesia is still almost total. It would be highly irresponsible of TSC to let you go off unsupervised.'

Catherine was smiling at him as if he were a small boy who had tried to run away from home but had then found that twenty-three cents and a toffee wouldn't get him very far. Doctor Hamid was standing with his arms folded and he, too, had a benign look on his face.

'I'm just hoping that Ms Kerwin's recovery hasn't been compromised,' said Kingsley Vane. 'I'm not at all sure why you took her away. She has a very serious brain trauma, and needs highly specialist care which only TSC is equipped to give her.'

Michael was tempted to tell him that he had been hiding in Natasha Kerwin's closet and had overheard Doctor Hamid saying that he was going to pull the plug on her. He could also have told him that he was convinced that he knew her – not just as an acquaintance, but intimately. It was even possible that – once – they had loved each other. But he decided to keep his mouth shut. He didn't exactly know why, but he thought it would be safer, both for him and Natasha Kerwin.

Most of all, he was thinking of Jack, in his wheelchair. Maybe Jack had suffered a relapse, because of the injuries that he had sustained in his truck accident. On the other hand, he had appeared to be perfectly fit before he had been found outside Natasha Kerwin's room. Maybe Doctor Hamid or Doctor Connor had tried to make him tell them what he was doing there, but he had refused, and who knows how they might have persuaded him to talk? Doctor Hamid was an expert in the finer points of physical pain, and Doctor Connor could untie people's most complicated inner thoughts as easily as if they were so many granny knots.

Kingsley Vane said, 'What I suggest you do, Gregory, is take Mrs Weston's Jeep back home, and go back to bed, and pray that she hasn't noticed that you've been AWOL for the past two hours. I think you can imagine how distressed she would be if she knew that you had tried to leave her.'

'And – please – come in to the clinic early tomorrow for a physical check-up,' put in Doctor Hamid. 'I just want to make sure that your little adventure hasn't caused you any spinal torsion, in particular.'

Catherine simply kept on smiling and said, 'See you tomorrow, then? Usual time? So long as you're not too tired.'

Michael hadn't taken his eyes off Kingsley Vane, and Kingsley Vane was staring back at him unblinkingly from under those hooded lids.

'That's why you didn't send anybody after me, isn't it?' Michael demanded. 'You must have been laughing your butts off, knowing that all I was doing was a round trip to no place at all.'

'Like I said, Gregory,' said Kingsley Vane, and here his voice grew even harsher, as if he had real grains of grit between his teeth, 'that road is for your own protection.'

'So – where *is* the way out? You said that I wasn't a prisoner. Supposing I just wanted to drive out of here and never come back? You can't legally keep me here against my will.'

'I'm afraid I can,' said Kingsley Vane. 'Don't you remember signing a durable power of attorney, in my favor? I am your attorney-in-fact, and that responsibility includes your health care.'

'What? What the hell are you talking about? I never signed any power of attorney!'

'You want me to show it to you?'

'Yes, believe it or not, I want you to show it to me.'

'Very well, come into my office when you have your appointment with Doctor Connor tomorrow, and I will gladly oblige.'

'No. You show it to me now. And I mean right fucking now!'

'I regret that I wouldn't be able to find it at this time of night, not without my PA. But I *will* show it to you tomorrow, I promise. And I assure you, Gregory, that it is in your very best interest. Your post-traumatic amnesia is extremely serious – more serious than Doctor Connor has admitted to you – and lately it's been deteriorating, instead of getting better. Why do you think you tried to abduct Ms Kerwin tonight? You thought that she was an old school friend of yours. You were sure that you knew her. But I'm afraid you couldn't have done.'

'Why? Why couldn't I?'

'Obviously I am not at liberty to tell you where she originally comes from, but geographically there was no chance that you two ever could have met before.'

'Geographically?' Michael repeated. At the same time, he saw another quick flash of light, and heard a blurting voice saying *'—you should-n't—'* and smelled again that elusive flowery perfume.

Kingsley Vane nodded gravely. 'You were born and raised more than a thousand miles apart from each other. I'm sorry, Gregory. I know this is all very difficult for you. But you must trust us to help you recover. Meanwhile...' He lifted his left wrist and looked at his Rolex. 'Meanwhile I must check on Ms Kerwin, and then go home and try to get some sleep.'

Michael couldn't think what else to say. Catherine reached out and touched his arm and said, 'Goodnight, Greg, what's left of it.'

Doctor Hamid said, 'Take good care.'

He climbed back into the Jeep and closed the door. He sat for a while behind the wheel, feeling stunned. Nothing made any sense any more. He *did* know Natasha Kerwin, he was absolutely sure of it. Yet Kingsley Vane had told him that his amnesia was getting worse, and Catherine had warned him against inventing memories just to fill in the gaps.

He started the engine and drove slowly out of the clinic gates. Henry was standing in his security booth, staring at him with what looked like a satisfied sneer on his face. Michael felt strongly inclined to give him the finger, but what would be the point of that? Henry might not even be real.

He drove down the road and parked the Jeep in Isobel's driveway, closing the door as quietly as he could. He let himself into the house and it was silent. He undressed quickly in his own room, and then crept naked along the hallway to Isobel's room.

Isobel was still sleeping, in exactly the same position in which he had left her. The closet door was an inch ajar, and inside he could see Belle's glossy black eyes staring at him. He closed the door, making sure that the catch clicked. Isobel mumbled and stirred and said, *'Emilio?'*

Michael lifted the covers and eased himself into bed next to her, wrapping his arms around her even though she felt so cold. He cupped her left breast in his hand and her nipple was crinkled tight and hard, like a raisin taken out of the fridge.

Thus in the winter.

He shut his eyes but after a few minutes he opened them again. He couldn't stop thinking about Natasha Kerwin and wondering how she was. He could see her face in his mind's eye, looking up at him. Her beautiful, perfect face. Pray God that he hadn't hurt her.

Stands the lonely tree.

He must have fallen asleep, because the next thing he knew Isobel was shaking his shoulder, and the bedroom was filled with sunlight.

'Wake up, Rip Van Winkle! Do you know what time it is?'

He lifted his head off the pillow, trying to focus on her. As he did so, he saw something totally impossible. He squeezed his eyes tight, and shook his head, and when he looked at her again, everything was normal.

'What's the matter, baby?' she asked him.

'Tired, that's all. Didn't sleep very well.'

She kissed him, poking the tip of her cold tongue between his lips. 'You should have woken me.'

She sat up in bed and looked around. When she saw all her clothes on the floor, she said, 'Did I drink too much last night?'

'A little, yes.'

'I mustn't do that, Greg. You won't let me do it again, will you? Doctor Hamid says it's bad for my substance.'

'Your substance? What the hell is your substance?'

'Damned if I know,' she said, standing up. 'I didn't ask him.' Michael kept his eyes on her in case he saw that impossible thing again, but he didn't. He didn't really know what it was that he had seen, or if he had seen it at all. It had probably been no more than an optical illusion – an indoor mirage created by the sunlight which was reflected from the multiple mirrors on the closet doors.

He climbed out of bed, too, and she came across to him and put her arms around his waist. 'Do you know what we remind me of?' she asked him, looking serious.

Michael shook his head. 'I have no idea.'

'Adam and Eve, before they found out what was going on.'

He kept his eleven o'clock appointment with Catherine. She was wearing a very severe gray suit, and black pantyhose, and her hair was pinned tightly in a French pleat. He had the feeling that she was angry about something, or out of sorts. Even her perfume smelled bitter. Maybe she was suffering from PMS.

'You're taking your Vinpocetine regularly?' she asked him, without looking up from her clipboard.

'Of course, yes. How's Natasha Kerwin?'

'Miraculously well, thank you.' Still without

raising her eyes.

'Is she conscious?'

'Yes, as a matter of fact. She's very weak, but that's only to be expected.'

'You mean that's only to be expected after being taken out of her bed in the intensive-care unit in the middle of the night and driven around Siskiyou County for two hours?'

Now Catherine lowered her clipboard and looked at him directly. 'Yes, that's exactly what I mean. But fortunately for you, the outcome has been unexpectedly positive. We should thank you, I suppose, for making up our minds for us.'

'I don't follow.'

'It happens every day in medicine. We have to make critical choices about how to treat people, and sometimes it's hard to know if we're going to do them more harm than good. In Natasha Kerwin's case, you took the decision out of our hands.'

'What the hell did *I* do? By the time we got back here, she looked like she was really, really sick.'

'She was. But now she's conscious, and she's talking, and we have every expectation of a speedy recovery.'

'And I did that?'

'In a manner of speaking, yes.'

Michael didn't know what to say to that. When he had last checked up on Natasha Kerwin, at the intersection with Summit View, he would have said that she was critically ill. In fact, he had brought her back to the clinic because he had been convinced that if he didn't, she would die.

211

'Can I see her?' he asked.

Catherine hesitated for a moment. 'I'm not too sure that's a good idea. Do you still think you know her?'

'Does that make any difference?'

'Not really. I'm just asking from the point of view of *your* recovery.'

'Mr Vane told me last night that I couldn't possibly know her. Geographically impossible, that's what he said. Apparently we were brought up more than a thousand miles apart.'

'That wasn't what I asked you. What I asked you was, do you still *think* that you know her?'

'What if I said no?'

'If you said "no" I would say that you were showing some signs that your neural pathways were mending. When you come to understand that a false memory is exactly that – *false* – that's a real step forward. That's even more important than remembering things that actually happened.'

'OK. So, can I see her?'

'Not today. She's not quite ready for visitors yet. But maybe tomorrow or the day after. Now ... can we get back to your recollection therapy? Do you remember your seventh birthday party?'

'My *what*? My seventh birthday party? No, I don't.'

'Well, try. You dressed up as somebody special. One of your superheroes. Can you remember which one?'

'No, I can't. Did my so-called sister tell you this?'

Catherine lowered her clipboard again. 'Greg

212

... you mustn't be so suspicious and so hostile. Everybody here is trying so hard to help you find your way back.'

'Are you? I don't know. I'm really not so sure about that.'

'*Try*, Greg. You have to try, otherwise you won't make any progress at all.'

'All right,' said Michael. 'Spider-man.'

'That's it!' smiled Catherine, lifting up her clipboard and ticking a box. 'That's exactly right! It was Spider-man.'

Michael watched her as she scribbled an additional comment. Then he said, 'That was only a guess, Catherine. I don't really remember it at all.'

After his session with Doctor Connor, Michael went for a physical check-up from Doctor Hamid.

Doctor Hamid said very little, but continued to smile while he checked Michael's blood pressure and heart rate and felt his spine for any obvious signs of displacement of his vertebrae.

'I think you are quite fine,' he said, as Michael buttoned up his shirt. 'Your usual CT scan is scheduled for tomorrow afternoon so I will be able to make one hundred per cent sure then that you have not suffered any setback in your healing process.'

'I can go now?'

'Of course. I will see you tomorrow.'

As Michael opened his consulting-room door, however, Doctor Hamid said, 'You will not try such an escapade again, will you?'

'I don't know. I'm not sure I can make any promises.'

Doctor Hamid swiveled around in his chair and took off his spectacles. 'The entire clinic is covered by closed-circuit television. You didn't think that we would be so lax in our security, did you? Perhaps I should not be telling you this, but we have been aware all of the time that you were attempting to take Ms Kerwin away.'

Michael stared at him in disbelief. 'You *knew*?'

'Of course we knew. We saw you the first time when you entered Ms Kerwin's room with Jack Barr, and our security people were watching when you came back with Lloyd Hammers.'

'Well, if you knew, why the hell didn't you stop me?'

'It was important for us to find out how far you were prepared to go.'

'But, for Christ's sake, I was putting Natasha Kerwin's life at risk. I thought it was worth it, to get her out of here before you pulled the plug on her. But if you knew that I couldn't get out of here, all you were doing was jeopardizing her recovery for no reason at all – except what? To find out how far I was prepared to go? I don't even understand what that means.'

Doctor Hamid said, 'Ms Kerwin was and still is in a very serious condition. She was involved in a catastrophic automobile accident in which she suffered extensive brain trauma. There seemed to be no point in keeping her on life support. Therefore we allowed you your little adventure for your sake – so that we could evaluate how attached you felt to Ms Kerwin and how

214

delusional you were.'

Michael closed the door and came back across the consulting room to stand right in front of Doctor Hamid's desk. 'I still don't get it. What about her relatives? What about her mom and dad? Didn't you ask *them* how they felt about taking her off life support?'

Doctor Hamid looked away to the left, and Michael thought: *Whatever you're going to say to me now, it's going to be a lie.*

'Ms Kerwin's parents have already given us permission to take her off life support. So whatever happened to her after that was academic.'

'But now she's recovering? That's what Doctor Connor told me, anyhow.'

'Yes. It seems as if she is.'

'So what exactly are you telling me?' asked Michael.

Doctor Hamid looked up at him again. 'I am trying to emphasize to you, Gregory, that you are here in Trinity for your own good. We are watching you in order to take care of you, and for no other reason. In our judgment, if you were to leave Trinity now, the consequences for you would be disastrous.'

'What do you mean, disastrous?'

Doctor Hamid said, 'I am sorry, Gregory. I have already told you more than I ought to, but I am a doctor and you are my patient and I care passionately about your welfare. I am simply saying that you should stay here for the time being in order to prepare yourself physically and mentally for the world outside.'

'Is there something wrong with me that you

haven't told me? I mean apart from the spinal injury, and the memory loss?'

'Again, Gregory, I am sorry. I am not at liberty to say any more. Sometimes, if patients know everything about their condition, it can have a negative effect on their recovery. Some cancer patients, for example, or those who suffer from multiple sclerosis.'

'So there *is* something you've not told me?'

'I cannot say that there is or that there is not.'

'Doctor Hamid – what the fuck is wrong with me?'

Doctor Hamid put his spectacles back on, and stood up. 'Please, Gregory. You should go now. I have another patient waiting.'

'I'm not leaving until you tell me.'

Doctor Hamid walked over to the door and opened it. 'I can say only this, Gregory. It is nothing that I or anybody else can cure. It is something that, in time, you will learn to accept.'

Michael glanced toward the waiting-room outside. The two white-faced security men were standing by the tropical fish tank in their black suits and their sunglasses, their hands cupped over their genitalia in the standard pose of all security men everywhere.

'No fuss, please, Gregory,' said Doctor Hamid, very softly.

Michael looked at him intently – trying to see if he were sending him a message with his dark brown eyes that he was not at liberty to say with his lips. All he could read was sympathy.

For some reason, Doctor Hamid felt sorry for him.

216

EIGHTEEN

Before he went home, Michael knocked on the half-open door of Kingsley Vane's office. Kingsley Vane's personal assistant Valerie was sitting at her desk with a half-eaten bagel on top of her in-tray, talking on the phone. She beckoned Michael to come in and take a seat.

'Of course I'll tell him,' she was saying. 'Of course I will. He'll be *delighted*.'

When she had hung up, she gave Michael a smile, all scarlet lipstick and horselike teeth. 'Mr *Merrick*,' she said. 'Mr Vane said that you'd be dropping in.'

'He told you why?' asked Michael.

Valerie reached over to her out-tray and picked up a brown Manila envelope. She passed it to Michael and said, 'Durable power of attorney. That was the one, wasn't it?'

Michael took the two-page document out of the envelope and read it. Gregory Merrick had appointed Kingsley Vane his attorney-in-fact, even if he became disabled or incompetent. At the foot of the document 'Gregory Merrick' had signed his name and two witnesses had added their signatures – *'Catherine T. Connor'* and *'A. Hamid.'*

He handed the envelope back. 'All above

board, I trust?' smiled Valerie.

Michael nodded, but at the same time he thought: *If I'm really Gregory Merrick, then yes, it's valid, even though I don't remember signing it. But what if I'm not?*

As he walked back to Isobel's house, he met Jemima and Angela coming up the slope in the opposite direction – Angela with her white sheepdog gasping at its leash and Jemima circling around on her bicycle.

'We *heard* about you, Gregory!' Jemima sang out.

Michael stopped, shielding his eyes with his hand. The sun shining on the snow was dazzling, and both girls looked blurry and unfocused, as if they had moved while they were having their photographs taken.

'Oh, yes? So what did you hear?'

'We heard you're getting married!'

'Excuse me?'

'That's what my mom was saying. We heard her talking to Mrs Steinman next door. She said you're going to marry that hoo-ha!'

Michael lowered his hand and shook his head. ''Fraid your mom's got it wrong there, girls. Me and Mrs Weston, we're just good friends, that's all. We're not getting married. And – please – don't call her that name any more, OK?'

'Hoo-ha! Hoo-ha! Mrs Weston's a hoo-ha!'

'You be careful there, Jemima,' Michael warned her. 'One of these days when you least expect it I'm going to come right up behind you and drop a spider down the back of your neck.'

'Hoo-ha! Hoo-ha!' sang Jemima, and Angela's sheepdog barked to join in.

Michael gave the girls a dismissive wave and continued to walk down to Isobel's house. When he let himself in, he found Isobel in the kitchen, rolling out pastry. Her hair was tied back and she had a smudge of white flour on the tip of her nose.

'You're back! How did it go?'

'Pretty much the same as usual. Catherine seems to think I'm not making sufficient progress, but for Christ's sake, some of the questions she asks me! What costume did I wear for my seventh birthday party? Can *you* remember what you wore for your seventh birthday party?'

'Yes, a pink frilly dress with a huge bow at the back. And pink ballerina shoes.'

'You're kidding me.'

Isobel came up to him and put her floury hands on his shoulders and kissed him. 'Yes,' she said. 'I'm kidding you.'

'I met those two girls,' he said. 'What are their names? The one with the bike and the one with the dog.'

'Jemima and Angela.'

'That's it. Jemima and Angela. According to them, we're getting married.'

Isobel stared up at him with those liquid brown eyes. Her full pink lips were slightly parted and he could just see the tip of her tongue between her teeth. He could see that she was deliberately trying to look seductive.

'Erm ... that's what their mom said, apparently,' Michael added, when she didn't answer straight away.

'We *will*, though, won't we?' she asked him.

'Get married? I'm sorry. Who said anything about getting married?'

'Don't you *want* to?'

Michael took hold of her wrists and gently took her hands off his shoulders. 'Isobel – we've never even discussed it.'

'You love me, though, don't you?'

Michael didn't know what to say to that. 'I'm not physically or mentally fit to get married,' he told her. 'I still need a stick to walk around with, and I can't remember what my name is. How can I marry you when I don't even know who I am?'

'That doesn't matter. Why should that matter? You're still *you*, whatever your name is. I love you, Greg. I love you so much. I need you. I really need the security of knowing that you're always going to *be* here.'

'Isobel – I don't intend to stay in Trinity for the rest of my life. As soon as Doctor Hamid has given me the all-clear, and as soon as I've gotten over this amnesia, I'm out of here. I really mean it.'

'You can't.'

'What do you mean, I can't? What's going to stop me?'

She started to reach up to touch his face, but then she suddenly realized how floury her fingers were, and so she simply stood there in front of him with both hands lifted in a gesture of helplessness. To Michael's surprise, he realized that she was close to tears.

'Greg, please marry me. Marry me and stay

220

here in Trinity. *Please.*'

'Isobel...' he began, but at the same time he was thinking: *Doctor Hamid said that it would be 'disastrous' if I left Trinity. Now Isobel's telling me that I simply* can't *leave Trinity. But nobody will tell me why.*

Apart from that, there was Isobel's physical coldness. How could he marry a woman whose skin always felt so chilly, and whose insides froze his semen into ice crystals?

And that wasn't the only thing that disturbed him about her. He was still baffled and confused by what he had seen when he had woken up and looked at her this morning. Or what he *thought* he had seen.

In spite of all that, he didn't like to see her so distressed. He put his arms around her and held her close and kissed her forehead and then her lips, and smiled at her and wiped the flour from the end of her nose with his finger.

'OK,' he said. 'I'll think about it. I promise.'

That afternoon, ragged gray clouds began to drift in from the south-west, and the inside of the house gradually grew dark and colorless, as if they were going back in time.

Michael came into the living room where Isobel was sitting in front of the television watching *Days Of Our Lives*.

'Just going out for my obligatory walk,' he told her. He nodded toward the television and said, 'How's life in Salem these days?'

'A whole lot more exciting than Trinity,' said Isobel. 'You *will* be thinking, while you're walk-

221

ing, won't you? About you-know-what?'

Michael didn't answer but blew her a kiss. He closed the front door behind him and headed down the slope toward Mrs Kroker's house. He wanted to thank Lloyd Hammers for his help last night, even though he hadn't managed to get away.

Not only was it gloomy outside, it was utterly still and silent. At ground level there was no wind at all, although the clouds were still moving, and a plume of snow was waving from the peak of Mount Shasta like somebody fluttering a long white scarf.

As he passed the house next door, Michael saw that their neighbor was standing in the window of his front room, wearing a mustard-colored cardigan. Michael didn't know his name, and he hadn't yet come by to introduce himself, but he was a stockily built man with slicked-back gray hair and a podgy, Slavic-looking face.

The strange thing was, he was pointing at Michael, and he appeared to have a disapproving frown on his face. Michael slowed down and then stopped and stared at him. The man continued to frown, and to point, as if he were accusing Michael of something. Michael pointed to himself, like Robert De Niro in *Taxi Driver*, and mouthed the words, 'You pointing at *me*?'

But the man didn't respond. He simply continued to point. After hesitating a few more moments, Michael continued walking. He glanced back once, but the man was still pointing at him. Michael felt distinctly uneasy. Another reason not to get married to Isobel and stay here in

222

Trinity.

When he passed the next house, he saw two people standing in their living-room window, a youngish couple. The man was wearing a pale blue sweater and heavy-rimmed Clark Kent glasses, while the woman appeared to be pregnant and dressed in a floral maternity smock. They, too, were pointing at him; and they, too, had stern, accusing frowns on their faces.

Michael was tempted to walk up to their front door and ring their doorbell and ask them why the hell they were pointing at him, but they looked so hostile that he decided against it.

He carried on. As he approached the next house, he saw that there was nobody standing in the living-room window, even though there was a light on, and a television screen flickering. It was a two-story house, however, and when he looked up he saw an elderly woman in one of the bedroom windows, pointing at him in the same way. He stopped and stared back at her, but she didn't flinch.

It was the same in every house on his way down the slope to the community center. In every one of them, somebody was pointing at him – single people, mostly, but some couples and even some families with children.

In the second-to-last house before he reached Mrs Kroker's, a man of about his own age was pointing at him – slim, pale, with floppy brown hair. Michael went up to his porch and pressed the doorbell. There was no answer, so he pressed it again. When there was still no answer, he knocked on the door with his knuckles.

'Come on, what are you afraid of?' he shouted.

The door suddenly opened, and Michael was confronted by a middle-aged woman with short gray hair. She was quite handsome, although she was wearing a sludge-green woolen dress which reflected under her chin and made her look as if she were ill.

'Yes? What do you want?' she asked him. From her accent, he would have guessed that she was Canadian.

'I just wanted to ask that fellow in the window why he's pointing at me.'

A pause, then, 'Why do you *think* he's pointing at you?'

'I don't have the first idea. And he's not the only one. Everybody in the whole damn street is doing it.'

'They're giving you a warning, that's why.'

'A warning? A warning about what, exactly?'

'Causing trouble. Asking questions that nobody wants answered. You think that word doesn't get around, here in Trinity, just because everybody keeps themselves to themselves? Well, let me tell you, Gregory Merrick, word gets around. Everybody here is hanging on by their fingernails, and the last thing they want is trouble.'

'Trouble?' said Michael. 'Believe me, I'm not out to cause trouble; and the only questions I want answered relate to my own personal health.'

'So where are you off to now?' the woman asked him, in the tone of a schoolteacher asking a pupil what he was doing out of class.

'I'm taking a walk, that's all. I have to take a walk every day. It's part of my therapy.'

'You're not going to see Lloyd Hammers, then?'

'I don't mean to be rude, but I don't see that it's any business of yours whether I do or not.'

'Of course it's my business. It's everybody's business. Everybody here is hanging on by their fingernails.'

'I don't understand what you mean.'

Instead of answering his question, the woman said, snappily, 'Are you going to get married then – you and Mrs Weston?'

Michael half-turned away from the door in exasperation, and then turned back. 'Again – I don't think it's any of your business. Who told you that, anyhow?'

'She did.'

'Well, we've talked about it, that's all.'

'I see. Maybe folks will stop pointing, if you do.'

Michael was about to ask her what possible connection there could be between him marrying Isobel and people in Trinity pointing their fingers at him when she abruptly closed the door, and noisily rattled the safety chain.

He stood in the porch for a few moments, but even if he managed to persuade the woman to open up the door again, he doubted if she would make any more sense. He turned around and went back down the driveway, conscious that the young man with the floppy brown hair was still pointing at him, even behind his back. He continued on his way to Mrs Kroker's house. Across the street, in the living-room window of the house next to the community center, he saw a tall ginger-haired woman in black, and she was pointing at him, too.

To start with, all of this pointing had been baffling, and even faintly ridiculous. With each successive house, however, it had become more irritating; and then annoying. Now it was beginning to make Michael feel seriously uneasy. They were pointing at him, these people, as if they were accusing him of some terrible crime – a crime for which they would expect him to be punished. He felt like a murderer desperately trying to escape from a vengeful crowd.

He rang Mrs Kroker's doorbell and Lloyd opened the door almost immediately.

'Lloyd!'

'Yes?' said Lloyd. Today he was wearing a plain black T-shirt and black jeans. A small gold crucifix was hanging around his neck.

'I'm back, Lloyd. As you can see for yourself, I didn't make it.'

'Did you want something?' Lloyd asked him.

'Well, for starters, is it OK if I come in? That's unless the gorgeous Mrs K is still in her night attire.'

'Did you want something?' Lloyd repeated.

'I only wanted to tell you what happened, that's all. That road that's signposted for Route Ninety-seven and Weed – that road doesn't go to Route Ninety-seven and Weed. It goes right around in a damn great circle and comes back here to Trinity.'

'I see.'

Michael stared at him intently. 'Are you OK, Lloyd? You haven't been smoking the old sensemarilla, have you?'

'Did you want something?' said Lloyd.

'Who is it, Lloyd?' called a woman's voice, from the living room. It wasn't Mrs Kroker. It was a very much younger woman. 'Can you close the front door, please – there's a terrible draft!'

'Lloyd,' Michael insisted, 'you need to know what happened. They were watching us the whole time on CCTV. They could have stopped us at any time they wanted to, but for some reason they didn't. Mr Vane said they let me do it as part of my treatment, but that didn't make any sense at all. Natasha Kerwin could have died.'

'OK,' said Lloyd. 'I'll see you around.'

'Aren't you going to let me in?' asked Michael. 'I want to talk to you about what we can do next. We really need to find out what the hell is going on here, Lloyd. When I walked down here, everybody was pointing at me, you know, like I'm some kind of leper or something. Every single person, in every house.'

'Lloyd – the door!' the woman's voice called out again, much more impatiently this time.

'I got it!' Lloyd called back.

He started to close the door in Michael's face, but Michael stepped forward quickly and jammed his foot in it.

'Listen to me, Lloyd. I need your help. I can't do this on my own. They've told me that Natasha Kerwin's beginning to recover. If that's true,

227

then I stand a much better chance of getting her out of here. But like before, I'm going to need some kind of diversion, which is where you come in.'

'I'll see you around, Greg,' said Lloyd. Michael looked at his eyes and the pupils were like pinpricks. He repeatedly pushed at the door, trying to close it, as if he wasn't aware that Michael's foot was wedging it open.

'Lloyd!' the woman shouted, and now the living-room door was thrown open and she came storming out into the hallway.

Her hair was curly, which it hadn't been before, but Michael recognized her instantly. It was his sister – or his so-called sister – Sue.

NINETEEN

Michael said, 'OK. What the hell is going on here?'

'You'd better come inside,' said Sue. 'We don't want Mrs Kroker to catch her death. Let him in, Lloyd.'

Lloyd opened the door wider and allowed Michael to step into the hallway.

'Who's that, at the door?' called out Mrs Kroker from the living room. 'Lloyd, are you going to answer the door? Lloyd, do you hear me? Lloyd!'

Sue ignored her and said to Michael, 'Come

into the kitchen. I think Mrs Kroker has had enough upsets for one day. Lloyd – go check on her, will you?'

'Sure,' said Lloyd. He went into the living room and closed the door behind him.

'Do you want to sit down?' asked Sue, pulling out a chair from the kitchen table.

'You're not really my sister, are you?' said Michael.

'No, Greg, I'm not. You do have a sister, but she and her family live in Guatemala, and there's no way she could have come to see you on a regular basis.'

'So – what? So you've just blatantly been *pretending* to be my sister? I mean, why? What's the point of it?'

'I'm sorry you had to find out this way,' Sue told him. 'I'm sorry that you had to find out at all – at least until you could have remembered for yourself that I'm not really your sister. It's all part of the therapy, having a family member to show you photographs and tell you stories about yourself when you were younger. It helps you to rebuild your inner perception of who you are.'

'But it's a *lie*, for Christ's sake! It's an out-and-out deception! Catherine Connor keeps telling me that I shouldn't create false memories ... but here you are, you're creating a false memory *for* me.'

'Not at all,' said Sue. 'I'm simply acting as a guide. Doctor Connor asks you questions about yourself, to see if she can reactivate your memories, while I actually show you what your life was like before your accident. She and I are both

229

therapists, in our different ways. It's an accredited technique, believe me.'

'So when I called you on the phone, was that you or not? The number had an Oakland area code.'

'That *was* me, Greg. But your call was diverted.'

'And when I spoke to my mother, that wasn't my mother?'

'No. It was one of our senior nursing staff.'

'So where did you get all of this background information about my life? Where did you get all those photographs from?'

'From your real sister, of course, and other people who knew you. School friends, colleagues from work, girlfriends.'

'Did I ever have a girlfriend called Natasha Kerwin?'

She shook her head. 'I'm sorry. Doctor Connor told me that you had a strong false memory that you used to know her, but no. I don't know how you could have gotten hold of that idea. Maybe she just looks like some girl you used to go out with.'

'So what about Jack? What happened to him? And Lloyd? Lloyd's gone all weird since last night. He hardly seems to know who I am.'

'Greg – so many of the people who live here in Trinity are in one form of recovery or another. Both Jack and Lloyd have suffered something of a relapse. Jack's was physical ... Lloyd's, as you can see, was mental. I'm not blaming you, but when you asked them to join you in abducting Natasha Kerwin, that put a great strain on both of them. We're sure they'll improve, in time.'

Michael said nothing for almost half a minute, staring at Sue and breathing heavily, as if he had a head cold.

Then he said, 'Bullshit.'

Sue shrugged and gave him a slanted smile. 'You can think what you like, Greg. But I'm sure Doctor Connor has told you that the more resistant you are to us helping you, the longer it's going to take for you to get your memory back.'

'It's still bullshit. I don't believe any of it.'

'Then what *do* you believe? Tell me – it could help.'

'I don't believe that my name is Gregory Merrick. I don't believe that I'm a marine engineer. I *do* believe that I know Natasha Kerwin. In fact I believe that Natasha Kerwin and me used to be friends. Maybe even more than friends.'

'OK. Is there anything else?'

'Yes. There's one more thing. I don't believe that if I leave Trinity it's going to be disastrous, which is what Doctor Hamid told me. And Isobel said that I *can't* leave, although she didn't say why. I believe that I *can* leave, so long as I can find the way out of here, and even if I'm still suffering from amnesia, I believe that I'll be able to survive.'

'You can see Natasha Kerwin tomorrow morning.'

'*What?*'

Sue nodded, and kept up that slanted smile. 'You can see her. You never knew her, but you obviously find her very attractive, which is why

231

your mind is telling you that you once had a relationship. Natasha is going to need a lot of support and encouragement to help her to recover, and who better to do that than you?'

'Are you serious?'

'Absolutely. And both Doctor Connor and I believe that it may help *you*, too. As you get to know Natasha better, you should gradually come to realize that you didn't actually have a relationship with her, after all, and that will strengthen your ability to distinguish between real memories and false memories.'

'But if I do that I'll have to stay here, in Trinity?'

'For the time being, yes.'

Michael thought: *If I do stay here for a few weeks longer, until Natasha Kerwin recovers, I can plan how to get her away from Trinity without us being intercepted, or driving around in a fifty-mile circle, like we did last night.*

'OK,' he said.

'You mean it? You'd really like to give it a try? In that case, you can see her at the clinic tomorrow, when you go for your appointment with Doctor Connor, and after that you can visit her whenever you like, until she's ready to come home with you, which shouldn't be more than three or four days.'

'You mean back to Isobel Weston's house?'

'Of course. You still need Isobel to take care of you, and in her own way she still needs you.'

Michael wondered if he ought to ask Sue about Isobel, and how cold she was, but then he thought: *No, don't rock the boat.* He didn't want anything to make Natasha Kerwin's doctors change their minds about allowing him to look after her.

He did say, though, 'I guess you know that Isobel wants me to marry her. Well – everybody else in Trinity seems to have heard.'

'Yes. She said that to Emilio, too. She'll get over it. It's only because she's feeling insecure.'

'So what should I say to her?'

'Tell her that you will, in the summer. Tell her that there's nothing more romantic than a June wedding.'

He walked back up to Isobel's house. It had grown so dark now that the street lights had switched themselves on, even though it was only quarter of four in the afternoon. The drapes were drawn tight across the living-room windows of every house he passed. He felt as if – having been accused – he was now being ostracized. In some ways that left him feeling even more isolated and even more unsettled than before. He had nobody to rely on any longer, like Jack or Lloyd, and everybody else seemed to be lying to him. Not only that, they all seemed to be telling him different lies, which made it impossible even to *guess* what the truth was.

'How was your walk?' asked Isobel, as he came in.

'Interesting,' he said. 'Educational, even.'

He sat down on the couch next to her to unlace his boots and she shuffled up close to him and ruffled his hair and kissed him. 'Did you think about you-know-what?'

'About supper, yes. I thought, I could murder one of Isobel's beef enchiladas.'

She gave him a playful slap and said, *'No* – I mean you-know-what with a capital M.'

'Sure, yes. And the answer is – yes. We could get married in the summer, couldn't we? June weddings, they're so romantic. And June is only five months away – less than that – four-and-a-half.'

Isobel pressed her hand over her mouth and her eyes filled with tears.

At last she took her hand away and said, 'You mean it? You really mean it? You'll marry me?'

'I couldn't think of any reason not to.'

She put her arms around him and kissed him again and again. 'Let's go to bed,' she said. 'Let's go to bed now! I'm going to suck you till you scream for mercy!'

The following day was just as gloomy and a thick wet snow was coming down. Michael sat in Doctor Connor's office watching it through the window behind her. It looked as if it were falling in slow-motion.

'Sue told me about your conversation at Mrs Kroker's house,' said Catherine. She looked a little more relaxed today, in an oatmeal-colored sweater and a brown skirt, and a pair of Ugg boots, stained with dark wet blotches from the snow. 'She said that you seemed to be very understanding about her pretending to be your sister.'

'Yes,' said Michael.

'She also said that you would be happy to help

Natasha Kerwin to convalesce.'

'Yes. Yes, I am.'

'She explained that it could be very good for you, too? That it could help you to get your memory back?'

'Yes.'

Catherine stood up. 'In that case, why don't we skip the question-and-answer session for today and go see her?'

'Really?'

'Yes, really. Come on.'

She left her office and walked ahead of him along the corridor that led to Natasha Kerwin's room. Over her shoulder she said, 'We're *so* excited how quickly she's recovered. You won't believe it when you see her.'

She knocked on the door and then pushed it open. Natasha Kerwin was sitting up in bed, propped up by pillows. She was still attached to the Veris monitor, but she looked very much better. In fact, she looked even more like the girl that Michael believed he had loved. She had a white gauze bandage around her head, but underneath it her straight blond hair was clean and brushed and shiny. Her eyes were bright, and although she was still quite pale, she had a touch of rose-petal pink on each cheek. Instead of a hospital gown, she was wearing a flowery cotton nightdress with a ruffled collar and puffy sleeves.

She was talking to Doctor Hamid and two nurses who were standing around her bed. Doctor Hamid was telling her, '—you *will*, Natasha, I swear to you – just as soon as we are happy that all of your vital signs are completely stable.'

When Michael and Catherine entered her room, Natasha gave them only a cursory glance. She had probably had doctors and nurses and orderlies walking in and out all day and two more weren't anything exceptional. But as they came up to her bed and stood beside Doctor Hamid, she turned her head slowly around and looked up at Michael, and this time her eyes widened and her mouth opened as if she were about to say something, but couldn't think of the words.

'Ah, Gregory, so pleased you could join us!' said Doctor Hamid. 'Do you see how much improved our patient is today? Natasha, this is Gregory – Gregory Merrick. Gregory, this is Natasha Kerwin. Of course, you met before, didn't you, Natasha, when Gregory accidentally came into your room. But perhaps you don't remember?'

Michael smiled and said, 'Good to meet you again, Natasha. It's great to see you looking so much better.'

Natasha closed her mouth and then opened it again but still didn't seem to be able to say anything.

'You *did* say she was talking?' Catherine asked Doctor Hamid.

Doctor Hamid laughed. 'I think our friend Gregory has stunned the poor girl into silence. Don't worry! She has been talking and joking with us all day, haven't you, Natasha?'

Natasha still didn't take her eyes away from Michael. He went up to her bedside and took

236

hold of her hand. Her fingers were very cold, almost as cold as Isobel's, so he cupped his other hand over them to warm them up.

'*It's you,*' she whispered, so softly that he could barely hear her.

'What did she say?' asked Catherine. The room was quite noisy, with the nurses chatting and the Veris beeping and Doctor Hamid leafing through his notes and clearing his throat as he did so.

'Nothing,' said Michael. 'I think she's a little overwhelmed, that's all.'

'*It's you,*' Natasha repeated. 'It really *is* you, isn't it?'

Michael put one finger to his lips and gave her an almost imperceptible shake of his head. Then he leaned close to her so that only she could hear what he was saying. 'Later,' he murmured. 'Don't say anything now. I'll come back.' He nodded then, to show her that he meant it.

Catherine said, 'Are you two having a *tête-à-tête* here?'

'Not really,' said Michael. 'I think she's mistaken me for someone else.'

'How about you? Have you really met her before?'

'I'm not too sure. I think I may have. She seems kind of familiar, but I don't know. Like you say, maybe she just *reminds* me of someone.'

All the same, the two of them continued to stare at each other with such intensity that eventually Catherine said, 'I think that's enough now, Gregory. We don't want Natasha to get overtired.'

'No,' said Michael. Reluctantly, he let go of Natasha's hand. He was convinced now that he *did* know her, although he still couldn't remember who she was. Since he didn't even know who *he* was, that was hardly surprising. But she had recognized him, which meant that whoever she was – a past lover or a work colleague or a friend or just a casual acquaintance – Kingsley Vane's assertion that it had been 'geographically' impossible for them to know each other had been yet another lie.

'You can see her tomorrow, after your session with me,' said Catherine, as they walked back along the corridor. 'With any luck she won't be so shy and retiring when she sees you again.'

Michael said, 'OK,' and nodded, although what he really felt like doing was shaking her and screaming at her to tell him the truth. The truth about himself, the truth about Natasha, the truth about Isobel – and most of all the truth about all of the residents of Trinity, who had assembled outside his bedroom window without leaving a single footprint in the snow and who had pointed at him so accusingly.

The woman in the sludge-green dress had said that they were hanging on by their fingernails. But hanging on to what? Their sanity? And what would happen to them, if they were to lose their grip?

TWENTY

Again that night Michael pushed his Vinpocetine capsules into the plughole of the bathroom basin, and rinsed them away.

He was beginning to remember more and more random fragments – songs, conversations, images of people running and laughing. None of these fragments had yet begun to reassemble themselves into a coherent picture of what his life had been like before his accident, but he was sure that his memory was gradually coming back. His *real* memory – not the memory that Catherine was trying to invent for him.

In particular he kept remembering sitting in the back of a car and driving along Fonderlack Trail, and feeling so desperately unhappy that he had to bite his lip to stop himself from crying.

And he could remember that poem. *Thus in the winter stands the lonely tree.*

And saying to somebody, *'Fifth highest peak in the Cascade Range.'*

And a girl, opening her eyes and looking at him, again and again, like an endlessly repeated loop of film.

'You shouldn't let me—'
'You shouldn't let me—'
'You shouldn't let me go to sleep like that.'

And then lights flashing, and metal screeching, and his whole world rolling upside-down, over and over. And another crash, so deafening that he could hardly hear it.

He was still staring at himself in the mirror over the bathroom basin when Isobel called out, 'Sweetheart – are you coming to bed?'

'Won't be a moment. I just have to brush my teeth.'

When he came into the bedroom, Isobel was sitting up in bed, bare-breasted, nipples stiff, with a suggestive smile on her face. He lifted the covers and climbed into bed next to her, and she immediately turned over and wrapped her arms around him. She parted her legs and he could feel her chilly wetness against his thigh.

'You're not going to make me jealous, are you, when your Natasha comes to stay with us?' she asked him, running the tip of her finger across his lips.

'Why should I? She's probably not the girl I thought she was. So Catherine says, anyhow.'

'But supposing she is?'

'I don't know, Isobel. I'm just trying to take things day by day. It would help if people around here told me the truth now and again.'

'I always tell you the truth, don't I? When have I ever lied to you?'

'You made out you didn't know Sue, just like Sue made out she didn't know you.'

Isobel kissed him, and slid her hand down between his legs to squeeze him. 'You know why we had to do that. That was part of your therapy. Sue said that it was the best way of helping you

240

to remember your childhood. But I swear on my life that I've never told you any other lies. I wouldn't. I love you too much. Besides, we're going to be married, aren't we?'

The next morning, at the very beginning of his therapy session, Catherine asked him if he remembered a family vacation in the Napa Valley when he was nine years old.

'You took a canoe out on to Lake Berryessa, you and Sue. Your *real* sister Sue. And the canoe capsized.'

Michael closed his eyes for a moment. He *did* remember taking a canoe out, on to a lake. He could picture it clearly. A sharp, sunny day, with a breeze making the waves slap against the side of the dock. But his companion in the canoe wasn't Sue. It was a blond-haired boy in a blue-and-white T-shirt.

Tim, that was the boy's name. *Tim Freeman*. And he was sure it wasn't Lake Berryessa. It was Lake ... what was it? It was Lake...

'You remember that?' Catherine asked him. 'You look like it's all coming back to you.'

Michael said, 'Yes ... it is. I remember that day distinctly.'

Lake Mendota, thought Michael. *It was Lake Mendota, and I was eleven that day, not nine. I've never even been to Lake Berryessa.*

'At last!' smiled Catherine. She reached across and patted him on the knee. 'At last you seem to be making some progress.'

'Yes,' said Michael. 'I do believe that I am.'

* * *

Afterward, Catherine took him to Natasha's room. Natasha was sleeping, with only a Korean nurse sitting in attendance, in a pale green uniform and clumpy black shoes.

'Mind if I stay here for a while?' asked Michael. 'Maybe she'll wake up.'

'That should be OK,' said Catherine. 'But I'll have to leave you now, I'm afraid. My next patient will be waiting.'

She left, and Michael pulled up a chair and sat close to Natasha's bedside. The nurse was writing out some long medical notes, punctuated by regular sniffs, and took no notice of him at all.

Natasha continued sleeping. After a while, Michael reached up and took hold of her hand. Chilly-fingered, like before, but her blood pressure was still very low, after all. She stirred, and whispered something, and then very abruptly opened her eyes. Those blue-gray eyes, the color of a lake after a rainstorm has just passed over.

'You came back,' she murmured.

Again, Michael raised his fingertip to his lips. 'Yes. I told you I would.'

'Doctor Hamid said I'll be coming to stay with you.'

'That's right. Just until you're well again.'

'I *am* well,' she said. 'There's nothing wrong with me at all.'

'Well, not much. Only the small matter of a serious skull fracture.'

'It's all healed up now.'

'I don't think so. Only yesterday it was still bleeding.'

'It's all healed up now,' she insisted. 'I'm fine.'

'You know who I am?'

'Yes, of course I do. You're Gregory.'

Michael looked at her for a long time without saying anything. She was speaking in a whisper but he was so shocked that she might just as well have screamed it at the top of her voice. If Natasha Kerwin knew him as Gregory, then maybe he really *was* Gregory. Maybe Catherine was right, and his mind had been inventing scenes from some imaginary childhood just to fill in the gaping holes where his early life should have been. Had he really taken a canoe out on to Lake Mendota, with a boy called Tim Freeman? Or had he been on Lake Berryessa, with Sue?

'Gregory?' he echoed.

'That's right. Gregory Merrick.'

'So how do we know each other?'

Those blue-gray eyes suddenly filled with tears. 'You really don't remember, do you?'

'I'm sure that we know each other. I'm certain of it. I told my therapist that I probably made a mistake, and that you just happen to remind me of a girl I once knew. But I'm totally convinced that it's you.'

'Oh, Gregory. Oh, Greg,' she said. The tears slid down her cheeks into the pillow and her mouth was turned down in misery. 'We were engaged. We were going to get married. We had a crash on the interstate.'

Michael said, 'Engaged?' He could hardly catch his breath. 'You and me, we were *engaged*?'

'Is everything all right?' the nurse interrupted, looking up from her paperwork. 'Ms Kerwin

243

must not become stressed, please.'

'No, no, everything's fine,' said Michael, even though he was close to tears himself.

Natasha gripped his hand tightly and said, 'Doctor Hamid said they only have to do three or four more tests, and then I can come to stay with you. I promise you, Greg, I'll tell you everything then. I love you, darling, even if you can't remember me.'

At that moment the door opened and Doctor Hamid came in, accompanied by one of his juniors.

'Ah! Gregory! How are you and Natasha getting along? Natasha? Is everything all right? You look as if you have been crying.'

Michael tugged a Kleenex out of the box beside the bed and handed it to her. Natasha wiped her eyes and said, 'No, honestly. I'm fine. A little over-emotional, that's all. I'm really looking forward to getting out of here.'

'Well, there's a good chance I may be able to release you tomorrow or the day after,' said Doctor Hamid. 'Meanwhile, Gregory, I am afraid I must ask you to leave us.'

'Sure, yes,' said Michael. He raised his eyebrows to Natasha as if to say 'sorry' and then he stood up and left the room.

Walking back along the corridor, he felt as if somebody had hit him on the head with a ball-peen hammer. If he and Natasha had both been injured in the same crash, there wouldn't have been any question that they knew each other, and their families must have told the clinic that they were engaged. So why had Kingsley Vane and

Catherine tried so hard to persuade him that he *didn't* know her? Was it for his sake, or was it for hers, or was there some other reason? And why had they suggested that Natasha came to stay at Isobel Weston's house with him? If Catherine's therapy was effective, he would remember sooner or later that he and Natasha had once been lovers, and engaged. And what was he going to do about Isobel? He had promised to marry *her*, even though he hadn't really meant it.

As he reached the lobby, the door to Kingsley Vane's office opened, and Kingsley Vane emerged with a sheaf of pink medical folders under his arm.

'Mr Merrick – Gregory – how are you?'

How do you think, you lying sonofabitch? You can take your 'geographically impossible' and shove it where it's geographically impossible.

'Fine. OK, thanks.'

'I just want to tell you on behalf of TSC how much we appreciate you and Mrs Weston taking Natasha Kerwin under your wing.'

'She seems to think that she's better already.'

Kingsley Vane gave him a toothy, humorless grin. '*Brain* trauma, Gregory, *brain* trauma! It affects the perception in so many ways. It's extraordinary how the smallest of cerebral contusions can affect our way of looking at the world around us. So easy to become paranoid, and think that everybody is deceiving us. So easy, too, to become over-optimistic, and believe that all's right with the world when we're teetering right on the very brink of catastrophe.'

'I see. OK. I'll do my best with her.'

'We're sure that you will, Gregory. And we're confident that it will help *you* immensely, too – clear up all of those doubts that you've been having about your identity. *Ex cineribus ad astra*, as the Romans used to say – out of the ashes and up to the stars!'

Two days later, a white Grand Cherokee drew up outside Isobel's house, closely followed by the black Escalade driven by the clinic's security men.

It was a bright, cloudless afternoon and the snow was beginning to melt, so that Trinity's silence was interrupted by a syncopated pattern of dripping. Michael opened the front door and waited while one of the clinic's orderlies unloaded a wheelchair and helped Natasha out of the passenger seat. The orderly covered her knees with a blanket and pushed her up the driveway, but although he was treating her like an invalid she looked brighter than ever, and she gave Michael an enthusiastic little finger-wave as she came up to the porch.

Isobel came up behind Michael and laid a hand on his shoulder – a little possessively, Michael thought.

'Welcome!' she said, as Natasha was pushed up to the door.

Natasha drew back the blanket and climbed out of the wheelchair. 'I could have walked,' she said. 'But Ramondo here insisted. It's the rules. Something to do with insurance.'

'I fetch your bag, meez,' said the orderly, and pushed the empty wheelchair back down the driveway. Michael and Natasha and Isobel went inside. Isobel had lit the gas log fire, and as usual the living room was so warm that it was stifling.

'It's very cozy in here!' said Natasha. She looked around the room, taking in the gloomy framed print of a log cabin that hung on the chimney breast, and the collection of Disney figurines on the mantelpiece. While Isobel had her back turned, she raised her eyebrows at Michael as if to say: *My God – kitsch is not dead!*

Michael helped her out of her pale blue nylon snow jacket. Underneath she was wearing a silky white turtleneck sweater and blue jeans. It looked to Michael as if she had lost a great deal of weight while she was undergoing intensive care, because she was very skinny, with small pointed breasts and bony hips. She kept her blue knitted hat on.

'How about some herbal tea?' asked Isobel. 'I have some home-made coconut cookies, too.'

'I'd love some regular tea if you have some,' said Natasha. 'No cream, though. Do you need some help with that?'

'Unh-hunh, no thanks. This is *my* house and you're my guest here, remember.'

Isobel went into the kitchen while Michael and Natasha sat down in front of the fire.

'Do I sense a little coolness here?' asked Natasha. 'And I don't mean the room temperature.'

Michael knew that there was no point in him lying. She would find out by bedtime, if not before.

'The thing of it is, Natasha, in the past week or

so, Isobel and I have gotten pretty close.'

'How close is that, exactly?'

'About as close as a man and a woman can get.'

'You've slept with her? You're *still* sleeping with her?'

Michael nodded.

'Does anybody at the clinic know about that?' asked Natasha. Michael was surprised that she seemed to be taking it in such a matter-of-fact way, considering they were supposed to be engaged. 'Doctor Hamid, or Doctor Connor?'

'I really don't know,' he said. 'I don't think so. I don't think they would have suggested that you come and stay here if they did.' He paused, and held out his hand toward her. 'I'm so sorry, Natasha. I totally didn't remember that we were engaged. I was sure that I knew you, but I had no idea how well.'

She took his hand and tried to smile but her eyes looked sad. 'It's not your fault, Greg. Doctor Hamid told me what happened to you.'

'Natasha—'

'No. Not Natasha. You always used to call me "Tasha".'

'Tasha?' Michael shook his head. It rang no bells at all.

'You can start calling me Tasha now, if you like. Maybe it'll help you to remember me. Maybe it'll help you to remember *us*.'

Isobel appeared in the kitchen doorway, carrying a tray with three mugs of tea on it. Michael glanced up at her briefly, but then he looked up at her again, and stared at her, because he was seeing the same optical illusion that he had seen three mornings ago, when he had first woken up – if it *was* an optical illusion, and not his mind falling apart.

For a few flickering seconds, he thought he could see the kitchen window right through her, as if she were transparent.

TWENTY-ONE

Tasha had been right. Isobel's jealousy crackled in the air like static electricity. She was smiling and polite and everything she said was welcoming, but it was obvious that she regarded Tasha as a threat.

She wrapped her arms around Michael at every opportunity, and made sure that she cuddled up close to him on the couch when they were watching television that evening. When it came to supper time, and they were sitting around the kitchen table eating macaroni cheese, she made her big announcement.

'We're going to be married in June. Did Greg tell you that?'

Tasha looked sharply at Michael and said, 'No, he didn't.'

'Well, it's only four months away now and I do so hope that you'll be able to come.'

'Yes. That would be lovely.'

Isobel said, 'It's strange, isn't it, how two

people can just click sometimes?' She popped her fingers by way of emphasis.

'Yes,' said Natasha. 'I guess it is.'

Michael didn't take his eyes off Tasha for the rest of the meal, trying to read her expression and work out what she was thinking, but she didn't look at him again.

Isobel had given Tasha the small third bedroom at the back of the house. Later, close to midnight, while Isobel had gone to take her bath, Tasha came into the living room where Michael was watching the news. She was wearing pink-striped cotton pajamas and she was barefoot, which made her look even more girlish and vulnerable. She smelled of some light flowery perfume.

She sat down beside Michael and tucked her legs up underneath her. 'We have to talk, Greg. I have some things I need to tell you. I don't know if I'm supposed to. Probably not. But I really think you deserve to know.'

Isobel called out, 'Greg? Do you want this bath? It's beautifully hot!'

'Give me a minute, OK?' Michael called back. Then, to Tasha, 'What things? What?'

'Ssh, I can't tell you now. But we both have to go up to the clinic tomorrow morning, don't we? We can talk while we're walking up there.'

'Greg! Come on, sweetheart, or it'll get cold!'

'OK, I'm coming!' said Michael.

He stood up, but Tasha took hold of his hand and held it tight. 'I still love you, in spite of everything. I mean it.'

Michael bent forward and kissed her on the

forehead. He was about to kiss her on the lips when Isobel appeared in the doorway, wrapped in a large red towel.

'Come *on*, lover!' she coaxed him, although the way she said it, it sounded more like an order.

Michael was woken up by somebody shaking his shoulder. He opened his eyes, and saw that Tasha was bending over him, silhouetted by the moonlight that was shining through the bedroom drapes.

'What is it?' he whispered. Isobel was fast asleep, and breathing steadily.

'There's some people outside my window, in the yard!'

'What?'

'A man and a woman and two little girls! In their night things! They're just standing there, staring!'

'Hold on,' said Michael. He lifted the cover and swung his legs out of bed. He was naked but he had left his clothes on the chair in the corner of the room, so he picked up his boxer shorts and stepped into them. Tasha was already at the door, waiting for him.

He followed her into her bedroom. She had drawn back the drapes and there they were, standing in the snow. Bill Endersby and his wife Margaret, with Jemima and Angela. Bill Endersby was wearing a white nightshirt, while Margaret was wearing a long white nightgown. Both Jemima and Angela were wearing patterned pajamas. All of their feet were bare.

'Who are they?' asked Tasha. 'It must be so

251

cold out there! What do they want?'

As if in answer to her question, Bill Endersby started to beckon.

'It looks like he wants us to join them,' said Michael.

'Oh God, they scare me,' said Tasha. 'Can't you make them go away? How can they stand out there in the snow like that, in the middle of the night?'

Tasha looked back out of the window. Bill Endersby was still beckoning. He wasn't smiling. In fact his expression was quite grim. He had his hand on Jemima's shoulder, and Jemima was beckoning, too. What made the scene look even more eerie was that Michael's and Natasha's reflections appeared to be standing in the yard next to their unwelcome visitors, like two ghosts.

'They've done this before, these people,' said Michael. 'The weird thing is, they never leave any footprints in the snow.'

'But why do they want us to go out there?'

'I don't know. I think the best thing to do is go ask them.'

He left the bedroom and went through to the kitchen. Natasha followed him, but she said, 'Don't, Greg! They really frighten me!'

'It's a couple of geriatrics and two kids, that's all. They may look creepy but what can they possibly do to us?'

With that, Michael unlocked the door that led out on to the back yard patio.

'Please be careful!' Natasha begged him.

Outside, the cold was intense. The moonlight

252

was bright but it had the strange effect of making the back yard look like a stage set made of cardboard. Michael stepped outside in his bare feet, just far enough to be able to see where Bill and Margaret Endersby and the two girls were standing.

Except that they were gone. There was nobody in the yard at all.

Michael took two or three more steps forward across the patio, looking around the side of the house to make sure, but all four of their visitors had vanished. And, just like before, they had left no footprints.

His bare feet were growing numb with cold, so he returned to the kitchen and closed the door and locked it. Natasha, wide-eyed, said, 'What did they say? Did they tell you what they wanted?'

'They weren't there, Tasha. They were gone. That's if they were ever there at all.'

'But that's *impossible*! I saw them with my own eyes, and so did you!'

Michael took the blue towel that was hanging by the side of the kitchen sink and bent over to dry his feet. 'People have been appearing outside the house ever since I moved in here,' he said. 'The first night I came here, I saw about a hundred of them standing in the road out front. I went out to see what they were doing, but there was nobody there. I was beginning to think that I was having hallucinations ... you know, that it was something to do with my amnesia.'

'They *were* there, Greg. I saw them, too. That was no hallucination. God, they scared me. I was

253

never so scared in my life.'

Michael held her in his arms. Through her cotton pajamas she felt as if she were all skin and bones. 'Listen,' he said, 'there's nothing else we can do tonight. But I think we need to talk to Catherine Connor tomorrow about what we both saw. None of those people at the clinic are telling us the truth – or not the whole truth, anyhow. Something is happening here in Trinity and it's not just people convalescing. Everybody here seems to be panicking about something, but I can't work out what it is.'

Natasha looked up at him. He thought that she was about to say something, but all she did was touch his bare shoulder as if she were reassuring herself that he was real.

'We'd better go back to bed,' he said. 'We can talk about this more in the morning.'

He kissed her, on the lips. She still didn't say anything, but there was something in her eyes that told him that she was hurting.

'Try to get some sleep,' he told her. She nodded, and went back into her bedroom and closed the door. Michael stood outside in the hallway for a few moments, and then returned to Isobel's room. Isobel was still sleeping, and when he climbed back beneath the sheets she didn't even murmur.

Michael lay there staring at the ceiling while the moon sank below the horizon and the room gradually filled up with darkness. He was beginning to feel that he had lost touch with reality altogether, and that there was no way he was ever going to be able to find his way back. Bits and pieces of memory were coming back to him, but they were like so much space junk, ill-assorted fragments tumbling over and over through an endless, airless vacuum.

The room grew darker still, and he fell asleep. He couldn't have been sleeping for more than twenty minutes, however, when he felt a quick, chilly draft and then somebody slipped into bed next to him. Somebody cold, and skinny, and naked.

He opened his eyes. He could see only blackness, but he could smell her flowery perfume, and he could feel her woolly hat and her hair against his shoulder.

'Tasha?' he whispered.

She put her arms around him and clung to him close. She was shaking.

'They're back,' she said, in such a breathy voice that he could hardly understand her.

'What?'

'They're back. Those people.'

Michael started to sit up. 'I'll go take a look,' he said. Beside him, Isobel shifted and half-turned over and said, *mmmfffff.*

'Don't,' said Natasha, clinging on to him even more tightly. *'Please don't.'*

'I don't think they can harm me,' Michael whispered.

'Just don't. Please. I don't want to lose you again.'

Michael hesitated and then he lay back down again. Natasha stayed close to him, holding him tight. Gradually, she stopped shaking, but she was still very cold. Isobel continued to breathe evenly, in what Michael hoped was a very deep sleep.

'What are you going to do?' he asked Natasha. 'You can't stay here all night.'

Natasha lifted herself up a little so that she could kiss him. It felt like a very chaste kiss, especially since her lips were so cold.

'*I need you,*' she said, and kissed him again, and this time her tongue slid into his mouth.

'We can't!' he hissed at her, taking hold of her wrist and trying to lever her away from him. But she kissed him again, much more greedily this time, and she began to pant, very quickly, as if she had been running. She twisted her hand free and scratched his bare chest, and then scratched him further and further down his stomach, until she worked her fingers under the waistband of his shorts.

'Tasha, we can't!' he repeated, but she took hold of his penis, which was already three-quarters erect, and massaged it up and down. Her hand was cold, and he knew that he shouldn't be doing this. Isobel could wake up at any moment. But then he thought: *Tasha is supposed to be my real fiancée, after all, and it was Isobel who made a play for me first.* He was also beginning to find that the danger of making love to Natasha while Isobel was sleeping so close beside him was highly arousing.

Natasha pulled the bedspread aside and climbed on top of him, guiding his penis between her emaciated thighs. She was so thin that he could almost close his hands around her waist. He

256

could feel her ribs, and her breasts were tiny, although her nipples were stiff. He took each of them between his lips in turn, and rolled them against the roof of his mouth with his tongue. Each time she let out a long, quivering exhalation of breath, which sounded almost as if she were dying.

Isobel let out another *mmmffff* and restlessly tugged at the sheets. Michael and Natasha froze and for over ten seconds they stayed utterly still. Natasha was as cold inside as Isobel had been, although her vagina was much tighter, and Michael was already losing all sensation in his penis. Even his testicles were beginning to feel cold, and his scrotum had scrunched up tight.

Isobel seemed to have settled down again, so Natasha started slowly to ride up and down on Michael's penis, making sure that her movements coincided with Isobel's breathing. Each time she lifted herself up so high that his glans almost slipped out of her, but each time she slid herself back down again at the very last moment until he could feel her prominent pubic bone pressing against his, so hard that it was painful.

After three or four minutes, however, she began to ride Michael faster and harder. With every stroke, Michael was pushing himself up into her so forcefully that he was lifting his buttocks clear off the bed. As the pace of their lovemaking quickened, both of them forgot about Isobel, and what would happen if they woke her up. All they were concentrating on now was that moment of sparkling ice-cold climax.

Which came. And came. And came again.

Natasha bent her head down and sank her teeth into Michael's left shoulder, to stop herself from crying out loud.

Afterward they lay in each other's arms, neither of them speaking. The bedroom was now utterly dark. Not even Belle's eyes gleamed at them from out of the closet.

As they lay there, however, and their thumping heartbeats gradually slowed down, they became aware that Isobel was no longer breathing as slowly and regularly as she had been before. In fact she was panting, and panting faster and faster with every second that went by.

Michael could feel the mattress gently quaking, and he could hear what sounded like somebody persistently licking their lips. After less than a minute, Isobel gasped, and shook, and then lay as still as Michael and Natasha.

The three of them lay awake in the darkness until it began to grow light outside. Then, without saying a word and without looking at Michael and Natasha, Isobel got out of bed and went to the bathroom.

Natasha kissed Michael and said, quietly, 'I think this is my cue to leave. I'll see you later.' She kissed him again, three times, and then she added, 'I love you, Greg. I love you so much.'

After she had gone back to her room, Michael lay on his own and thought about what had happened. Most of all, he thought about how cold Natasha had felt, just the same as Isobel. How could any woman feel as cold as that, let alone *two* of them? He was beginning to become convinced that maybe they weren't cold at all, and that the iciness he felt when he made love to them was caused by some kind of physical or mental aberration from which *he* was suffering.

Isobel came back into the bedroom. She walked around the bed and stood in front of him, naked. She had the most complicated expression on her face: part jealousy, part arousal, part amusement, but wholly superior.

'Did you enjoy that?' she asked him.

He could have retorted, 'Did *you*?' but he kept his mouth tightly closed. The situation was thorny enough already without him making it worse; and apart from that he liked her too much, and he thought that he had probably hurt her quite enough already.

'I don't mind you fucking her, sweetheart,' said Isobel. 'In fact, she could share our bed with us every night, if you like. We could have some really good fun. But don't forget that you're mine. That's the whole reason you're here.'

'I thought I was here so that you could help me to get better.'

'Of course. But you know what William Blake wrote? "I am in you and you in me, mutual in divine love."'

'But you said that I was yours. Like I *belong* to you, or something.'

Isobel sat down beside him on the bed. She reached out and touched his face with her finger-tips, as if she were blind, and trying to discover what he looked like.

'You have to, Greg. You know that I couldn't survive without you.'

'Bill and Margaret Endersby were outside in

the yard again last night, along with Jemima and Angela. Tasha was totally freaked out and that's why she got into bed with me.'

'Just a nightmare, Greg, that's all.'

'Two people can't have the same nightmare, Isobel.'

'I know,' she said, enigmatically, and kissed him.

TWENTY-TWO

Breakfast the next morning was silent and uncomfortable. Outside the kitchen window they could see nothing but thick pearly fog. It was a sign that the day would probably be sunny later on, because the snow was evaporating, but at that time of the morning it looked as if the end of the world had arrived, and that zombies would soon come swaying out of the gloom.

Michael had only a single mug of strong black coffee. He had no appetite for Isobel's pancakes with maple syrup, although Natasha asked if she could have one. Isobel sat opposite the two of them, looking from one to the other without saying a word, and eating her own pancakes as if she were punishing them, cutting them sharply and noisily with the edge of her fork.

'About last night—' said Michael.

Isobel raised her left hand to stop him, and shook her head. 'I don't want to talk about last night, Greg. Love is never having to explain yourself.'

'But I swear to God that the Endersbys were out there. And Jemima, and Angela. You wouldn't make up something like that.'

Isobel didn't answer. She finished her pancakes and then she got up and stacked her plate into the dishwasher.

'I probably won't be here when you two get back from the clinic,' she said. 'I'm having lunch with George Kelly and Hedda and Diana Quick.'

'OK,' said Michael. Long pause. 'Hope you enjoy it.'

'Thanks for the breakfast,' said Natasha, who had still only half-finished her pancake. Isobel said, *'Hm!'* and stalked out of the kitchen.

After breakfast, Michael and Natasha put on their coats without saying a word and left the house, heading for the clinic. Trinity was always quiet, but in the fog it was utterly silent, and the houses looked as if they were all unoccupied. Even the trees appeared as if they were paralysed.

Thus in the winter stands the lonely tree.

Michael took Natasha's hand. She was wearing thick blue woolen gloves so he couldn't tell how cold she was.

He coughed, and then he said, 'You had some things you wanted to tell me.'

'Yes, I do,' she nodded. 'Like I said last night, I'm not sure that you're supposed to know any of this, but I really think that you deserve to.'

Michael said, 'Listen, Tasha, before you say

anything, I've made up my mind that you and I need to get the hell out of here – and the sooner the better. Whatever's going on here, it's just too weird. Maybe it's us. Maybe we're seeing things that aren't really there. But I think we need a second opinion on that, and the only way that we can get it is to leave. Like, *today.* As soon as Isobel's gone off for lunch, we'll take her Jeep and find our way back to civilization. There has to be a road out of here somewhere.'

Natasha stopped, and stood still. Her breath smoked in the fog. The silence around them was so complete that Michael could have believed that he had gone deaf.

'We *can't,*' she said. 'That was what I was going to tell you.'

'Why can't we? Isobel said the same damn thing to me. *You can't.* But she didn't tell me why.'

'Oh, God,' said Natasha, and her eyes filled with tears. 'Doctor Connor and Doctor Hamid should have told you. I don't know why it has to be me.'

'What? What is it, for Christ's sake? Do I have some kind of disease? That's it, isn't it? I thought it was! Plague? Bird flu? Everybody here in Trinity, we're all in quarantine. They're keeping us here to stop us infecting the rest of the country.'

'It's not that,' said Natasha. 'You're not infected with anything.'

'Then I'm crazy. My mind's gone, and I'm imagining all of this. In reality, I'm sitting in a padded cell in some nuthouse somewhere, being fed with a plastic spoon.'

'You're not crazy, either,' said Natasha, 'but your name isn't Gregory Merrick. You're not the person that the clinic has been trying to make you believe that you are.'

'Well, hallelujah!' said Michael. 'Who told you that?'

'Doctor Hamid. He gave me a long talk the day before I left the clinic.'

'That's incredible. That's really incredible. I never believed for one moment that I was Gregory Merrick. For one thing I never felt like a Gregory – and besides that I know absolutely squat about marine engineering. I never recognized myself in any of those photographs that my pretend sister Sue showed me.'

He paused while Natasha took a crumpled tissue out of her coat pocket and wiped her eyes. Then he said, 'So ... if I'm not "Gregory Merrick", who am I?'

Natasha sniffed and blew her nose. 'Your real name is Michael Spencer. You're thirty-one years old and you're a soil scientist.'

'*At last!*' said Michael. He felt as if he were checking his lottery ticket and all his numbers were coming up, one after another. 'That makes *so* much sense! I know all of this stuff about erosion and landscape and soil chemicals, but I couldn't understand how. So where do I live? Where's my family? What's my background? I can't believe this ... it all totally fits together. It's amazing.'

Although Michael was becoming so excited, Natasha sounded more and more miserable.

'Your dad and your stepmom live in Madison, Wisconsin,' she told him. 'That's where you grew up.'

'My stepmom? What happened to my mom? Were they divorced?'

Natasha shook her head. 'Your mom died when you were seven. She had cancer.'

Michael suddenly thought of sitting in the back of the car on Fonderlack Trail, feeling so sad that he could cry. That must have been when his mother passed away.

'OK,' he said, 'that makes sense, too. Come on, Tasha, please don't get so upset. Do I have any brothers or sisters?'

'You have an older sister, Jennie. She's married and she lives in Wauwatosa. You graduated from the University of Wisconsin and worked for a company in Sheboygan for two years but then you got a job in San Francisco with Kennedy Jenks Consultants. Which is where you met *me*.'

Michael wrapped his arms around her and hugged her. Although her dark blue coat was so thick, she still felt painfully thin. 'Come on, Tasha,' he told her. 'Everything's going to work out fine. I just don't understand why the clinic wants me to believe that I'm somebody else. What's the point of it?'

'The point of it is...' Natasha began, but then she tightly gripped the lapels of his overcoat and pressed her face against his chest and he heard her making a high, keening sound in the back of her throat.

All he could do was hold her close and wait for her to recover. As the sun rose higher the fog was beginning to shine, and the two of them were surrounded by radiant gold, as if they were standing in Heaven.

After a few moments Natasha looked up at him and her face was a mess of tears.

'You're dead,' she said.

'Excuse me?'

'You're dead, Michael. We crashed on the interstate on the way back from seeing my sister in Seattle, and you were killed.'

One corner of Michael's mouth began to lift up in a smile, but then he stopped smiling.

'I'm dead. I'm breathing and talking and walking about and eating food and drinking wine and making love, but I'm dead.'

'Yes, Michael, you are. And that's why you can't leave Trinity. You can only continue to breathe and talk and everything else so long as you stay here.'

'Tasha, I am patently not dead. How can I be dead? That accident was nearly three months ago, and if I was dead, I'd be rotten by now. You wouldn't be able to get near me, for the smell.'

'It's the mountain, that's what Doctor Hamid told me.'

'The mountain? What are you talking about?'

'Mount Shasta. It's one of the most powerful sources of spiritual energy in the country. Even *you* told me that, just before we crashed. They built the clinic here, and the community of Trinity here, so that they could use that energy. If you stay close to Mount Shasta, no more than five or six miles away, you can go on living even when you're dead.'

265

'Doctor Hamid told you this?'

'Yes,' Natasha whispered.

'Didn't it occur to you that Doctor Hamid might be talking a whole lot of horse manure?'

'Why would he invent a story like that?'

'I don't know. To keep me here, for some reason?'

'Michael ... they tried to make you believe that you were Gregory Merrick because they wanted you to forget about Michael Spencer and start a new life. Well ... an *afterlife*, that's what Doctor Hamid called it.

'He said that the clinic takes people who have died in accidents and uses the spiritual energy that comes from Mount Shasta to keep them conscious and active for as long as they can.'

Michael said, 'Tasha ... for Christ's sake ... do I look dead? Do I *feel* dead? How about last night, in bed, did I feel dead then?'

'No, of course not. You're going to be OK, so long as you stay here, close to Mount Shasta.'

'This is lunacy. I can't think why Doctor Hamid told you all of this. What did he think you were going to do, keep it a secret and never tell me? Did he seriously think that you were going to *believe* it? You don't believe it, do you? Because I don't fucking believe it.'

Natasha gave him a helpless shrug. 'He asked me to help them to convince you that you were Gregory Merrick. He said that you would be more likely to believe it if it came from me. He said that Doctor Connor has been trying to erase all of your memories of being Michael Spencer, but the problem is that you keep remembering things. Like *me*, for instance.'

'Why do I have to be Gregory Merrick? What's wrong with being Michael Spencer?'

'Because Michael Spencer is officially dead. His body was flown back to Madison and he was cremated.'

'But whoever they cremated, that wasn't me. They must have had a body, but who was it? They wouldn't have cremated an empty casket.'

'I don't know, Michael. Doctor Hamid only told me that legally you don't exist any more.'

Michael didn't know what to say to her. He could only stand there while the fog faded away and the snowy peaks of Mount Shasta reappeared above the treetops, pristine and aloof. *I own you*, said the mountain.

Natasha said, 'I'm so sorry, Michael. Maybe it would have been better if I hadn't told you, but I love you so much.'

'You love me even though I'm dead? Jesus! I don't know whether we'll have to arrange a wedding or a wake.'

'But so long as we stay here...'

'What? Stuck in this one-horse community for the rest of our lives? That's if we're ever going to die. Me – I'm dead already, apparently, but what about *you*?'

'Michael, I don't want to lose you. Not ever. I'd rather stay here in Trinity than lose you.'

'So we really can't leave? Or *I* can't leave, anyhow?'

'It's the energy. Doctor Hamid explained it to me, but I didn't really understand it. He said that there are centers of spiritual energy in different

267

places all around the world – usually volcanoes, like Vesuvius and Mount Fuji. He said that Mount Shasta is one of the most powerful.'

'And this energy is what's keeping me alive? Or undead, at least? Jesus, you're making me feel like a fucking vampire!'

Natasha said, 'No, Michael. There's nothing unholy about it, not like vampires.'

'Oh, great! Thank heaven for small mercies!'

'You probably don't remember, but you told me yourself that the Modocs believe that one of their gods came down from the sky to live on top of Mount Shasta. If this god thinks that some-body has died too soon he brings them back to life. That's what Doctor Hamid told me. It's, like, everybody has been put on this Earth to complete some specific journey, right? And if they die before they've completed it...'

'I'm stunned, Tasha. I don't know what to say to you. How can you believe this crap?'

'The god thing is only a legend, Michael. That was how the Modocs explained how dead people carried on living. But Doctor Hamid says he has scientific evidence that the energy around Mount Shasta can actually do that. Look at you, Mich-ael. You're dead but you're standing right here in front of me. If you need proof, go look in the mirror.'

'Tasha, listen to me. I am not fucking dead. If you really believe that I'm dead, how come you got into bed with me last night? I don't think I'd feel very comfortable about having sex with a dead person, even if it was you.'

Natasha released her grip on his lapels, and

looked up at him, her arms by her sides. 'I know you're dead but I'm not scared of you, Michael. Not at all. Those people in the back yard, *they* scared me, but you don't. I love you. You might have died but now you're living an afterlife and I want to share it with you.'

Michael said, 'I think we need to get out of this place, right now, before we both go stark raving bananas. Come on – let's forget about the clinic and go.'

He held out his hand but Natasha stepped away from him and furiously shook her head. 'No, Michael. I don't want to lose you a second time.'

'Nothing will happen to me, Tasha! I'm not dead. I don't look dead and most of all I don't *feel* dead. Now, let's go!'

'No, Michael. Please.'

'In that case, I'll go on my own.'

Natasha burst into tears again – not just sobbing but out-and-out crying. 'Please, Michael, *no*! I'm begging you!'

Michael took a deep breath and then he held her close again. 'All right,' he said, 'I'll make you a deal. We'll go up to the clinic and we'll talk to Doctor Connor and Doctor Hamid. You can tell them that I know that I'm supposed to be dead.'

'But I promised Doctor Hamid that I never would tell you, ever.'

'I know you did. But think about it. This is all beginning to sound like a double-bluff. They've been having a whole lot of trouble making me believe that I'm Gregory Merrick, right? Because my real memories keep on inconveniently bobbing up. So instead they thought they'd make me believe that I was dead. And the way to make it all sound more plausible was to have *you* tell me, as if you weren't supposed to. But don't you think they kind of overdid it, huh? All of that background detail about Vesuvius and Mount Fuji and the Modocs and Skell?'

He stopped, and then repeated, *'Skell.* That's right. That's the name of the sky god who lives on top of Mount Shasta. Skell. How about me remembering that? Pretty good recall for a dead guy, wouldn't you say?'

Natasha said, 'Can't we just leave it, and forget it, and carry on living together, the way we always meant to?'

'What – with all of those people staring into our bedrooms in the middle of the night? And sharing a bed with Isobel, even though she's convinced that she and I are going to be married? We have to get out of here, Tasha. It's a nightmare, this whole community. It's like the worst dream you ever had.'

'Yes,' said Natasha. 'Maybe it is.'

'What does that mean? What are you trying to say to me?'

Tasha pulled herself away from him, and took two or three paces up the snowy sidewalk. Because of the sunshine, Michael couldn't clearly see her face.

'Haven't you asked yourself, *whose* dream? If it's a nightmare, Michael, who's having it? You or me? Or somebody else altogether?'

TWENTY-THREE

He caught up with her and grabbed her arm but she twisted it away.

'You're just like you always were! All you ever think about is you!'

'You've just told me I'm dead, for Christ's sake! Don't you think I'm entitled for a few moments to think about the implications of that?'

'There are no implications, Michael. You're dead and that's it. Well, you were dead, but now you're alive again, and I still love you, and if we stay here in Trinity we can go on living together. Is that so hard for you to get your head around?'

'Yes,' said Michael. He waited a few seconds, and then he slapped himself very hard across the face. 'I felt that,' he said. 'I am one hundred per cent not dead.'

Natasha waited for him patiently and said nothing. Michael turned around and looked at Mount Shasta. Could it really be keeping him alive, that mountain?

'All right,' he said. 'Let's go see Catherine, and Doctor Hamid. Let's get this whole insane situation sorted out.'

'I'm really nervous,' said Natasha.

'What do you have to be nervous about? They

may be a little peeved that you told me I was dead, but what can they do to you? Nothing. They can't do much to me, either, if I really am dead. What are they going to do – kill me?'

They walked up the hill and in through the clinic gates. Henry the security guard watched them as they passed his booth with slitty-eyed suspicion. When they entered the shiny marble lobby they found that Doctor Connor was already there, wearing a smart cream suit, and talking to the receptionist.

'Ah, Gregory!' she smiled. 'And Natasha, too. How have you two been getting along?'

Michael turned around as if he were looking for someone. Then he turned back to Catherine and said, 'Oh! You're talking to *me*?'

'Of course,' said Catherine, with a wary tone in her voice.

'But you said "Gregory". My name isn't Gregory. It's Michael.'

Catherine looked sharply at Natasha. 'What makes you think that?'

'What do you *think* makes me think that? Tasha's told me everything. She's even told me that I've allegedly passed away.'

Catherine said, 'You'd better come into my consulting room. Brenda – would you page Doctor Hamid for me? Please tell him it's urgent.'

They followed Catherine into her consulting room. Catherine sat down behind her desk and said, 'Please – sit.' Natasha took a chair but Michael remained standing, with his arms folded.

'So now you know that you're not really Gregory Merrick?' asked Catherine.

'Yes.'

'I hope Natasha made it clear to you *why* we were trying to give you a new identity. We were doing it entirely for your own protection – both physical and psychological.'

'I don't believe you, Catherine. For some reason which is totally beyond me you've been trying to keep me here in Trinity. First of all you try to make me think that I'm this Gregory Merrick character, and when that little stunt doesn't pan out, you try to make me believe that I'm dead.

'What really makes me angry is that before we had our accident Tasha and I were going to be married, even though you tried to make me believe that I was deluding myself and that I didn't even know her at all. I love her, and you've really upset her. How the hell can you and Doctor Hamid be so goddamned callous? You're supposed to be doctors. You're supposed to look after people, not make them feel worse!'

Catherine remained quite calm. 'Michael,' she said, 'if you knew how much care this clinic has lavished on Natasha over the past few months, you wouldn't be raging at us like this, you'd be thanking us.'

'But you're still trying to make me think that I'm dead.'

At that moment, there was a quick rap at the door and Doctor Hamid came in, with a stethoscope around his neck.

'Oh, you've come to listen to my heart, have

273

you?' Michael challenged him. 'Just to make absolutely sure that I'm dead.'

Catherine said, 'Natasha told him. I was afraid that she would.'

'I love him,' said Natasha. 'You couldn't expect me to keep a secret like that forever.'

Doctor Hamid went over and stood behind Catherine's chair. The sunlight shining through the window made him look even darker than ever, with his black hair curled up into two Satanic horns.

'But now you understand, Michael, why we have been trying to keep you here in Trinity. If you leave this vicinity, you will die. It's as simple as that.'

'Why didn't you tell me this before? If it's true that I'm dead, which I don't believe for a moment, why did you tell me all of those lies?'

'Because we wanted you to live a peaceful and happy afterlife, without ever pining for the life you had before, and to which you can never return. Michael Spencer is dead and gone. Gregory Merrick is after-living, here in Trinity, in the benevolent influence of Mount Shasta.'

'What about all of the other residents of Trinity?' Michael demanded. 'Are they all dead, too? I keep seeing them outside of Isobel's house, in the middle of the night, wearing nothing but their nightclothes, and none of them ever leave any footprints in the snow. And all of them seem to be frightened of something.'

Catherine tapped her forehead. 'That's just your own imagination, Michael, adjusting itself to the new reality of afterlife.'

'But Tasha saw them, too. Are you trying to tell me that she's dead as well?'

'You're both recovering from appalling mental and physical traumas. It's quite normal for you to see people and objects that aren't really there. You'll find that it passes, in time. It's simply a form of hallucinosis, such as alcoholics get if they abruptly give up drinking.'

'And what about Jack Barr and Lloyd Hammers? Are *they* dead? And what the hell happened to them, after I tried to take Tasha away from here? Jack wound up in a wheelchair and Lloyd talked to me like he'd been brainwashed.'

Catherine gave him a faint smile and shook her head. 'I'm afraid I'm not at liberty to discuss other patients with you, Michael.'

Michael looked down at Tasha, who was biting her thumbnail and looking increasingly unhappy.

'All right,' he said. 'So where do we go from here?'

'Obviously, now you know the truth, there's no point in us carrying on with our Gregory Merrick therapy. We'll just have to work on rebuilding your identity as Michael Spencer, so long as you're prepared to do that. It's going to be lot harder, and a lot more distressing, but it's the only way left open to us.'

Michael said nothing for nearly ten seconds, keeping his eyes on Natasha. She glanced up at him two or three times, and it was obvious that she was very close to tears.

At last he said, 'I think what we're going to do is, we're going to skip the therapy for today and go back home. We really need to talk this over between us.'

'Very well,' said Doctor Hamid, 'but I will need to examine Natasha tomorrow. She needs another brain-scan and she still has a long way to go.'

Michael opened the door and Natasha stood up and took hold of his arm. As they were leaving, however, Michael turned and said, 'Tell me, Doctor Hamid – if Natasha and I get married, like we intended – can dead men become fathers?'

Doctor Hamid lifted both hands, as if to say, *who knows? such a thing is in the lap of the gods.* But then he said, 'Physically, there is no reason why not. For a man who is technically dead, Michael, you are in a state of very good health. We have Mount Shasta to thank for that.'

Michael thought about that, and then left, without asking any more questions, closing the door behind him.

Natasha said, anxiously, 'What now?'

'Now we get in the Jeep and go. We can be three hundred miles away by the time it gets dark.'

'You really don't believe you're dead, do you?'

'Of course not. Not for a moment. What do they think I am, some kind of retard?'

'But why do you think they're so anxious to keep you here in Trinity?'

'I have no idea, Tasha, unless it's to keep Isobel satisfied.'

'Don't,' said Natasha, turning away.

Michael tried to take hold of her hand but she wouldn't let him. 'Listen,' he said, 'I'm really sorry. That was a shitty thing to say. But come on – let's get out of here. Let's put all of this behind us. From now on we can forget about Trinity and you can start helping me to remember Michael Spencer.'

'Michael – I'm absolutely terrified that they're telling us the truth.'

'Here,' he said.

He gently held her chin in his hand and lifted her head up and kissed her. At first she kept her eyes open but then she closed them, and when he had finished kissing her she kept them closed, and let out a long, soft breath.

Kissing her, he knew for certain that he was Michael and she was Tasha and that they had been in love for a very long time.

They didn't say any more, but left the lobby hand-in-hand and went out through the doors and down the steps and out through the clinic's front gates. Henry the security man watched them leave with his iguana-like eyes but again Michael resisted the temptation to say anything to him or give him the finger. He didn't want anybody at the clinic to have the slightest suspicion that they were going to make another attempt to get away.

Isobel was still out when they got back to the house. She had left them a note saying *'Back around 4:00 probably. Help yourselves to cold chicken in the fridge.'*

Michael went into Isobel's bedroom, opened the closet and pulled out two navy-blue sports bags that he had seen on the bottom shelf. Belle the doll was sitting in there, with her glossy black eyes, staring at him. He picked her up and twisted her head around so that she was facing backward.

'There,' he said, 'now you really *do* look like you're possessed.'

He handed Natasha one of the sports bags and said, 'Pack as much as you can as quick as you can.'

'They don't know we're going to leave, do they?'

'I have a feeling, that's all. Catherine has a way of looking at you and telling what you're thinking. Come on, let's hustle!'

They crammed as many of their clothes into the sports bags as they could and zippered them up. Michael took the keys to Isobel's Jeep off their hook, and then he gave the house a last look around.

'What's the matter?' asked Natasha.

'Nothing. Some of the strangest things happened to me here, that's all.'

They left the house, closing the front door quietly behind them in case they attracted attention from the neighbors, and climbed into the Jeep – again, closing the doors as quietly as they could.

Natasha said, 'You're still sure about this?'

'When I kissed you, back at the clinic, did I feel like I was dead?'

He didn't wait for an answer, but started the engine and shifted the Jeep into gear. He was just about to pull out of the driveway when a flash of reflected sunlight caught his eye. He looked up the slope and saw that the black Escalade was driving down toward them, quite fast. With a crunching slither of ice and snow, it stopped right in front of them, blocking their exit.

'You see?' said Michael. 'I told you that Catherine was a mind-reader.'

The doors of the Escalade opened and the two white-faced security men climbed out. They came walking up the driveway in their dark glasses and their long black overcoats, not hurrying, as if they were weary parents who were telling their children for the umpteenth time not to run off again.

'What do we do now?' asked Natasha.

Michael said, 'We survived one crash, I'm sure we can make it through another.'

With that, he shifted the Jeep into reverse, and backed up the driveway with whinnying tires until the rear bumper hit the garage doors. There was a deep boom of sheet-metal, like stage thunder.

'*Michael!*' Natasha squealed.

But Michael shifted back into drive, and stamped on the gas pedal. The two security men realized at once what he was doing, and both of them jumped clear, one of them falling backward into the snow. The Jeep slewed down the driveway, across the sidewalk, and collided with the Escalade, denting its driver's door so that it was almost bent double, shattering two side windows, and pushing it out into the road at an angle of forty-five degrees.

The security men shouted and started to run toward them, but Michael immediately backed up again, and they had to retreat, scrabbling up the icy driveway like two frantic skaters. Back in drive, Michael spun the wheel and steered the Jeep around the rear end of the damaged Escalade.

He headed down the slope toward the community center. He had no idea where the road out of Trinity might be, but he knew it wasn't the road that was signposted for Route 97 and Weed, and it wasn't the road that passed by the intersection with Summit View, so maybe by process of elimination it was down this way, and out of Trinity on the other side.

Natasha twisted around in her seat so that she could see what the two security men were doing. 'I don't think they're coming after us,' she said. 'It looks like they can't get their doors open.'

As they approached the community center, however, he saw that two people had come out of their house and were walking quickly down their driveway toward the road, waving their arms in the air. He recognized them as the woman in the sludge-green woolen dress who had given him such a hard time when he had knocked on her door, and the young man who had been pointing at him out of her living-room window.

'What the *hell* are they doing?' he said.

'I don't know,' said Natasha. 'It looks like they want us to stop.'

'Well screw that. We're not stopping for nobody, nohow.'

By the time they had reached the traffic circle outside the community center, however, the woman had stepped right out into the road, still waving her arms. The young man followed her. Michael blasted the Jeep's horn, twice, and shouted, 'Get out of the goddamn road!' even though he knew that they couldn't hear him.

The woman was so close now that Michael could see the determined expression on her face. She stopped right in the middle of the road and continued to wave her arms as if she were signaling to a ship at sea.

Michael slowed down to a crawl. Even when the Jeep's front grille was less than three feet away from her, the woman didn't flinch, and kept on waving. Michael brought the Jeep to a halt, almost touching her.

'Get – out – of – the – goddamned *road*,' he repeated.

'Michael,' said Natasha, in a whisper. 'Look. Look behind us. Look over there.'

The front doors of all the houses in the street were opening up, and the residents were all coming outside and walking toward them, although none of them were waving. Some of them he recognized, like Walter Kruger and George Kelly and Hedda and Lloyd Hammers, too. Then he saw Katie Thomson, followed closely by her mother Bethany, and the large woman who had appeared at Isobel's last get-together in a crimson corduroy dress, but whose name he had forgotten.

Michael turned around. Behind them, the roadway was gradually filling up with more and more residents, so that it was impossible for them to back up. It was like the night when he had seen scores of them standing outside Isobel's front yard.

He turned back again. From the front door of George Kelly's house, he saw Isobel coming out, too. She was too far away for him to be able to see the look on her face, but he could imagine it. Angry and hurt, and deeply puzzled. He had promised to marry her in June, after all.

'How did all of these people know that we were trying to leave?' asked Natasha.

'I have absolutely no idea,' said Michael. 'I don't see the clinic having the time to contact them all, do you?'

'Oh God, Michael. What are we going to do?'

The residents had now begun to gather around the Jeep, so close that they could have touched it, and some of them had their hands reaching out, as if they were about to do so, but for some reason were holding off. They simply stood there, staring in through the windows at Michael and Natasha, most of them expressionless, but a few of them frowning, as they had when they pointed at Michael from their living-room windows.

Michael checked his rear-view mirror. Walking down the slope toward them, with much more determination than they had before, came the two security men, their long black coats flapping. *Shit*, he thought. *Now we're totally screwed.* It wouldn't have surprised him if they were both armed.

Natasha said, 'It's no good, is it? We're going to have to stay here.'

Michael glared through the Jeep's windshield at the woman standing right in front of him, still waving her arms. He took a deep breath, and then he blasted the horn, again and again. She continued to stand her ground, so he began to inch the vehicle forward, pumping his foot on the brake pedal, until it was actually pressing up against her stomach.

'You can't,' said Natasha. 'Michael, you *can't*!'

TWENTY-FOUR

Michael ignored her. Ever since he had woken up in Trinity-Shasta Clinic, all he had heard was people telling him 'you can't.' But inside of himself, he knew that he was the kind of person who *could*, and *would*, and always had done, regardless of the consequences.

His amnesia had made him cautious and suspicious and careful, even frightened. Without a memory that he could trust, he had felt completely defenseless. But at least he knew his real name now and who he was – even if all the rest of his recollections were broken bits and pieces that didn't yet fit together. Now he was ready to get the hell away from Trinity and go back to his life in the real world outside, no matter how difficult it turned out to be.

It could be that Catherine Connor and Doctor Hamid had been telling him the truth, and he *was* dead, and he couldn't survive beyond the spiritual influence of Mount Shasta. But maybe that was what his destiny had always been, and he would just have to accept it. *Kismet*. Nobody lives forever, especially if they're dead already.

He used the footbrake to nudge the Jeep forward again and again, so that step by step the woman had to give ground. Each time he nudged it a little harder and a few inches further, until she stopped waving her arms and pressed her hands flat against the radiator grille to save herself from losing her balance and falling over backward.

There was a loud bang on the passenger door, and then another on Michael's side, and then another, and another, as the residents of Trinity started to beat against the Jeep with their fists. At the same time, they started to howl – an eerie, high-pitched sound like wolves. They beat harder and harder on the sides of the Jeep until Michael and Natasha were almost deafened.

Michael glanced in his rear-view mirror again and saw that the two security men were only a few yards away now, and had started to jog. Looking toward the front, he could see the woman's contorted face as she strained vainly to keep him from advancing any further. And all the time the drumming and the howling grew louder and louder.

Michael inched forward yet again, and now the crowd screamed at them and started to shake the Jeep violently from side to side. Natasha had to grip both armrests to stop herself from being thrown against the door and hitting her head against the window.

'Michael! They're going to kill us!'

Michael blasted the horn just one more time. The woman in front of him stared at him un-blinking as if she were *daring* him to do what he wanted to do. She shouted something at him which he couldn't hear, but which he was sure was *go on, then, if you've got the stones!*

One of the security guards shouldered his way through the crowd and appeared beside his win-dow. He made a twisting motion with his wrist to indicate that Michael should switch off the Jeep's ignition. Michael shook his head, and it was then that the security man reached inside his coat and lifted out a gun.

For a fraction of a second, Michael had the odd thought: *If this man knows that I'm already dead, why is he threatening me with a gun?* But then his survival instinct went into overdrive, and he kicked down the gas pedal as hard as he could. The Jeep surged forward with a chorus of screams from its tires, and the woman instantly disappeared from sight like a conjuring trick. Michael could feel her bumping underneath the floor as they ran over her.

He kept his foot down as they roared up the slope. None of the residents made any attempt to get out of his way, and he hit at least seven of them with a barrage of thumps. He thought that he had collided with Lloyd Hammers and possibly with George Kelly, too, but he couldn't be sure. All he could see when he looked in his rear-view mirror were bodies that were rolling over and over down the slope like bundles of rags.

'*What have you done?*' cried Natasha, in a

shrill, breathless scream that was almost inaudible.

'What did you expect me to do? That mob were going to tear us apart! And that security guy pulled a gun on me!'

'Oh God, I don't believe this is happening! I don't believe this is happening!'

Michael checked his mirror again. It looked as if at least two of the residents that he had hit were being helped to their feet.

'Take a look,' he told Natasha. 'I don't think anybody got badly hurt.'

Natasha turned around but by now the crowd had disappeared from sight around a curve in the road.

Michael steered with his left hand and laid his right hand on top of hers. 'It's going to be OK – I mean it! They were standing right in the middle of the goddamned road and wouldn't get out of the way! What the hell did they expect?'

Natasha was about to say something more but then obviously couldn't find the words. She dabbed her eyes with a tissue and blew her nose and then sat silent, with her head bowed, staring at the floor.

'Come on, Tasha. We'll be miles away from here soon.'

'Oh – even though you don't know how to get to the interstate?'

'I know it's not back that way, so it's a pretty reasonable guess that it's *this* way.'

They were passing the last few houses in Trinity, and Michael noticed that people were peering out of their windows at them as they

286

drove by. One man in a fluorescent yellow jacket was shoveling snow from the sidewalk outside his house and he turned around to stare at them and kept on staring until they were out of sight.

Natasha said, 'It's like everybody in Trinity has heard what we're doing.'

The road became narrower, until it was nothing much more than a ribbon of gray tarmac between the rocky verges and the pine trees.

'Do you think they'll send the police after us?' asked Natasha.

'I don't know, Tasha. In a way I almost hope they do. At least the cops will take us back to civilization. And you have to admit that was a really threatening situation back there. Even if I did hurt anybody, I think it was justifiable, don't you?'

Again, Natasha didn't answer. Michael glanced at her a few times as they drove. She was biting at her knuckle and her eyes were filled with worry. He had tried to make light of hitting all those people but he knew how serious it was, especially if he had killed one or more of them. But of course that wasn't all she was worried about. She was worried what was going to happen as they drove further and further away from Mount Shasta.

They drove for about ten minutes without talking. Natasha tried the Jeep's radio, but all she got was crackling and white noise, with only an occasional blurt of country music.

'Same as the last time,' said Michael. 'Maybe it's all of this so-called spiritual energy.'

'Are we headed in the right direction?' asked Natasha.

'Sun's behind us, and off to the left, so we should be going north-west. I'd be happier if it were going *due* west, but we'll just have to see.'

As the narrow road continued for mile after mile, however, the shadows of the pines that lay across it started to tell Michael that it was gradually turning north-eastward, and then almost due east. After they had been driving for about an hour, the pines began to thin out, and flickering through their branches they could see the white snowy peaks of Mount Shasta, much closer than they had appeared from Trinity.

'Shit,' said Michael. 'We're heading totally the wrong way.'

'What happens if we just keep going?'

'I guess we'll wind up someplace eventually. But we're really low on gas, and I don't exactly relish the idea of getting stranded way out here in the Cascade mountains in the middle of the night.' He checked the thermometer on his side mirror. 'It's already five degrees below.'

'Well, what are we going to do? We can't turn back, we'll just wind up in Trinity again.'

'We'll drive on a few miles further, OK? There's all kinds of climbing and winter sports centers around Mount Shasta. We're bound to run into one of them, sooner or later.'

They kept driving. The needle on the gas gauge was almost touching red. Even if they U-turned now, they wouldn't have enough fuel to get back to Trinity, and the sun was sinking lower and lower behind them. In less than two hours, it would be dark.

'What's that up ahead?' said Natasha, suddenly.

The road began to climb steeply, with a rocky overhang on the left-hand side. About a hundred yards ahead of them, though, the road rose high enough to reach the same height as the overhang, and there, set back among a small clearing in the trees, stood a large pine cabin. The windows were lit, there was smoke coming out of the chimney, and there was a battered white Dodge Ram parked outside.

'Think we just made that by the skin of our teeth,' said Michael. He turned into the driveway and parked at a tilt behind the Ram, making sure that the Jeep's parking brake was fully applied. They climbed the wooden steps in front of the cabin and crossed the veranda. There was all kinds of junk out here: two broken kitchen chairs, several small barrels, a heap of snow chains, and a rusty diesel generator.

Michael went up to the front door, but he didn't have the chance to knock. As he raised his fist, the door was abruptly opened up by a lean middle-aged man with long gray hair.

'Lost, or something?' he demanded. His voice was very sharp and hard, so that every word was like a whip crack.

'Yes, to be honest,' said Michael. 'Nearly out of gas, too.'

'Where you aiming for?'

'I-Five, hopefully.'

'Hopefully is the understatement of the year, mister. You couldn't be going more wronger if

289

you tried.'

'Do you think you could give us some directions? And maybe point us toward the nearest gas station?'

The man looked at Michael with pinprick eyes. 'Come from Trinity, then? Was you staying there, or just passing through?'

'Just passing through. Took a wrong turn past Weed.'

The man shook his head. 'Nobody passes through Trinity, mister. Not even by accident.'

'All right. We *were* staying there, for a while, but we decided it was time to leave. But really – all we need is gas and directions.'

'You'd better come along in.'

Michael turned to Natasha and pulled a face to show her that they really had no choice. In any case, Natasha was looking very tired and she was shivering, out there on the veranda. A cold katabatic wind was blowing down the slopes of Mount Shasta and making the trees sound as if they were whispering amongst themselves. *Escaped from Trinity, those two. What are their chances?*

Michael put his arm around Natasha and guided her in through the cabin door. Inside it was very warm and smelled strongly of dry wood and smoke. The man closed the door behind them and turned a key in it, although he left the key where it was, in the lock.

'Come and park your asses by the fire,' he said.

The stone fireplace stood at the end of the room, with a couch on one side and two armchairs on the other, all of them draped with

290

Modoc throws in colorful geometric patterns. Apart from these, the room was very sparsely furnished, with only two side tables with old-style brass lamps on them, and a chest of drawers with a clock on top of it. A framed tapestry on the wall said *Memories Are Best Forgotten*.

'Want a drink?' the man asked them. He was wearing a red checkered shirt and jeans with red suspenders; and with his long wispy hair and pointy nose he reminded Michael of the late David Carradine. In fact, he could almost have *been* David Carradine, returned from the dead and living in isolation on Mount Shasta. 'Beer? Whiskey? Soda? Or if you're feeling cold, miss, Nann won't mind stirring up a hot chocolate for you.'

As if on cue, a woman came out a side door beside the chest of drawers, wiping her hands on her apron. She was short and plump, with a round face, and she looked as if she were partly Native American. Her hair was tied back in a glossy black ponytail, and she was wearing a necklace of elaborately painted beads.

'This is Nann,' said the man. 'Actually "Nann" is short for "Nannookdoowah" which is Modoc for "strange child". Her hair was red when she was born, for some reason. Some of the elders in her tribe thought that she had been baptized in blood by Kumush, the creator god.'

He held out a dry leathery hand and said, 'Samuel Horn, that's me. Local handyman. No job too pissant. Snowshoe repairs and maintenance a specialty. Broken your frame, feller? Need your rawhide webbing re-waterproofed?

I'm your man.'

'Michael Spencer, and this is Tasha Kerwin.'

'Trying to get away, then?' asked Samuel Horn. He sat down on one of the armchairs and took a pale blue pack of Bugler tobacco out of his shirt pocket.

'Just looking for a change of scenery, that's all,' said Michael.

'Yeah, same as I did,' said Samuel Horn, without looking up from the thin cigarette that he was rolling one-handed.

'You lived in Trinity, too?'

Samuel Horn nodded, at the same time as licking his cigarette paper.

'Were you a patient at the clinic?'

'That's right. Gunshot wound. Like, *serious* gunshot wound. When I was pretty much recovered, though, they billeted me with this woman to convalesce. Sheila, her name was. Ex-librarian or something like that. She was OK, I guess, but I was never an indoors kind of guy. She wanted to sit and play Scrabble and Monopoly while all I was pining to do was come out and breathe some fresh air and maybe shoot something.'

Nann came out of the kitchen with two bottles of Budweiser and a mug of hot chocolate for Natasha. 'You want maybe something to eat? Sandwich, cookie?'

'No – no, thanks,' said Michael. 'It's very kind of you to offer.'

'We all share the journey,' said Nann. 'We should all help each other on the way.'

Samuel Horn lit his cigarette with an old Zippo

lighter and leaned back in his chair. 'Nann – she's got a saying for everything, don't you, Nann? Even going to the crapper.'

'So you left Trinity and came here?' asked Michael.

'That's right. I had lived here and worked here for twenty-odd years, and I knew plenty of people who would give me shelter for a while, Nann included. Mainly, though, I didn't want to risk going too far away from Mount Shasta.'

'Why was that?' asked Natasha.

'Well ... I don't know if them doctors at the clinic told you the same story as they told me. It all sounded so crazy that I could never decide if they was shooting me a line or not. But ... like I say, I didn't want to risk it.'

'They told you that you were dead, is that it?'

Samuel Horn sucked in smoke, and then nodded.

'You were dead,' said Michael. 'Your gunshot wound killed you, but somehow you were brought back to life by the spiritual energy that surrounds Mount Shasta. You have an afterlife. But be warned – if you ever stray too far from that spiritual energy, that's the end of your after-life and you go back to being dead.'

'Pretty much, yes.'

'So you believed them? You believed the doctors when they told you that story?'

Samuel Horn smoked for a while, letting the smoke drift out from between his lips and disappear up his nostrils. After a very long pause, he said, 'I don't know, Michael. Not for sure. You did say your name was Michael? I'd give anything to know if it's true or not. "You died, Samuel, but now we've given you *Life: The Sequel*." But let's put it this way: I don't intend to be the lab rat who finds out whether it's true or not. If it *is* true, I'll never know it, will I, because I'll have bought my second farm, so to speak.'

He paused a while longer, and then he squinted at Michael sideways and said, '*You* don't believe it, though, do you? Otherwise you wouldn't be trying to head for I-Five. All I can say is, you're a much braver man than me.'

Nann came back in from the kitchen with a tray of snacks: corn chips and chili salsa, pretzels, cubes of cheese, slices of salami and pickles. She sat down next to Samuel and said, 'I would never let Samuel leave the mountain.'

'So you believe in its spiritual energy?' asked Natasha.

Nann nodded her head vigorously. 'I was brought up always to believe in the power of Shasta, although my father always called it Uytaahkoo, the White Mountain. It is where Skell the sky god came down to greet Kumush the creator when Kumush returned from spending six days in the underworld.

'Kumush brought with him a bag of loose bones. Some of the bones he had dropped on his way up to the surface, and these stayed in the darkness underground to become demons and spirits. But with the few bones that he had left, he fashioned the first Modoc people.'

'Kind of like God did, with Eve,' put in Samuel Horn.

Nann said, 'Kumush went back up to live in the sky, but Skell remained on Shasta to protect us. *That* is the power of Shasta. *That* is its spiritual energy. Each man and woman must walk every step of the journey for which Kumush created them, and if they fall before they can complete it, then Skell will pick them up, and breathe life back into them.'

Michael said, 'That's a very colorful story, Nann.'

'I used to be a teacher of very young children, on the reservation. I know all of the Modoc legends.'

'Believe me, you make just as much sense as any of those doctors at the clinic. But what I'm thinking is that ... *Me*, I'm not Modoc, am I? It wasn't Kumush who created me, and therefore I doubt if Skell would have bothered about me when I died. So the only conclusion that I come to is that I'm not dead, after all. I'll bet that *you're* not dead, either, Samuel! I mean, let's get real! Two dead guys sitting around drinking beer and eating Doritos?'

'I don't know,' said Samuel. 'You go for it, if you think that you'll make it. I'll give you some gas and I'll show you how to get to the interstate without having to go back through Trinity.'

'I can't pay you for the gas, Samuel. I only have credit cards, and I'm not even sure they're good for anything.'

'Don't worry about that. If you make it, then come back and pay me in cash. If you don't make it, then take it as a parting gift.'

'And what if I *do* come back – which I'm

pretty damn sure that I will. What about you?'

Samuel sucked the last quarter-inch of his cigarette and then crushed it out in a Modoc pottery ashtray. 'Can't answer that, Michael. I've been here a long time now, breathing in the fresh air and mending snowshoes and shooting things. Sometimes what you've got is as good as it's ever going to get.'

'I thought Nann was the one with a saying for everything.'

Samuel gave a philosophical shrug. 'Come on,' he said, 'let's get you that gas.'

TWENTY-FIVE

Samuel came out of his ramshackle shed carrying two five-gallon jerrycans, and topped up the Jeep's tank. It was beginning to grow dark now, although the summit of Mount Shasta was still reflecting the orange light of a sun that had dropped below the horizon. The temperature was falling fast.

When he had emptied the two jerrycans, Samuel came back from his shed with a two-gallon red plastic gas container. 'You'd best take this, too, just in case you run out again and you can't find a gas station to take your credit card.'

'Thanks, Samuel. I won't forget this.'

Michael went back into the cabin to collect Natasha. 'You are sure that I cannot fix you something to eat before you go?' asked Nann.

'We're fine, I think,' said Michael. 'How about you, Tasha? I'm just looking forward to stopping at some crappy roadside diner on the interstate and ordering a cheeseburger.'

Samuel took Michael out on to the veranda, laid his hand on his shoulder and pointed east. 'Keep on driving about three miles, until you reach a fork. Take the right-hand fork and then about six or seven miles further along you'll come to a T-junction. If you take a left there, you'll be heading almost due south. After about twenty miles or so you'll hit a little place called Lookout, and just past Lookout you'll be joining I-Five. The good old Cascade Wonderland Highway, which I haven't seen in more years than I care to remember.'

Michael gripped Samuel's hand between both of his. 'I really do appreciate this, Samuel. You've been a godsend.'

'Well – you know what I'm hoping, don't you?' said Samuel. 'I'm hoping you're going to come back and pay me for that gas.'

'You'd better believe it.'

Michael helped Natasha up into her seat, and then climbed behind the wheel. As he backed down their driveway, he gave Samuel and Nann a blast on the horn, and a wave. He had met them less than two hours ago: he didn't know why he felt so emotional at saying goodbye.

Natasha said, 'Here goes nothing.'

'We're going to make it,' Michael assured her. 'I just have this feeling that everything's going to work out. Think of it. We could be in San

Francisco by midnight.'

They drove in silence until they reached the fork, and Michael turned right. The road sloped quite sharply downhill, between pines that crowded so close that their branches brushed and scraped and rattled against the sides of the Jeep, as if even the trees were trying to stop them.

After about fifteen minutes, however, they reached the T-junction.

'Left here,' said Michael. 'Then straight on till we get to Lookout, and the Wonderland Highway.'

'We could still turn back,' said Natasha.

'No,' said Michael.

'What happens if you die while you're driving?'

'I'm not going to die, Tasha. I didn't die the first time and I'm not going to die a second time, either.'

'Oh God, please let that be true.'

'Sweetheart, sometimes you just have to have faith in yourself. Listen to me – I'm starting to sound like Nann now. Before you know it I'll be saying "follow your dream".'

He made an acute left-hand turn and headed south. This road was wider and better-paved, and almost completely straight. The trees on either side of the road began to thin out, too, although there was no sign of civilization yet. No roadside shacks, no signposts, no lights up ahead of them, although they did see an airplane at a very high altitude, flashing its lonely way across a plum-colored sky.

'How are you feeling?' asked Natasha, after

they had driven over five miles away from Mount Shasta.

'I feel *fine*,' Michael told her. 'I feel perfectly myself. No breathlessness. No temperature. No heart palpitations.'

It was then that he saw the first lights twinkling up ahead of them.

'There!' he said. 'That must be Lookout! We've almost made it, sweetheart. We're almost there!'

Only two or three minutes later, he looked to his right, and less than a mile away, in the darkness, he could see the red-and-white lights of traffic streaming up and down the interstate.

'They were lying, those bastards! Those unscrupulous, conniving bastards! "If you leave Trinity, you'll die." Oh, for sure! "And if you unscrew your navel, your ass is going to fall off."'

He felt an extraordinary surge of freedom. It was only now that they were heading back to the outside world that he realized how restricted he had been while he was in Trinity, and how much Catherine Connor and Doctor Hamid had played on his fears and his weaknesses to keep him there.

He pressed his foot down on the gas, and the Jeep's engine surged. The lights of Lookout began to spread out wider and sparkle brighter as they sped toward them.

So I'm dead, am I? he thought, triumphantly. *I have never, ever, felt so alive!*

'Michael,' said Natasha.

'We're almost there, Tasha! And I never felt better! Dead? What a goddamned joke!'

'Michael,' Natasha repeated, and this time she tugged at his sleeve. 'Michael, stop.'

'We're nearly there! We're nearly in Lookout!'

'Michael, stop. Please.'

'What's the matter? If you need to go to the bathroom, we'll be there in two minutes! There's bound to be a bar or something.'

'*Michael!*' said Natasha, in a whispery shriek. '*Stop the Jeep now! Look at me!*'

Michael glanced at her quickly. At first sight, there didn't seem to be anything wrong with her. She was very pale, and the wide-eyed way she was staring at him was more than a little unnerving. But then he looked at her again, and he saw that there was a dark curved line down the left side of her face. Not only that, she had red-and-white fireflies crawling backward and forward across her hairline.

At first Michael couldn't understand what he was looking at. But then he realized that the dark curved line was the door-frame behind her, and the red-and-white fireflies were the lights of traffic on the interstate. He could see through her. She was half-transparent, and with each passing second the dark curved line grew clearer, and the fireflies glittered more brightly.

He stepped on the brakes and the Jeep slid with a sharp crunch of shingle into the side of the road.

'Oh, Jesus,' he said.

Tasha held up both hands, and turned them this way and that. They were half-transparent too, as if they were nothing more than clear plastic gloves with pink fingernails painted on them.

She pulled down one sleeve of her sweater, and her arm was the same, all the way up to the elbow. He could see *inside* her sleeve.

Her hair was still clearly visible and so was the outline of her face – her eyes, her nose, and her lips. He could even see the tears that were glistening on her cheeks. But he could also see right through her neck, to the Chaps label inside the back of her orange cable-knit sweater.

It was then that it struck him, so hard that he physically felt as if he had been hit by a speeding truck – *bang*. It wasn't him who was dead – or if he was, they hadn't driven far enough away from Mount Shasta for him to die for a second time. It was Natasha. After he had brought her back from his first escape attempt, she hadn't made a miraculous recovery at all. She had died, but somehow the clinic had revived her.

What had Catherine said to him? *'It happens every day in medicine. We have to make critical choices about how to treat people, and sometimes it's hard to know if we're going to do them more harm than good. In Natasha Kerwin's case, you took the decision out of our hands.'*

They had been trying to make up their minds whether they ought to take her off life-support or not – 'pull the plug on her', as Doctor Hamid had put it. But by abducting her like that, he had effectively killed her, and solved the problem for them.

'You took the decision out of our hands.'

He put his arms out to her and held her as close as he could. She still felt solid, inside of her coat, and when he buried his fingers in her hair he could still feel the weight of her head. But she was colder than ever, and she was shuddering, and she didn't seem to be able to speak any more.

Michael closed his eyes for a moment, just to feel her close to him. No wonder the clinic hadn't sent their security guards after him, or called the police. They had known all along that this would happen, a certain distance away from Mount Shasta, and they knew what he would have to do.

He made sure that Natasha was as comfortable as possible, and then he shifted the Jeep into gear and U-turned back the way they had come. As he drove, his eyes filled up with tears, and sometimes the road ahead of him seemed to jiggle and dance in his headlights.

He didn't look at Natasha again until he turned in through the clinic gates. He didn't recognize the security guard on duty, an African-American with a shiny shaven head, but the guard waved them through without stopping them and demanding to see their identity cards. He must have been told to expect them.

Michael pulled up outside the front steps. Natasha appeared to be sleeping, with her head against her left shoulder, so that he had to lift her hair to see her face clearly. With a mixture of relief and sadness, he saw that she looked completely normal. She was still very cold, but no longer transparent.

He shook her gently. 'Tasha.'

She stirred, and opened her eyes. Without

saying anything she sat up straight and looked around.

'We're back,' she said.

He nodded. 'I'm sorry,' he told her. 'If only I'd known.'

She held up her hands and looked at them. 'I can't believe it. I feel like I dreamed it.'

'I wish you had.'

'It's me who's dead, isn't it?' she said.

'I have no idea. I don't understand any of this. How are you feeling?'

'Tired. Very tired. But I'm all right otherwise.' She looked at him and touched his lips with her fingertips and tried to smile. 'It isn't your fault, Michael. I should have guessed it was me, and not you. In fact I think I did.'

'So why did they tell you that it was me?'

'I don't know, Michael. But Doctor Hamid did say that he would have something important to explain to me, at my next appointment.'

'He didn't give you any inkling what it was?'

Natasha shook her head.

'All right,' said Michael. 'I guess we'd better go in and see him now, if he's there. I want him to take a look at you, and make sure that you're OK. And then I think he owes us an explanation, don't you?'

Natasha clung on to his sleeve. 'No, Michael. *Please*. I don't want to hear it.'

At that moment, the front doors of the clinic opened up and Doctor Hamid came out, on his own, in a gray three-piece suit. He stood there for a moment, with his hands resting on his hips, looking down at them.

'Talk of the devil,' said Michael.

Doctor Hamid started coming down the steps. As they both watched him, Natasha said, 'I knew there was something wrong with me. I *knew* it.'

'Well, you were very, very cold. In bed last night, you were freezing.'

'I'll tell you how cold I was. I breathed on the bathroom mirror and there was condensation on it. But I did believe them when they told me that *you* were dead. I thought maybe it was both of us.'

Doctor Hamid came up to the Jeep and stood beside it with a serious expression on his face. Serious, but more regretful than angry. He made no attempt to knock on the window or to shout out to them. He just stood there, waiting.

Eventually Michael opened his door and climbed out.

'Welcome back,' said Doctor Hamid.

Michael looked around. 'No cops?' he asked.

'No reason to call the police, Michael. Nobody was hurt.'

'Are you kidding me? I must have run over at least half-a-dozen people. I'm surprised there were no fatalities.'

'You shouldn't have tried to get away like that, Michael. We are trying to take care of you here. We are trying to take care of *all* of these people in Trinity. Acting with defiance only makes matters worse.'

'I'm not dead, am I?'

'No, Michael, you are not dead. You came very close to death, I must say, after your accident, and it was only highly skilled surgery that saved you.'

'But Natasha?'

'It is very chilly out here, Michael. Why don't you come inside?'

Michael turned to Natasha, who was hugging herself in the passenger seat, shivering.

'OK,' he agreed, 'but this time I want the truth. You got me? Any more cock-and-bull stories and I'm out of here, and I'm getting in touch with the media, even if I have to leave Tasha behind.'

Doctor Hamid raised one eyebrow. 'You won't do that, Michael, when you hear what I have to say to you.'

Michael went around, opened the passenger door and helped Natasha out of the Jeep. Doctor Hamid climbed back up the steps and they followed him.

Inside his office it was warm and smelled of leather chairs. 'Please, sit down,' he told them. 'You must both be exhausted. Would you like anything to eat or drink?'

'We came here for the truth, Doctor, not refreshments.'

'Of course,' said Doctor Hamid. He was about to sit down when there was a knock at the door and before he could answer it, Kingsley Vane stepped in.

'You don't mind if Mr Vane joins us, I hope?' asked Doctor Hamid. 'He knows very much more about TSC's overall strategy here in Trinity than I do.'

Michael shrugged and said, 'Whatever. So long as we don't get any more lies.'

Kingsley Vane gave Michael a serpentine

smile and sat down opposite him, crossing his legs and tugging fastidiously at the knees of his sharply creased pants. Michael took hold of Natasha's cold hand and held it tight.

'Am I right in thinking...?' he began, although he had to stop then and swallow, because he had a catch in his throat. 'Am I right in thinking that after I brought her back the last time, Tasha passed away?'

Kingsley Vane steepled his hands and said, 'It depends on your definition of "passed away", Gregory – I'm sorry, I apologize – *Michael*.'

'How many definitions of "passed away" are there? I thought "passed away" meant "dead". Period.'

'Mostly it does,' said Doctor Hamid. 'But not always. Almost every belief system agrees that human beings have a spiritual existence as well as a physical existence. A *soul*, if you like. What happens to this spiritual existence after the physical existence has expired has been a subject of great philosophical and scientific argument from the very earliest times.'

'OK, we get it,' said Michael. 'Now can you just cut to the chase and tell us exactly what is going on here in Trinity?'

'Go ahead, Goresh,' said Kingsley Vane. 'I think under the circumstances he has earned the right to be put in the picture. Many of our companions have questioned what we are doing here, but Michael is the very first to have challenged us so robustly. He may not like what he hears, but the truth is often much harder to bear than lies.'

'For Christ's sake,' said Michael. 'Just *tell* us.'

'Very well,' said Doctor Hamid. 'The native tribes who lived around Mount Shasta always believed that the volcano was a place of great spiritual significance. In the 1960s, it attracted many New Age pilgrims, who were also convinced that it was a hub of psychic energy. Because of this, a series of studies was undertaken by the Western Ecological Research Center. They discovered that unusually powerful geomagnetic energy emanates from Mount Shasta, although at first they did not understand that this might have a significant effect on humans.'

'Like resurrecting them?' said Michael. 'Bringing them back to life when they're supposed to be dead?'

Doctor Hamid nodded. 'This effect was discovered in 1997 when the US Geological Survey sent out a small team to measure seismic activity around the volcano, because they were concerned about the possibility of an imminent eruption, like Mount St Helens. While the team was high on the summit, there was an avalanche, which can be very frequent on Mount Shasta during the spring, and a young researcher called Paula Ferris was buried and killed.

'Her body was brought here to the Trinity-Shasta Clinic, which in those days was only a small medical center for the local population. During the night when she was brought here, the nurse on night duty saw her walking along the corridor.

'The nurse followed her to the front door, which was locked. Ms Ferris said that she felt

307

perfectly well, although she didn't know where she was, and wanted to leave. The nurse managed to calm her down, and asked her to wait in reception while she called for one of the doctors. Another nurse came to assist, and sit with them.

'While they waited for the doctor to arrive, Ms Ferris insisted several times that she was fine, although both nurses thought that she felt extremely cold. Ms Ferris then said that she had left her purse in the room where she had woken up, and asked if one of the nurses would fetch it for her.

'When the nurse went to the room, she found that Ms Ferris's body was still lying on the gurney on which the paramedics had brought her into the clinic.'

Michael stared at Doctor Hamid in perplexity, and then looked at Natasha, and then turned back to Doctor Hamid.

'What are you saying? If her body was still lying on the gurney, who was sitting in reception?'

'Here at TSC, we call it a "semi-substantial",' said Kingsley Vane. 'It's a combination of the human soul and the spiritual energy which surrounds Mount Shasta. Semi-substantials can walk, talk, think, eat – do everything that their physical beings could do when they were first alive.

'Colloquially, I suppose, you would call them ghosts.'

TWENTY-SIX

'Is that what I am?' asked Natasha. 'A *ghost*?'

Kingsley Vane said, 'I'm sorry, Natasha. Normally, it's something that would have been broken to you very gently.'

'I don't believe this,' said Michael. 'How do you break it gently to somebody that they're a ghost?'

'Because, in their semi-substantial manifestation, people still feel that they are alive,' said Doctor Hamid. 'They have the same personality that they had when they were alive, and physically they can do everything that they used to before they died – except of course for leaving the benign influence of Mount Shasta.'

He turned to Natasha, and then he said, 'Natasha, my dear, when you had your accident you suffered catastrophic brain damage. There was very little hope that you would ever fully recover your mental faculties. You would never have been the same Natasha that you were before – or the same Natasha that you are now.

'But – so long as you remain here in Trinity – there is no reason why you cannot enjoy a full and happy afterlife.'

'Is *everybody* in Trinity a ghost?' asked Michael. He suddenly thought of Isobel's coldness, and how she had crystallized his semen, and how he thought he had seen the outline of the kitchen window right through her. 'Isobel Weston's a ghost, isn't she?'

'We do prefer to call our residents "semi-substantials",' said Kingsley Vane. '"Ghosts" conjures up images of imaginary beings walking through graveyards, carrying their heads under their arms.'

'But they can walk through the snow and leave no footprints. And they seem to be able to walk through walls.'

'Yes, they can. They are, after all, *semi*-substantial.'

'*All* of them? Walter Kruger and old Mrs Kroker and Bethany Thomson and Katie Thomson and that miserable guy who lives next door to me?'

'Not all, Michael. There are some like you, who are still alive, but who are recovering from serious accidents. We find it beneficial to let them convalesce in our residents' homes, in as normal a domestic environment as possible.'

'Normal? What the fuck is normal about living with a ghost? I've even been *sleeping* with a ghost, for Christ's sake!'

'Yes,' said Kingsley Vane, with the air of a weary school principal, 'we *are* aware of that. But Doctor Connor did explain to you when you first moved in with Mrs Weston that the arrangement was intended to be one of mutual benefit – to help *her* as much as it helped you. Your relationship has been extremely helpful for Isobel's equilibrium.'

'Her equilibrium? More like her goddamned libido!'

'Mrs Weston was and is a very highly sexed woman, Michael. That was what led to her death. You are not to tell her this, but she was the victim of her very jealous husband.'

'Oh ... so she didn't fall down an elevator shaft at some conference? She only thinks she did because you told her so?'

'She *did* fall down an elevator shaft, yes, but under slightly different circumstances than she remembers.'

'Jesus,' said Michael. 'Don't you people ever tell the truth about anything?'

'As I said, Michael, we're taking care of men and women who have been through the ultimate trauma – death. They know that they're dead, and they know that their physical bodies have either been interred or cremated. We adjust their memories to eliminate their most disturbing recollections, using the same procedure that we used with you – a combination of therapy and beta-blockers like propranolol.'

'Where's *my* body?' asked Natasha.

'Still here,' said Kingsley Vane. 'The morticians will be coming tomorrow to collect you and take you back to your family, for your funeral.'

'Can I see it?'

'That is not a good idea, Natasha,' said Doctor Hamid. 'It is better for you to think that *this* manifestation sitting here in front of me is you, and that your physical existence is just a memory. To see yourself dead – that is not at all

311

healthy.'

'Healthy?' said Michael. 'That would be hilariously funny if it wasn't so goddamned tragic.'

Kingsley Vane stood up. 'You should get yourselves back home now, Michael. You must both be very tired, and you're both going to need some time for reflection.'

'Just tell me this,' said Michael. 'Who else is alive, besides me? Jack Barr? Lloyd Hammers? Anybody else?'

'Jack Barr and Lloyd Hammers are both alive, yes.'

'So what happened to them? I asked Doctor Connor but she wouldn't tell me.'

'Nothing dramatic. They were very seriously injured, both of them, and occasionally they have relapses.'

'Oh – like whenever they try to help me find out what the hell's going on here?'

'As I said, Michael, they occasionally have relapses.'

'How come I didn't have a "relapse"?'

Kingsley Vane didn't answer that. Instead, he said, 'There are plenty more residents in Trinity who are still alive. At least one in every household. We like to call them "companions". Our semi-substantial residents help them to convalesce, and in turn they help our semi-substantial residents to lead a full and enjoyable afterlife.'

'Like I'm supposed to be doing with Isobel Weston? And Tasha, too? I'm not so sure that Isobel's very happy about Tasha living with us, to tell you the truth. She's been looking a little transparent lately in the past couple of days.'

Kingsley Vane and Doctor Hamid exchanged meaningful looks. 'Stress,' said Doctor Hamid. 'That can affect the semi-substantial state. It would be helpful if you could try to reassure Mrs Weston that you are not going to abandon her.'

'But I'm alive,' said Michael. 'Supposing I abandon Trinity altogether? I know the way out of here now, and now I know that I'm not going to die if I take it.'

'Ah, but you won't,' smiled Kingsley Vane. 'If you abandon Trinity, you will also have to abandon the lovely Natasha. You can't take her with you, Michael, as you know. Worse than that, if we can't find her another companion...'

He left his sentence hanging, and gave a dismissive shrug.

'What are you talking about?' Michael demanded. 'If you can't find her another companion – *what*?'

'In spite of popular belief, Michael, there is no such thing as a "haunted house".'

'What does that mean?'

'It means that ghosts – if you want to call them that – are incapable of existing for any length of time in isolation. They cannot haunt a house unless there is somebody living there who is aware of their existence. Ghosts haunt *people*, not buildings. That is one of the most important discoveries that we have made here at TSC. Without human interaction, semi-substantials simply fade and disappear. It's rather like that old conundrum about the tree falling in the forest – if there is nobody around to hear it, does it make a noise? In the case of semi-substantials, absolutely not. If there is nobody around to experience their presence, they *have* no presence. They vanish.'

'So you're telling me that if I leave Trinity—'

'Natasha's future is in your hands, Michael. The decision is entirely yours.'

They drove back to Isobel's house without saying a word to each other, but as soon as they stepped inside the front door, Natasha clung on to Michael and let out a terrible sob of anguish. Michael held her tight. He could understand exactly how she felt. She was grieving for the dead Natasha, and so was he.

They were still standing together in the hallway when Isobel appeared out of the living-room door. She was wearing a very low-cut black sweater and a triple string of pearls. She stood looking at them for a long time before she said, 'Well, well! The wanderers return! Very noble of you, Greg. You could have just kept on going.'

'The name's Michael,' Michael told her. 'Or maybe you knew that already.'

'No,' said Isobel. 'They only told me that your name was supposed to be Greg and that you allegedly came from San Francisco. But they did warn me that they were concerned about you.'

'Oh, yes?'

She came forward and stood very close to them. Natasha kept her face pressed against Michael's chest and didn't turn around.

'Yes,' said Isobel. 'They said you were remembering things about your past life, before you had your accident. Only a few stray things, apparently, but enough to worry them. Me too, of course.'

Michael frowned to show that he didn't understand what she meant.

'You were my new companion, sweetheart. You were the one who was going to warm my bed for the rest of my days and keep me alive. Of course I was worried about you. I didn't want you suddenly waking up to who you really were and walking out on me.'

At this point, Natasha turned around and confronted her. 'So where was I supposed to come into this? They knew that Michael and I were going to be married.'

Isobel shook her head in amusement. 'Where do you *think* you came into it, sweet cheeks? If Greg – if *Michael*, sorry – if Michael remembered who he was, and realized that he was alive and well, the chances are that he would have left Trinity, and worst of all he would have left *me*. And as it happens, I love him.

'They gave you wonderful treatment, Natasha. You can't fault the clinic for that. But you were too badly brain-damaged for them to be able to save you. To begin with, they had no intention of bringing you back as one of us, and giving you an afterlife. But when Michael started to remember things...'

Michael said, 'It's OK, Isobel. I get it. They gave Tasha an afterlife and arranged for her to live with us to make absolutely sure that I would stay here.'

'Exactly,' said Isobel. 'Which is why we all need to get along. You, me and Natasha. I wasn't very happy about it at first, I have to admit. But we can have some amazing times together, can't we?'

'You know that I don't love you, Isobel, don't you, and I never will.'

Isobel gave him a tight, hurt smile. 'People can *learn* to fall in love, Michael.'

'Well, we'll have to see about that. Meanwhile we're very tired and we're both going to go to bed. Our own beds.'

'You know that it was my idea, Michael. You ought to be grateful.'

'What was?'

'Giving Natasha an afterlife. Usually, if companions start to ask too many questions, they give them the treatment.'

'What treatment?'

'It's a form of lobotomy, as far as I know. That's what they did with Jack Barr and Lloyd Hammers. They wanted to do it to you, but I begged them not to. You wouldn't be any good as a lover if they did that to you. They did it to Emilio, and he was useless after that.'

Michael held Natasha close to him. 'So they brought Tasha back to life so that you could continue to get your jollies in bed?'

'Oh, come on, Michael. What we have together, it's much more than that. I thought we were close friends, too.'

'Yes, Isobel. So did I.'

Sometime in the small hours of the morning,

long after the moon had set, Michael thought he heard a crunching sound, like car tires rolling over frozen snow. He lifted his head from the pillow and listened, but all he could hear was a thin wind blowing from the east, and the persistent rattling of the TV antenna. He went back to sleep and dreamed that he was sitting in the back of a car, silently weeping.

A few minutes before seven o'clock the next morning, the doorbell rang – one of those sharp, jangly rings that leave the taste of salt in your mouth. He heard Isobel coming out of her bedroom and shuffling in her slippers along the hallway. She unlocked the door and then he heard voices. He could feel the cold draft from outside blowing under his bedroom door.

After a few seconds, the front door was closed again, but whoever was calling on them, Isobel must have let them in, because he heard the voices again: Isobel's, and another woman, but much less distinct. Then there was a tentative rapping at *his* door.

'Michael? Are you awake?'

Michael climbed out of bed and opened the door. It was Isobel, in her robe. Her hair was all messed up and she was wearing no make-up.

'What is it?' he asked her.

'Somebody to see you. Doctor Connor.'

'Catherine? What does she want at this time of the morning?'

'You'd better come find out.'

'Wait up one second.'

Michael pulled on his jeans and struggled into a sweater. Then he walked barefoot into the

317

living room, where Catherine was standing in front of the fireplace. She was wearing a black coat and a black beret and black leather gloves and her expression was almost theatrically grave.

'What?' said Michael. 'What's happened?'

'Do you want to sit down?' Catherine asked him.

'No. No, I don't. Just tell me why you've come here.'

Catherine said, 'Very early this morning the Highway Patrol found Isobel's Jeep by the side of the road, about a mile north of a small town called Lookout.'

Michael said nothing, although he felt a cold flood of apprehension, because he could guess what was coming next. He thought of those tires that he had heard in the middle of the night, crunching over the snow.

'The Jeep's engine was still running, but there was nobody in it. Only some women's clothing in the driver's seat. An orange sweater, a pair of jeans, and underwear. They also found a pair of sneakers on the floor.'

Without a word, Michael left the living room and went to Natasha's bedroom at the back of the house. The bed had clearly been slept in, but the covers were pulled back and it was empty. He looked around the room while Catherine watched him from the doorway. Natasha had left a few clothes in the closet, and some lipstick and moisturizer on top of the bureau, but that was all. No sign of a note.

'I'm sorry,' said Catherine.

Michael didn't answer her, but stayed where he

was, in the middle of the room, staring at Natasha's empty bed. All that was left of her now were creases in the sheets where she had turned over and the indentation of her head in the pillow.

'We'll have to talk,' said Catherine.

'About what? About the fact that you should have let her die when she was supposed to die, and not turned her into a ghost?'

'Michael – you don't seem to understand how difficult this is. We're trying to balance along a high-wire here.'

'How do you think Tasha felt, when she found out that the only reason you gave her an afterlife was so that she could be a hostage, to keep me here? She loved me, Catherine, as much as I loved her, and what she's done ... well, I think that proves it, don't you?'

'I'm so sorry, Michael.'

Michael turned to face her. 'I bet you are. How are you going to keep me in Trinity now?'

Isobel was standing in the hallway, hugging herself tightly as if she were freezing cold – which of course she was.

'Come up to the clinic later,' said Catherine. 'There's a few more things you need to know. Maybe we can appeal to your better nature.'

'My better nature?' said Michael, in disbelief. 'The woman I was going to marry has sacrificed herself so that I can walk away from you people – and you seriously think that you can appeal to my better nature?'

'Michael – I've told you how sorry I am. Everybody at TSC is really upset about what's happened. But there are some very much larger issues at stake.'

'Oh, really? Such as what?'

'I can't tell you now. But come up to the clinic when you're ready and we'll talk it through.'

Michael took a deep breath. He suddenly realized that he was very close to crying. He looked at Isobel and Isobel's cheeks were shiny with tears. He didn't know whether she was weeping because she felt sorry for Natasha, or whether she was sorry for herself, because now there was nothing to stop Michael from leaving her.

He was on the brink of losing his temper – not only with Catherine, and everybody at the clinic, and Isobel, too, but also with himself. Although he knew that the clinic had manipulated his mind, he still felt that he should have been mentally stronger, and remembered who he really was, and what had happened to him. It wouldn't have saved Natasha from being killed when they first crashed, but it would have saved her the pain and humiliation of being brought back to life, and dying for a second time.

However, he said nothing, except, 'OK. Give me a chance to take a shower.'

Catherine held out her arms to him, as if she were offering him a conciliatory hug, but he ignored her. After a few moments she left the house, and Isobel closed the door behind her. Michael heard her saying, 'I'll see you later, Isobel. Take care of him.'

Isobel came up to him and said, 'I'll make you some coffee.'

'No, thanks.'

'I don't know what to say to you. I really don't.'

'You don't have to say anything, Isobel.'

'But I blame myself. If I hadn't been so selfish...'

Michael laid his hands on her shoulders. 'Forget it, Isobel. When it comes down to it, we're all doing what we can to survive.'

'That's what Neale Donald Walsch said. "Our choices are largely based on survival. But if life is eternal, life is not a question."'

'Neale Donald Walsch? The guy who wrote *Conversations With God*?'

'That's right.'

'The same Neale Donald Walsch who plagiarized somebody's account of a miraculous happening at his children's Christmas pageant, and then said that his memory must have been playing tricks on him?'

Isobel smiled at him through her tears. 'There's not much wrong with *your* memory, I'm sorry to say.'

TWENTY-SEVEN

He delayed his return to the clinic for as long as he could.

Whatever it was that Catherine had to say to him, he wasn't at all sure that he wanted to hear it. His grief at losing Natasha was physically painful, as if his lungs had been filled up with molten lead, which had then chilled hard, so that he could hardly breathe. At the same time, however, he felt a strange sense of relief. She hadn't been the real, warm Tasha after all, and he wasn't sure that their relationship could have lasted very long – especially knowing that she had been revived only to keep Isobel alive and satisfied.

He stood in his room, staring out of the window at nothing at all, and Isobel left him well alone. She didn't even switch on the TV.

A few minutes after 11:00 am, two vehicles drew up outside the house – Isobel's Jeep and a black Toyota Landcruiser. The doorbell rang and Michael went to answer it. One of the white-haired security men was standing outside, holding out the keys to the Jeep.

'The Highway Patrol brought it back,' he said, in a back-vowel, Oregon accent. 'They said that they didn't need to keep it for forensics because there was no suspicious circumstances. Nobody reported missing or nothing.'

'I see,' said Michael. He took the keys and went to shut the door. As he did so, however, the security man said, 'Keeping our eyes on you, sir. Trust we won't have no more disturbances. Don't want anybody hurt. Namely you.'

'Don't count on it,' said Michael. After he had closed the door, the security man stood outside for well over a minute, not moving. Michael waited, too, standing in the hallway watching the security man's distorted image behind the hammered glass window. In the end, he turned around and walked away, but Michael definitely felt that he had been making a point. *We're here, we're always going to be here, and we're watching you.*

In a way, it was the security man who made him decide what he was going to do next. Around midday, he put on his coat and laced up his boots and got ready to leave the house. He also picked up a book of matches from the Black Butte Saloon in Weed.

Isobel came into the hallway and said, 'You're off to see Doctor Connor, then?'

He nodded.

'I don't suppose it's any use, my telling you again how much I love you?'

'You don't love me, Isobel. You love being alive, and you love making love. That's all.'

'You're very cruel, Michael.'

'Yes. And doesn't it turn you on? You don't mind if I take the Jeep, do you?'

'It depends how far you're thinking of going.'

'Just to the clinic. To begin with, anyhow.'

'And what does that mean? "To begin with"?'

'You'll see.'

He climbed into the Jeep, started the engine and drove off up the slope, leaving Isobel standing in the porch. As the clinic wall came into sight, his heart was beating so hard that it was painful, and he thought he could understand how suicide bombers must feel, as they approached their targets.

He stopped outside Henry's booth, waiting for Henry to come out and challenge him, but when Henry saw who it was, he simply scowled and waved him through. Michael turned into the parking lot, and saw that the black Toyota Landcruiser was parked there, too. God was on his side so far, anyhow. He parked as close to the front entrance as he could.

When he went inside the clinic, the receptionist told him that Catherine was still engaged with another patient, so he sat in the waiting room, next to the tropical aquarium. The two security men were hunched on a couch on the opposite side of the room, going over a duty roster together, by the sound of it. One of them glanced up at him over his sunglasses, but he quickly looked down again when Michael gave him a hard, challenging stare.

A young gingery-haired man on crutches came out of Catherine's office, and Catherine beckoned Michael inside.

'I can only repeat what I said to you this morning,' she said, as they sat down. 'What your Natasha decided to do ... it was selfless beyond all imagination. But you and she could have led a very fulfilling life together here in Trinity.'

'Oh ... you think?'

'So many of our residents do, you know. Living here in Trinity, in their afterlife, they can continue all of the important work that they were doing before they died.'

'Go on,' said Michael, suspiciously.

'You may have thought that you recognized some of the residents here. That's because most of them, in their physical life, were leading scientists and mathematicians and authors and artists.'

'Walter Kruger,' said Michael. 'I *thought* I knew who he was. Nuclear physicist, who discovered the Kruger particle. But he must have died years ago.'

'Two thousand five, to be exact. But they brought him here to the clinic and we gave him his afterlife. Then of course there's your own Isobel Weston. A remarkable literary figure. And the list goes on. When geniuses die, they take with them all of their knowledge and all of their inspiration and all of their remarkable way of looking at the world. It's all gone. It's all lost. It's a tragedy.

'But then Kingsley Vane approached the government and suggested that whenever a genius dies, we should bring him or her to Mount Shasta and resurrect them as semi-substantials, so that we can carry on taking advantage of everything they have to offer us. Walter Kruger invented the narrow-band accelerator three years after his physical death from old age, and Susan Kirschbaum synthesized Malgon, the anti-malaria drug, eighteen months after she died of breast cancer.

'In the past few years, some of the greatest advances in science and medicine and engineering have come from this community. Trinity is literally a hotbed of inventiveness.'

'Deathbed, more like,' said Michael. 'But all of these geniuses ... what about their companions? Where do *they* come from? Don't tell me they *all* come from auto wrecks on the interstate, like me, and Tasha, and Jack Barr, and Lloyd Hammers?'

'Not all of them. Some of them come from

other situations, like Bethany Thomson, who was involved in a house fire, or Kevin Moskowitz, who was badly crushed by a crane.'

'But a lot of them come from auto wrecks?'

'The majority, yes. Car crash victims are much more likely to have suffered severe concussion or post-traumatic amnesia, and so it's much easier to help them fit into this community.'

In a sudden flood-tide of recollection, Michael saw the halogen headlights in his rear-view mirror, and felt the pick-up truck bumping into the back of his Torrent. He could remember Tasha screaming *'Oh my God! He's going to kill u*s!' and then the Torrent rolling over and over.

And at last he was able to pick out of his consciousness the single question that had been irritating him like a sharp fragment of shrapnel ever since he had first opened his eyes and found himself in the Trinity-Shasta Clinic.

'Those auto wrecks. They're deliberate, aren't they?'

Catherine looked down and sideways, but she didn't answer.

'Where else are you going to find people to volunteer to be companions?' Michael persisted. '"Come to live in a small, dull community for the rest of your life, where nothing ever happens except really weird shit like your neighbors gathering outside of your house in the middle of the night and staring at you. Come to live with dead people. They walk, they talk, they'll even bake cookies for you. But they're as cold as the Arctic Circle and they'll never let you leave."'

Catherine at last said, 'Michael – you have no

idea how important this community is. Our country depends on Trinity to keep us ahead! Imagine what it would have been like, if we could have given Albert Einstein an afterlife! Or Niels Bohr! All of you companions, you're doing such a service for America!'

'And that's what you meant when you said you were going to appeal to my better nature?'

'Yes, Michael, it is. Please stay here. Please stay with Isobel. Please try to forgive us for what happened with your Natasha. She was technically dead already and we were only trying to do what was best for all concerned.'

Michael stood up, and went to the window. Outside, he could see the first signs of a thaw. Patches of grass were beginning to appear through the snow, and the icicles along the gutter were all dripping.

'I wonder what it felt like,' he said. 'Driving along, and gradually becoming transparent. There must have come a point when she went blind, because the light could shine right through her optic nerves.'

'Yes,' said Catherine. 'I suppose that would have happened, yes.'

'And then she just vanished, as if she had never been, leaving nothing but her clothes and her shoes?'

'Yes. But that always happens when people die, doesn't it?'

Michael suddenly turned away from the window, crossed over to Catherine's desk, and picked up her letter-opener, which was shaped like a silver dagger. Before she could snatch it away from him, he wrapped his arm around her neck and heaved her upward, so that her chair tipped over sideways on to the floor. He dug the point of the letter-opener into the side of her neck and hissed at her, 'You fucking killed her! You killed her the first time, by ramming us on the inter-state, and then you brought her back to life and you killed her again! What she suffered, because of you! What *I've* suffered, because of you!'

'Michael,' said Catherine, in a strangled voice. 'Michael, don't.'

'Don't what? Don't kill you, like you killed Tasha? Don't hurt you, the way you hurt her?'

'What do you want me to do? What do you want me to say?'

'I don't want you to do anything, or to say anything. You're going to come outside with me now and we're going to go see Kingsley Vane's office, and we're going to ask his personal assistant to print me out all of the names of all of the companions you have living in Trinity.'

'They're all confidential,' Catherine gasped. 'She's not allowed to do it.'

'Well, we'll see about that.'

Michael frogmarched her across to the door. 'Open it!' he told her, and she reached out with her left hand and pushed down the handle. Michael kicked the door wide and forced her out into the reception area.

'Help me!' shouted Catherine, and immediately, the two security men jumped up from the couch. One of them reached into his coat and tugged out a gun – the same security man who had threatened Michael when he tried to escape from Trinity with Natasha.

'Put it down!' Michael ordered him.

The security man aimed his gun at him, holding it two-handed, but then Michael tilted his elbow higher, as if he were preparing to stab Catherine through the neck.

'Put the gun down on the table – now! Or I'll kill her. You think I'm joking?'

The security man hesitated for a moment more, but then he carefully set the automatic down on top of a stack of magazines.

'Right now – back off!' said Michael. 'Go on – right back to the wall!'

He dragged Catherine across the room, and then he reached down and picked up the gun, which was surprisingly heavy. Once he had done that, he pushed her roughly away from him, cocked the gun and pointed it at them.

'OK – now we're all going to go into Kingsley Vane's office and we're going to stand there quietly in the corner while I ask his assistant to do me a favor.'

Catherine said, 'Michael, this isn't going to do anybody any good. Please. I'm sure we can come to some kind of a compromise.'

'Catherine – Tasha is dead and you killed her. How can we reach a compromise about that? Now, let's get going, before somebody gets hurt. Namely you three.'

They walked down the corridor until they reached Kingsley Vane's office. One of the security men knocked on the door and when Kingsley Vane's personal assistant Valerie called out, 'Come!' they all trooped inside.

When Valerie saw that Michael was pointing a gun at them she immediately reached across her desk for her phone, but Michael snapped at her, 'Valerie! Don't even think about it!'

'What's going on?' asked Valerie. 'Doctor Connor – you're not hurt, are you?'

Catherine said, 'I'm all right, Valerie, don't worry. Michael is a little stressed out, that's all. I think for the time being we need to do what he says.'

'Well, you got that right,' said Michael. 'Now, Valerie – I want you to do me a big favor. I want you to print out all of the names and addresses of the companions you have here in Trinity.'

'What? I can't do that! All of that information is highly confidential.'

Michael walked up to her desk and pointed the gun in her face so that it was almost touching the tip of her nose.

'You have a choice here, Valerie. Either you print out all of those names or addresses or I'm going to redecorate this office with your brains.'

'I can't,' she said, with her nostrils flaring.

At that moment, the door to Kingsley Vane's office opened up, and Kingsley Vane himself stepped out, in his shirtsleeves and suspenders, fastening up a cufflink as he came, and smelling of aftershave. He looked around and said, 'What's going on here? Jesus, Michael – what are you doing with that gun?'

'Michael wants some information from us,' put in Catherine, quickly.

'What information?'

'He wants to know the names and addresses of

330

all our companions.'

Kingsley Vane looked at Michael and said, 'What do you want those for?'

'That's my business. Now, are you going to print them out for me, or am I going to start shooting people – because, believe me, I will.'

Kingsley Vane looked toward Catherine, and Catherine gave him a hard look which meant *he means it*.

'All right,' said Kingsley Vane. 'Valerie – give him what he wants, will you?'

Valerie turned to her computer screen and frantically started typing, her long red nails clicking on the keyboard.

Kingsley Vane said, 'Michael ... I hope you realize that this will be a serious breach of national security, and what the consequences could be.'

Michael was beginning to feel strained, and his voice was shaking. 'Catherine's explained to me exactly what you're doing here in Trinity, yes. You're giving our country's greatest thinkers another lease of life, after they're dead.'

'Quite right,' said Kingsley Vane, and he was about to continue when Michael interrupted him.

'She also told me the means that you've been employing to achieve this miracle – including vehicular assault and vehicular homicide, false imprisonment, maladministration of prescription drugs and generally lying your fucking heads off.'

Valerie's printer beeped into life, and five sheets of paper were spat out into its print tray, one by one. Michael picked them up and quickly scanned them. He found his own name, and Jack Barr, and Lloyd Hammers, as well as George Kelly's companion, Hedda, she of the upswept spectacles.

'OK,' he said, folding up the sheets of paper and tucking them left-handed into the inside pocket of his coat. He looked around the office, and saw another door, at the far end, on the right-hand side of the window.

'What's in there?' he asked Valerie.

'Nothing. Just stationery, and the clinic's computer server.'

Michael crossed the room and opened it up. She was right. The room was windowless, with nothing but shelves stacked with paper and files and envelopes, and a tower server.

'All right, all of you,' he said. 'Take out your cells and put them on to Valerie's desk, then get in here.'

'Michael,' said Kingsley Vane, but Michael stiffened his arm and pointed the gun directly at him.

'Don't tempt me,' he said. 'Get in here.'

The two security men took out their cells and left them on Valerie's desk. Then all of them crowded into the stationery store. Kingsley Vane was the last.

'You *will* regret this,' he said. 'I promise you.'

Michael said nothing, but closed the door and turned the key in the lock.

TWENTY-EIGHT

Now he knew that he had no time to lose. He tucked the gun into the back of his jeans and went out through the front entrance, down the steps, and across to Isobel's Jeep. He opened up the tailgate and lifted out the two-gallon gas container that Samuel had given him, still full of gas. Then he hurried back up the steps and across the shiny reception area.

The receptionist was talking on her headphones and polishing her nails purple and she didn't even notice him, or the bright red container that he was carrying.

He went right down to the end of the corridor, to the room where Natasha had been treated. He went inside and shut the door behind him. Unscrewing the cap from the gas container, he sloshed fuel into the bathroom, and across the floor, and finally emptied it over the bed, so that the mattress was soaked. Coughing because of the fumes, he opened up the door again and stepped out into the corridor.

There was nobody in sight, so he took the book of matches out of his pocket, folded all the matches over and struck one of them, so that the whole book flared up. He tossed it into the room and quickly shut the door.

He heard a soft *whoomphh* and the sharp crack of the window in the door breaking, but by then he was already halfway back along the corridor. The receptionist was still on the phone as he pushed his way out of the clinic and jogged back to Isobel's Jeep.

Henry didn't even look up from his newspaper as Michael sped past him, and down the slope.

He slewed to a stop at the first house he came to. He checked the name on his list and then he climbed out of the Jeep and went up to the front door and rang the doorbell.

It seemed to take several minutes before anybody answered. Eventually, an elderly man with wild white hair and enormously magnifying spectacles opened the door.

'Yes? Can I help you?'

'Professor Marowitz?'

'Yes, that's me. What do you want?'

'I've come from the clinic, Professor. There's an emergency. I don't have time to explain the whole thing now, because I have to warn everybody in the whole community. It's Mount Shasta. The US Geological Survey says that it's about to erupt, literally at any minute, and Trinity's right in the path of the predicted volcanic mudslide. We all have to get out of here, fast.'

'But we need to stay *near* to Mount Shasta,' said Professor Marowitz. 'I mean, if we don't—'

'Don't worry about that,' Michael told him. 'We'll actually be going closer to the mountain, not further away. We just have to evacuate

Trinity, as a precaution. You know what happened when Mount St Helens blew. More than fifty people got killed.'

'So what are we supposed to do?'

'You have a companion here, right? Jane Buchanan? Get her to drive you down to the community center. We're going to form a convoy, and I'll lead you all out of here.'

Doctor Marowitz said, 'Very well, then.' He turned around and called out, 'Jane! Jane! Get yourself down here, will you? We have a crisis!'

'Make it as quick as you can,' Michael told him. 'Mount Shasta could erupt at any moment.'

He went to the first five houses in the street, telling the same story. When he walked away from the fifth house, he saw that smoke was rising from behind the clinic wall, and immediately afterward he heard the shrilling of fire-alarm bells.

When he knocked at the sixth house, a young woman answered, in her early thirties. She was very pale, with plum-colored circles under her eyes.

'Lily French?' he asked her, checking his list.

'No ... Audrey O'Sullivan. I'm only staying here temporarily. I saw you at the last community meeting, didn't I?'

'Sure. More than likely. But we have an emergency on our hands here.'

When he had told her about the imminent eruption, she said, 'How are you going to warn everybody here, just on your own?'

'Well ... I was hoping that if I gave you a page out of my list, you could maybe warn six or seven other people. Then I'll ask more residents to do the same.'

'OK. Yes. I'll see you later then, down at the community center.'

During the next forty minutes, Michael's evacuation gained more and more momentum, with residents hurrying from door to door, warning their neighbors that Trinity was in danger of being buried under thousands of tons of volcanic mud. Nobody questioned it. In 1980, the mudslides from Mount St Helens had reached the Columbia River, more than fifty miles away. The afternoon echoed with the sound of vehicle doors slamming and engines starting up, like the beginning of a motor race.

The sense of panic was heightened by the thick black smoke that was now billowing up from the clinic, and the honking and wailing of fire trucks, which had just arrived from Weed Volunteer Fire Department. It was difficult for Michael to judge how far the fire had spread, but the chilly air was thick with the acrid smell of burning timber.

He managed to call on more than twenty houses himself, but he handed out his list of names, mostly to companions, and the rest of the community were alerted by their neighbors, from Summit View to the loop where the Endersbys lived. By the time he returned to Isobel's house, there were more than a hundred cars and SUVs parked around the circle outside the community center, and even more lined up along the side of the slope beyond it.

As he parked in the driveway, Isobel came running out of the house. She had a thick cream sweater wrapped tightly around her and she looked distraught.

'Where have you *been*, Michael? John came around from next door and said that Mount Shasta was going to erupt, and that we all had to evacuate. I was going to go with him if you didn't come back.'

For a split-second, Michael was tempted to tell her that there was no danger of Mount Shasta erupting, and that she should stay here in Trinity, where she would survive. But he looked behind her, and she had left no footprints in the snow, and he asked himself whether it was really survival, to live like that, for who knows how long, as a ghost?

Apart from that, he wasn't in a forgiving mood today. Rightly or wrongly, this was the day when he was going to punish this community for taking away the woman that he had loved so much, and wrecked his own life, and the lives of so many others.

'It's true, Isobel,' he said. 'We need to get out of here now.'

'But my house ... all of my ornaments ... all of my things.'

'You'll have to leave them. The chances are that the mudslide won't reach this far, but if it does, then nobody here is going to survive. Even semi-substantials, like you. They'll be buried.'

Isobel looked around at her house, and then back at Michael.

'Come on,' he said, even though he knew that

337

those two words would be her death sentence.

She went back and closed the front door, and then she climbed up into the passenger seat. Michael backed into the roadway and headed for the community center.

'There's a fire at the clinic?' asked Isobel, twisting around in her seat. 'I saw smoke, and heard sirens.'

'Bad one, by the look of it,' said Michael. 'Could have been caused by a stray lump of magma, from the mountain.'

'Oh, my God. I just pray this doesn't happen. A friend of mine lost her house when Mount St Helens erupted. All her horses, too.'

Michael negotiated his way slowly past the community center, and the shoal of vehicles parked outside it. He switched on his flashers and blew his horn, and put down his window so that he could wave his arm, indicating that everybody should follow him.

'Where does this go to?' asked Isobel, as he headed along the same road that he had taken when he had tried to escape with Natasha.

Michael pointed ahead of them, where the white peaks of Mount Shasta floated serenely above the pine trees. 'You don't have to worry. Look. We're actually going a little nearer to the mountain, but out of the path of any mudslide.'

He checked his rear-view mirror. All of the vehicles that had assembled outside the community center were following him now, in a line that seemed almost endless.

'How do you know where we're supposed to be going?' said Isobel, after they had been driving for more than twenty minutes. 'Where are all of these people going to spend the night?'

'Don't worry,' said Michael. 'The USGS people told me exactly where we need to head for. The Forestry Service will look after us. You know – feed us, give us someplace to sleep.'

He checked his mirror again. The long line of vehicles was still behind him, like a freight train wending its way through the woods.

'So when did they tell you this?' asked Isobel, after a while.

'Who?'

'The people from USGS. When did they tell you this?'

'At the clinic, when I went to see Catherine Connor.'

'Why didn't *they* come around and warn us? I would have thought they would have had megaphones, you know, and toured around the streets. Why did they leave it to you?'

'I don't know. I guess they thought that the local people might take more notice if *I* warned them. Same thing happened before Mount St Helens blew. The USGS had a hell of a job persuading the local authorities to keep the area closed off.'

There was another long silence between them, and then Isobel said, 'I don't think I believe you, Michael. You've just persuaded almost the entire population of Trinity to follow you God knows where. What are you up to?'

Michael looked at her and smiled, and then he laid his right hand on top of her left hand. Her fingers were as cold as ever. 'I'll tell you what

I'm up to, Isobel. I'm saving lives.'

'I still don't believe you.'

'Would you believe me if I told you that I loved you?'

Another long silence. Then, 'No. But you can lie to me, if you like.'

'All right, then. I love you.'

'Say it again.'

'I love you, Isobel Weston. Essayist, poet, literary genius.' He almost added 'nymphomaniac' but bit the tip of his tongue before he could say it.

They started to climb the gradient that passed by the house that Samuel Horn shared with Nann. As they went by, Michael saw that Samuel's battered old Dodge Ram was still parked outside, and that the lights were shining in the living room.

'My God, I couldn't live here,' said Isobel. 'Talk about isolated.'

They continued up the hill. Michael thought that Samuel must be able to hear this long procession of vehicles going past his house, especially since they were going uphill. He wondered if he would guess where they were all going, and why.

He took a sharp right turn at the fork, and one by one the rest of the cars and crossovers and SUVs followed his example.

'The Pied Piper of Mount Shasta,' said Isobel, turning around to see them all following.

They drove down the narrow road with the pine branches brushing and scratching at the sides of their Jeep. A high bank of cumulus cloud had risen into the sky from the south-west, and it was beginning to grow gloomy. By the time they reached the T-junction it was almost dark, and Michael switched on his headlights.

'Are you sure we're going the right way?' asked Isobel. 'I would have thought that Mount Shasta was over *there*, to the left, and behind us.'

'Don't panic,' said Michael. 'We're heading left right now.'

After they had turned the corner, he put his foot down on the gas until they were speeding along at nearly fifty, and the rest of the procession kept up with him. As the clouds thickened, it grew darker and darker, and after about fifteen minutes it started to rain. Michael switched on the windshield wipers and they mournfully squeaked from side to side.

'How much further?' asked Isobel. 'I'm sure we're driving *away* from Mount Shasta, not toward it.'

The lights of Lookout appeared up ahead, and on their right Michael could see the traffic on the interstate.

'Not long now,' he told her.

They drove for another five minutes, and then Isobel said, 'Michael, I'm not feeling too good.'

'What's the matter? Motion sickness? Let me turn the heat down and open a window.'

'No, it's not that. I feel ... please, I think you'll have to stop.'

'There's a town up ahead, Isobel. We can stop there.'

'I need to stop now, Michael. Really. I feel like

341

... my God, I feel like I'm...'

He turned and looked at her. Her face was so transparent that she could have been made out of glass. Just as he had been able to see the twinkling lights from the interstate around Natasha's hairline, he could see them through Isobel's forehead, as if she were wearing a living crown of thorns.

'I'm *going*,' Isobel whispered. 'I can feel myself going. So *weak*, Michael, it's like I'm just draining away.'

He could just about make out the dark hollows of her eyes, and the glistening movement of her lips, but that was all.

'You did this on purpose, didn't you?' she breathed.

He checked his rear-view mirror. The Ford Explorer that had been following him closely had slowed down to less than twenty miles an hour, and it was weaving erratically from side to side across the road with its tires howling. All the way back, as far as he could see, vehicles were slowing down or pulling into the verge. Some of them were driving off the road altogether, and jolting across the rocks, and into the trees.

He stopped the Jeep, and the Explorer stopped behind him, and the SUV behind that stopped, too. He could hear a succession of knocking noises, as vehicles ran into each other.

Isobel lifted her arm toward him, as if she wanted to touch his face, but the sleeve of her thick white sweater appeared to be completely empty.

'I love you, you bastard,' she said, with her

very last breath.

Michael said nothing, but sat there and watched her sweater softly collapse. It dropped on to the seat on top of her sweatshirt, her bra, her thong and her empty jeans. Isobel, or the ghost of Isobel, was gone.

He sat there for a while. He didn't know how he felt. He could have cried but he didn't really want to – not for Isobel, anyhow. Eventually he opened his door and climbed out and started to walk back along the halted procession of vehicles. Several other drivers had got out of their SUVs, too, and were standing in the road, stunned by the disappearance of their passengers. These were the living. The semi-substantials had all vanished, leaving nothing but their clothes and their shoes.

He was almost halfway down the line when he came across Jack Barr. Jack had messed-up hair and he was wearing a droopy pair of Hawaiian shorts. He blinked at Michael, and then he slurred, '*Hi*, dude! I thought I recognized you.'

They hugged and clapped each other on the back.

Jack said, 'How the hell did this happen? Like, where did they go, all of these people? That was just about everybody who lived in Trinity! Fricking *gone*, man!'

'Back to where they should have stayed, when they died for the first time,' said Michael. 'In their graves, or their urns, or wherever.' He tapped his forehead with his finger and said. 'In here, Jack. *In memoriam.*'

* * *

343

He turned the Jeep around and drove back the way that they had come. Some of the other vehicles were already doing the same, presumably because they had no place else to go tonight but Trinity.

Michael knew that he couldn't go back there, ever, and he couldn't carry on driving south, not yet. He had no money and his credit card was in the name of Gregory Merrick. Besides that, he couldn't yet remember where he lived. There was one place where he could go, however, and ask for at least one night's shelter.

He parked up behind Samuel's Dodge Ram, jammed on the parking brake hard so that the Jeep wouldn't roll back down the slope, and climbed out. As he made his way up to the porch, several vehicles sped along the road behind him, on their way back to Trinity.

He walked along the boarded porch, and as he did so the front door opened, and there was Samuel.

'Hi, there, Michael,' he said. 'You came back a darn sight quicker than we thought you would.'

'I'm sorry. I don't yet have the money to pay you for the gas.'

'Oh, don't you worry about that, my friend. All in good time.' He sniffed the air, and looked around. 'Whole lot of traffic out on the road tonight. What's that about?'

'Armageddon, I think you could call it.'

Samuel gave him a complicated, narrow-eyed look, with his head tilted slightly to one side. 'Maybe you'd better tell me about it. Do you want to come on in?'

344

'That would be great. I'm bushed.'

As he entered the living room, where the fire was crackling, Nann came out of the kitchen with a wide smile. 'Pleased to see you back so soon, Michael! How about a beer, or a hot drink, maybe?'

'A beer, please. My mouth feels like the bottom of a birdcage.'

Nann said, 'Sure. But I got a surprise for you first.'

'Really? What kind of surprise?'

Both Samuel and Nann turned their heads toward the far end of the living-room. Michael hadn't noticed that the door there had silently opened, and that someone was standing there, waiting for him to see her.

Michael turned around, too. It was Natasha, smiling at him shyly, wearing a white cotton hat and a long white cotton nightgown.

'Tasha,' he said. 'I thought...'

He was incapable of saying any more. All he could do was walk over to her and hold her. She felt just as thin as she had before, and just as cold, but it was still Tasha, and here she was. She even smelled of that same flowery perfume.

'I thought you were gone,' he said, at last. 'God, that was some trick you pulled there.'

She touched his forehead with her ice-cold fingertips. 'I came here to Samuel and Nann's and Samuel helped me. I didn't want you to think that you had to stay in Trinity because of me.'

'But I might have left Trinity and never come back here. You didn't even leave a note.'

Natasha smiled and shook her head. 'I knew you'd come back. You had to pay Samuel for the gas.'

She paused, and then she said, 'You can still go, you know. I'll be fine here, with Samuel and Nann. They can be my companions.'

Michael shook his head. 'No. I love you, Tasha, and I'll go on loving you until *I* die.'

'Hooo-ee,' said Samuel. 'Then you can *both* be ghosts. I'll drink to that.'

EPILOGUE

Siskiyou Daily News, Thursday, February 27

Following last week's devastating fire at the Trinity-Shasta Clinic in Trinity, medical director Kingsley Vane announced today that the facility would be closed for at least the foreseeable future.

Mr Vane and several members of his staff were lucky to escape with their lives when fire swept through the building. Seven critically ill patients were rescued by firefighters from Weed Volunteer Fire Department.

Weed police and fire investigators are working on the theory that the fire was set deliberately by a previous patient who suffered from a severe mental imbalance.

Mr Vane commented today that the intensive care at TSC had been 'revolutionary'. He said that 'regretfully, we have now lost our chance to become immortal'.